MOSCOW NOIR

MOSCOW NOIR

EDITED BY NATALIA SMIRNOVA & JULIA GOUMEN

Published by Akashic Books
©2010 Akashic Books

Series concept by Tim McLoughlin and Johnny Temple
Moscow Noir map by Sohrab Habibion

ISBN-13: 978-1-936070-06-0
Library of Congress Control Number: 2009939039
All rights reserved
Printed in Canada
First printing

Akashic Books
PO Box 1456
New York, NY 10009
info@akashicbooks.com
www.akashicbooks.com

ALSO IN THE AKASHIC NOIR SERIES:

Baltimore Noir, edited by Laura Lippman
Boston Noir, edited by Dennis Lehane
Bronx Noir, edited by S.J. Rozan
Brooklyn Noir, edited by Tim McLoughlin
Brooklyn Noir 2: The Classics, edited by Tim McLoughlin
Brooklyn Noir 3: Nothing but the Truth
edited by Tim McLoughlin & Thomas Adcock
Chicago Noir, edited by Neal Pollack
D.C. Noir, edited by George Pelecanos
D.C. Noir 2: The Classics, edited by George Pelecanos
Delhi Noir (India), edited by Hirsh Sawhney
Detroit Noir, edited by E.J. Olsen & John C. Hocking
Dublin Noir (Ireland), edited by Ken Bruen
Havana Noir (Cuba), edited by Achy Obejas
Indian Country Noir, edited by Sarah Cortez & Liz Martínez
Istanbul Noir (Turkey), edited by Mustafa Ziyalan & Amy Spangler
Las Vegas Noir, edited by Jarret Keene & Todd James Pierce
London Noir (England), edited by Cathi Unsworth
Los Angeles Noir, edited by Denise Hamilton
Los Angeles Noir 2: The Classics, edited by Denise Hamilton
Manhattan Noir, edited by Lawrence Block
Manhattan Noir 2: The Classics, edited by Lawrence Block
Mexico City Noir (Mexico), edited by Paco I. Taibo II
Miami Noir, edited by Les Standiford
New Orleans Noir, edited by Julie Smith
Orange County Noir, edited by Gary Phillips
Paris Noir (France), edited by Aurélien Masson
Phoenix Noir, edited by Patrick Millikin
Portland Noir, edited by Kevin Sampsell
Queens Noir, edited by Robert Knightly
Richmond Noir, edited by edited by Andrew Blossom,
Brian Castleberry & Tom De Haven
Rome Noir (Italy), edited by Chiara Stangalino & Maxim Jakubowski
San Francisco Noir, edited by Peter Maravelis
San Francisco Noir 2: The Classics, edited by Peter Maravelis
Seattle Noir, edited by Curt Colbert
Toronto Noir (Canada), edited by Janine Armin & Nathaniel G. Moore
Trinidad Noir, Lisa Allen-Agostini & Jeanne Mason
Twin Cities Noir, edited by Julie Schaper & Steven Horwitz
Wall Street Noir, edited by Peter Spiegelman

FORTHCOMING:

Barcelona Noir (Spain), edited by Adriana Lopez & Carmen Ospina
Cape Cod Noir, edited by David L. Ulin
Copenhagen Noir (Denmark), edited by Bo Tao Michaelis
Haiti Noir, edited by Edwidge Danticat
Lagos Noir (Nigeria), edited by Chris Abani
Lone Star Noir, edited by Bobby Byrd & John Byrd
Mumbai Noir (India), edited by Altaf Tyrewala
Philadelphia Noir, edited by Carlin Romano

MOSCOW

Ostankino

Elk Island

Babushkinskaya

Leningradsky Avenue

Silver Pine Forest

Birch Grove Park

Pure Ponds

Lubyanka

Kursk Station

Perovo

Kiev Station

Zamoskvorechye

New Arbat

Prazhskaya

TABLE OF CONTENTS

PART III: FATHERS AND SONS

PART IV: WAR AND PEACE

INTRODUCTION
CITY OF BROKEN DREAMS

Translated by Marian Schwartz

W hen we began assembling this anthology, we were dogged by the thought that Russian noir is less about the Moscow of gleaming Bentley interiors and rhinestones on long-legged blondes than it is about St. Petersburg, the empire's former capital, whose noir atmosphere was so accurately reconstructed by Dostoevsky and Gogol. But the deeper we and the anthology's authors delved into Moscow's soul-chilling debris, the more vividly it arose before us in all its bleak and mystical despair. Despite its stunning outward luster, Moscow is above all a city of broken dreams and corrupted utopias, and all manner of scum oozes through the gap between fantasy and reality.

The city comprises fragments of "utterly incommensurate milieus," notes Grigory Revzin, one of Moscow's leading journalists, in a recent column. The word "incommensurability" truly captures the feeling you get from Moscow. The complete lack of style, the vast expanses punctuated by buildings between which lie four-century chasms—a wooden house up against a construction of steel—and all of it the result of protracted (more than 850-year) formation. Just a small settlement on the huge map of Russia in 1147, Moscow has traveled a hard path to become the monster it is now. Periods of unprecedented prosperity have alternated with years of complete oblivion.

The center of a sprawling state for nearly its entire history, Moscow has attracted diverse communities, who have come to the city in search of better lives—to work, mainly, but also to beg, to glean scraps from the tables of hard-nosed merchants, to steal and rob. The concentration of capital allowed people to tear down and rebuild ad infinitum; new structures were erected literally on the foundations of the old. Before the 1917 Revolution, buildings demolished and resurrected many times over created a favorable environment for all manner of criminal and quasi-criminal elements. After the Revolution, the ideology did not simply encourage destruction but demanded it. The Bolshevik anthem has long defined the public mentality: "We will raze this world of violence to its foundations, and then/We will build our new world: he who was nothing will become everything!"

Back to the notion of corrupted utopias: much was destroyed, but the new world remained an illusion. Those who had nothing settled in communal apartments. After people were evicted from their private homes and comfortable apartments, dozens of families settled in these spaces, whereupon a new Soviet collective existence was created. (Professor Preobrazhensky, the hero of Mikhail Bulgakov's *Heart of a Dog*, happily avoided this "consolidation." In the novel, set in post-revolutionary Moscow, the professor transplants a human pituitary gland into a dog in hopes of transforming the animal into a person. The half-man who results from this experiment immediately joins up with the Reds. The test is a failure. In Bulgakov's opinion, he who was "nothing" could not become "everything.") That form of survival existed in Moscow until very recently, and from the average westerner's standpoint, nothing more oppressive could ever be devised: an existence lived publicly, in all its petty details, like in prison or a hospital.

The story of the Cathedral of Christ the Savior is a fairly graphic symbol of how Moscow was "built." The church was constructed in the late nineteenth century on the site of a convent, which was dismantled and then blown up in 1931, on Stalin's order, for the construction of the Palace of Soviets. The Palace of Soviets was never built (whether for technical or ideological reasons is not clear), and in its place the huge open-air Moskva Pool was dug out by 1960; it existed until the 1990s, when on the same site they began resurrecting the Cathedral of Christ the Savior, symbolizing "new Russia."

The more you consider the history of Moscow, the more it looks like a transformer that keeps changing its face, as if at the wave of a magic wand. Take Chistye Prudy—Pure Ponds (the setting for Vladimir Tuchkov's story in this volume)— which is now at the center of Moscow but in the seventeenth and eighteenth centuries was in the outskirts and was called "Foul" or "Dirty" Ponds. The tax on bringing livestock into Moscow was much higher than the tax on importing meat, so animals were killed just outside the city, and the innards were tossed into those ponds. One can only imagine what the place was like until it finally occurred to some prince to clean out this source of stench, and voilà! Henceforth the ponds were "clean."

There are a great many such stories. Moscow changes rapidly as it attempts to overcome its dirt, poverty, despair, desolation, and evil; nonetheless, it so often ends up right back where it started.

A noir literary tradition does not yet really exist in Russia in general or Moscow in particular. Why? Possibly due to the censorship of czarist Russia, to say nothing of the Soviet era. In 1887, Vladimir Gilyarovsky, a writer, journalist, and great stylist of Moscow life, prepared an anthology of short sketches about Moscow's gloomiest locales and their inhabitants, *The Stories of the Slums*. However, the book was not to see the light of day. The censorship committee banned the book and its pages were burned. As an aide to the main administration chief wrote in response to Gilyarovsky's request to allow the book to go to press, "Nothing will come of your troubles . . . This is sheer gloom without a single glimmer, the slightest justification, nothing but a condemnation of the existing order. Such truth cannot be written." There was no further writing "without a glimmer or justification" for another hundred years or so, and for a long time even Ludmilla Petrushevskaya, a Russian State Prize laureate and living classic (one of whose artistic directions could well be classified as noir), had to write her plays and stories about the shady aspects of life without hope of publication.

Any discussion of Moscow's noir sources demands mention of a novel by the brothers Arkadi and Georgi Vainer, *Era of Mercy*, about the postwar (1945) struggle between the police and the "breeding dregs." Experienced operative Gleb Zheglov and frontline soldier Vladimir Sharapov, who is, unfortunately, a novice at investigations, face the sinister "Black Cat." The book was adapted into a famous television miniseries, *The Meeting Place Cannot Be Changed*, which many Muscovites know by heart.

The atmosphere closest to noir is found in works devoted to the Stalinist era, such as Vasily Aksyonov's *Moscow Saga* and Aleksandr Solzhenitsyn's *First Circle*: the patrol wagons that spirit "enemies of the people" off into the night, never to return home, for they will be shot without trial or investigation; the torture chambers; the betrayals; the fear; the suicides; and the "House on the Embankment" as an icon of Stalinist noir. Inevitably, our anthology is haunted by this Stalinist ghost as well, in the stories of Sergei Kuznetsov and Dmitry Kosyrev (a.k.a. Master Chen).

True noir is not only contained within Moscow's central districts, replete with the atmosphere of multiple destructions and even more ghosts (Pure Ponds and Zamoskvorechye, the settings for the stories by Vladimir Tuchkov and Gleb Shulpyakov), but also the residential neighborhoods where, despite the dream of broad streets, bright-colored buildings, and ample green space, poverty still reigns and the typical apartments with their cheerless electric light and thin walls never let their inhabitants forget for a minute that there is no exit. This is Perovo in Maxim Maximov's story, and Andrei Khusnutdinov's Babushinskaya, where Paul Khlebnikov, editor in chief of the Russian *Forbes*, met his death. In the forested areas at the city's edge maniacs are at work, but in the largest of them, Elk Island National Park, there is a piece of land one kilometer square that, due to a strange combination of circumstances, is not protected by a single police unit. This is where thugs go to settle scores, this is where they bring their dead bodies, and this is where the dramatic events in Alexander Anuchkin's story "Field of a Thousand Corpses" unfold. Naturally, noir is train stations too, where people congregate after they have lost hope, where it's easy to be completely anonymous and get lost in the crowd; train stations play leading roles in the stories by Anna Starobinets and Alexei Evdokimov. Actually, almost any place in Moscow longs to be the setting for a story of crime and violence.

This anthology is an attempt to turn the tourist Moscow of gingerbread and woodcuts, of glitz and big money, inside out; an attempt to reveal its fetid womb and make sense of the desolation that still reigns.

Natalia Smirnova & Julia Goumen
St. Petersburg, Russia
March 2010

PART I

CRIME AND PUNISHMENT

PART I

THE MERCY BUS

BY ANNA STAROBINETS

Kursk Station

Translated by Mary C. Gannon

I'm waiting for mercy. It should be here any minute now. There it is, turning the corner. Soon it will stop and open up its doors to me and others like me. Just a few more minutes and we'll be warm.

Right now it's cold, though. It's real cold. Especially for me. At least they get to lie on the sewage grates, or sit nearby on the bare asphalt, their backs up against the gray panels of the train station. They get the choice spots. Hot steam rises up from under the ground, saturating their stinking rags and bodies, their hair and their skin. The steam is so hot that it even melts the icicles hanging down from the roof of the building. Droplets run down the icicles like pus. It's warm there, beneath the overhang.

On the other hand, I don't envy them. When they get up they're going to feel ten times worse, with their clothes soaking wet and all—it's minus thirty degrees. True, they'll be getting right onto the bus, but who wants to be soaking wet in a bus?

A shapeless old hag in sagging purple tights is asleep, breathing gently. The rest are awake. They watch with no expression as the bus approaches. The cripple shuffled off, the hem of his soft leather overcoat trailing behind him on the frozen ground, his shiny black dress shoes worth a thousand dollars each. Unbelievable, he hadn't even wanted them! Foxy Lee had it all figured out. "At the station you can just trade with one of them," she'd said, but she hadn't considered that these retards might turn down such a good deal, clutching their rags with iron grips.

I had to force the trade on him. I can be pretty convincing sometimes, particularly when I'm right.

By the way, never pick a fight with a bum at Kursk station. It's like trying to battle with a giant rotten apple, or a bag of garbage.

True, they were too small for him, the shoes. But that's no big deal, he can break them in. Or sell them. The rest of the duds were too big for him. But that's how they wear them around here.

None of his friends went after him. No one tried to stop me while I was slugging him either. The expressions on their swollen steamy faces were hard for me to make out, even under the streetlight, but I think they were looking kind of hostile.

So just in case, I keep to the edge of the group. I'm safer here, near the entrance gates and the cops. Because, first of all, they're afraid of the cops. Second, they're too lazy—no, lazy's not the right word, they're too *comatose* to cover the fifty-meter distance to where I'm standing.

Of course, the cops tried to shoo me away. There were two of them. I gave them each a hundred bucks (I didn't have any smaller bills on me). They stared at me, and then at the bills, with their blank fish eyes, and finally they laid off. Understandable, I guess. It's not every day you see a piss-covered bum around Kursk station with a wad of greenbacks in his pocket. A minute later one of them came back. He sniffed back his snot, his nose violet from the frost, and stared hungrily at the bridge of my nose.

"Got any ID?"

I gave him another hundred. Breathing hard, he examined it under the yellow light of the streetlamp, then stuffed it inside his jacket. He shifted his weight from foot to foot. His gaze slid like sewage water down my unshaven face, broken nose, lip soaked in blood, and my dirty rags covered in brownish-yellow stains, before slithering back up to my face, where it paused for a moment on my misshapen gray hat with earflaps. Something caught his attention there, either the cut of the hat or the locks of hair that were left uncovered, too shiny and clean for the likes of me. I pulled my hat down over my forehead to reassure him. He had already forgotten about it, and his eyes shifted over me mechanically, until he focused on the bridge of my nose again.

"Where'd you steal the money?"

Now that was going too far.

"I earned it," I told him. But my voice came out sounding choked and hoarse, like a crow cawing.

"I'm taking you down," the cop said colorlessly, and suddenly—I swear—his teeth started chattering, maybe from the cold or, most likely, from hunger, the greedy bastard.

I gave him another hundred bucks, promising myself that *this* was the last time. I really didn't want any problems with law-enforcement officers, but arrogance has its limits, even from a cop. And four hundred is definitely the limit. If he tried to get any more out of me, I'd kill him.

Again, he studied my contribution, then hid it away. He sniffed. Coughed uncertainly.

"Any more questions, officer?" I croaked, pulling the mitten off my frozen hand so that it would be easier to shoot if he said yes, and cursing myself for the servile "officer," which had rolled off my lips like a token rolling out of the broken turnstile at the john in Kursk station.

By the way, don't ever take a piss at Kursk. Unless, of course, you like pissing into a reeking hole in the cold in front of other people for fifteen rubles.

A passenger train pulled into the station with a shriek and a groan. The cop squinted lazily at the train and then stole a glance at my bare fingers—too clean, too smooth, and my nails were too manicured. He was thinking hard about something, which was obviously not easy for him. He wrinkled his low forehead, and his eyebrows twitched like cockroaches. Finally the twitching stopped.

"Who are you?" he asked, and looked me in the eye for the first time, intently and with some degree of intelligence. He was obviously on the brink of some kind of realization.

I felt the icy handle of the gun in my pocket. To be honest, I don't like guns. I'm a bad shot, anyway. On the other hand, even a fool can shoot. Right. First you just cock it back . . .

Foxy Lee hadn't wanted to give me the gun. That put me on my guard. She kept pushing me gently toward the door, shaking her red mane of hair and mumbling, "You won't be needing that. Come on! You don't need it." Then she caught my stare and her face crumpled up like she was hurt. "You don't believe me, do you? Just like before!"

I thought she was going to start bawling. But she didn't. She handed me the gun, barrel first, and frowned. *That's not how you do it. Handgrip first*, I said to myself automatically, and took the gun from her, feeling ashamed again.

"Just don't do anything stupid," said Foxy. "If anything happens, one of my guys will be at the station. He'll help you."

Suddenly I felt uncomfortable.

"One of *your* guys? What does that mean?"

"Ours," Foxy corrected herself playfully. "Our guy. A friend." She put her arms around my neck. Her hands were cool and her fingertips were slightly moist.

"I'll get along fine without your friends." I wanted to pull away, but she wouldn't let me.

"Don't be jealous," Foxy whispered into my ear. "It was a long time ago."

That made me even more mad. *A long time ago*, what the hell is that supposed to mean? When Stary picked you up at the train station you were seventeen, a filthy, skinny little red-head. You're twenty-one now. Only twenty-one, girl! So what the hell does that mean—a long time ago?

She stroked my cheek. Her fingers smelled sweetly of flower-scented hand cream and blood.

"I'll be with you," said Foxy. "If that's what you want."

I nodded and said I did. I was angry and I wanted her, and I kissed her red hair, and her thick blond eyelashes, her little palms and those fingers—cold, moist fingers that she hadn't managed to wash very well. I kissed them and inhaled their scent, animal-like and childish at the same time.

"Listen to me, buddy!" the cop said, his voice rising. "Who the fuck are you?"

". . . two . . . three . . ." I whispered.

"What?!"

I decided to count to seven, my favorite number, and then shoot.

". . . four . . ."

People started filing out of the train that had just pulled in, making a wide semicircle around the spot where I stood with the cop. Some character in a leather jacket with a shaved head shuffled by, looking furtively at us. Then he stopped and stared.

"Keep moving!" the cop barked at him.

The guy walked straight toward us.

"Let me see your ID," the cop demanded, taken aback.

"Cn I've a wrd ith you, offcr?" mumbled the guy in leather, completely unfazed but slurring every sound. He gestured to the cop amiably.

The cop turned to me and then to the leather guy—and froze.

"C'mon, c'mon," the leather guy said, still slurring his words, but this time in a more commanding tone. "Git ovr here, offcr."

Suddenly, the eyes of the officer took on the expression of an animal, a mix of sharp sadness and surprise, and he silently strode over to the leather guy the way a dog goes to its trainer when it has mixed up its commands.

The fellow in leather whispered a few brief words into the cop's ear. The cop looked at me from under his brow, nodded dejectedly, and sauntered off into the darkness.

"Offcr!" the leather guy called after him quietly.

"Aren't you frgetting smethin?"

The cop's back slumped.

"Didn ya take smthin tht didn blong to ya?"

The back didn't so much as stir.

"Git outta here," the guy in leather said, softening, and the cop rushed off, his boots crunching on the frozen crust of snow.

"Watch it, buddy!" The guy in leather advised me good-naturedly, then winked and moved away.

"Thanks," I replied politely, but he didn't turn around.

Buddy. Uh-huh, right.

* * *

And so I'm waiting for mercy. It should be here soon.

Here it is now. It just came around the corner, stopped next to the train station, and opened its doors to me.

Mercy, as everyone knows, is blurry and abstract. It can assume many different forms: from a coin at the bottom of your pocket to a blank check, from a plastic doggie bag to a benefit concert, from a kiss to artificial respiration, from a Validol pill to a shot in the head, from the ability to love to the ability to kill.

The mercy granted me is concrete. It takes the form of a dirty white bus. It is given to me for one night—this cold, dark, terrible, final, happy, damned night—and I will accept it without hesitation.

On this cold night, when you can freeze to death in an hour.

On this dark night, when you can disappear without a trace in a minute.

On this terrible night, when they're looking for me high and low: in apartments and bars, in subways and airports, at hotels and movie theaters, in nightclubs and casinos, on the streets and in stairwells.

On this final night they are looking for me so they can kill me.

On this happy night, when they won't find me because no one will think to look for me here, on the Mercy Bus that saves the homeless from hunger and cold.

Mercy is what I need on this damned night.

That is why I fall before the open doors of the bus. I cough, I snort, and I wheeze. I crawl on all fours as though I don't have the strength to stand up, and I stretch my trembling hands toward them—toward three people in blue jackets, with red crosses on their sleeves and the word Mercy on their backs, and gauze masks pulled tight over their faces. I babble, my tongue tripping on the sounds.

I crawl at their feet, touching their shoes and begging: ". . . Help . . . save me . . ." I sniff, then grovel: "Save me . . ."

Foxy taught me to do that. "There aren't many seats on the bus," she said. "They only take the ones who are in really bad shape. They drive you around the city all night, keep you warm, feed you, and in the morning bring you back."

"Only the ones who are in really bad shape."

"Only the ones who are completely down-and-out."

"Only the ones who will die without them."

Well, at least I wasn't lying when I groveled. Without them, I really would die. Stary's men would kill me. They'd hunt me down and kill me like a witless animal.

Besides, the cops would be after me soon too.

"I'm fucked, man . . ."

And the merciful guys in masks pick me up by the arms and haul me into the bus. Now I am safe. I will be safe all night long, until morning. In the morning I'll get on the 7:01 train.

The men in masks seat the swollen, dirty, frozen, decomposing half-people. The Mercy Bus drives off.

Foxy Lee, my girl, my little train-station slut, my sweet guardian angel, found me a safe lair to hide in. Safe and stinking.

God almighty, what a stench! I'd give every greenback in my possession for a mask—the kind those brothers of mercy have. Gimme a mask, man, gimme a mask!

The windows of the bus are draped in thin threads of frost, adorned in snowy cobwebs, covered from the inside with a frozen glaze. That thin glaze is all that separates the stinking, sticky warmth of our bus from the piercing cleanliness of the city. Out there it is easy and painful to breathe. With each breath, your nostrils seem to stick together. Out there my killers are looking for me, swearing and cursing, inhaling and exhaling the frozen air.

Here, inside, trying not to breathe through my nose, I scrape out an ugly peephole in the perfect pattern of the frosted window, and I look out.

We crawl along past the Atrium, and the engine roars and trembles in helpless convulsions. The mall glows with neon. Half-naked mannequins pose in shop windows, and others just like them, only dressed up in fur coats and winter jackets, surge through the glass doors to the twenty-four-hour cash registers. In the glare of headlights, streetlamps, and billboards, in a red snowstorm, the people, their faces rust-colored, look like frolicking devils. Their cars, parked seven rows deep, form the seven circles of hell—a honking Moscow hell, where traffic jams happen even at midnight.

Still, this place seemed by far the best location for the Merciful Monsters Charity Ball. The idea for the ChaBa (Charity Ball) belonged to me and me alone, though I had planned to rent a cushy theater like the MKhAT, or a concert hall, or at the very least a fancy nightclub.

Stary was the one who wanted to have the Charity Ball in the Atrium. Stary and Foxy Lee spent a lot of time in the Atrium. Foxy liked buying perfume, lotion, high heels, clothes, lingerie, bedding, shampoo, cookies, and sauces in nearly industrial quantities. Stary, I can't deny it, waited for her patiently, no matter how long it took. He even made excuses to his bleary-eyed bodyguards: "She had a tough frickin' childhood, so frickin' cool it! And cover your frickin' traps when you yawn, goddamnit!" While Foxy was shopping, he liked to kill time in a restaurant, eating sushi and washing it down with tequila, before going to a movie. He thought of himself as a film buff. From time to time, along with his lovers and security guards, Stary would take one of his subordinates to the Atrium. The invitation was the boss's seal of approval and guaranteed promotion, prosperity, and impunity to the recipient for some time to come.

This period usually lasted no more than two months. When his shelf life ran out, the favorite was thrown onto the garbage heap (that is to say, demoted to personal chauffeur of the second secretary's assistant, or fired, or wiped off the face of the earth, depending on Stary's mood).

From the beginning of November, I accompanied Foxy and Stary to the Atrium. Toward the end of December I was still the favorite, although I sensed that my time was running out. Late that month, Stary called me to the Atrium, sent Foxy off shopping, knocked back a double shot of tequila, and announced: "A friend of mine used to light a candle at the Cathedral of Christ the Savior if things were going good for him. I always thought that a candle wasn't enough. But I kept quiet because he was doing all right and I wasn't. Now my friend's in prison. It'll be a long, long time before he gets out. And now things are going good for me."

Stary *was* doing all right. He had found a cozy place for himself on the Pipeline. His perch was nonetheless precarious enough that he was ready to bail out any minute (the Pipeline didn't quite belong to him yet, at least not completely). He didn't experience any discomfort in his backside, however (because the Pipeline did not entirely belong to someone else). He sat placidly and listened to the faint gurgle of the black blood of Russia as it flowed abroad.

"I'm swimming in oil! She's black and she's mine!" Stary said this with carnivorous relish, as though he was talking about a naked and capricious African princess who gave herself to him at night with shrieks, tears, and moans. It tormented and affronted me in the most idiotic, awkward, and ridiculous way. When the boss used this expression, which he did very often, an ill-fated black princess appeared before my eyes: moist, nimble, shapely, and bearing a certain resemblance to Halle Berry. A second later, her image was replaced by that of a red-haired girl. The one Stary really did fuck. Foxy. Does Foxy moan when she comes? Does she close her whitish fox eyes, or do they go large and glassy, like those of a stuffed animal? These questions preoccupied me a great deal.

"Are you listening to me?"

"Yes, boss, of course!"

What does she smell like? What does she taste like?

"So, anyway, I'm doing pretty good. And I'm a superstitious man, so I think I owe something to the Big Guy. But I'm not going to light up any candles. Because candles won't cut it. I think I should do something for charity."

What about the shape of her nipples? What color are they? And what about her freckles? Freckles sprinkled her pale skin like gold dust. Does she have them all over?

"You seem like a smart guy. So I want you to think up some kind of charity event. A real tearjerker. Something to make everyone bawl. So that I seem like a father to everyone, you know what I mean? So they'll think of me afterward when the time comes. You know, elect me. You get it. So, think something up. You got imagination."

That's when I created the ChaBa.

It was the end of December, my time was almost up, Stary was eating sushi, and Foxy was throwing money to the wind. I thought up the idea for ChaBa in a whirlwind of inspiration and despair. I thought of ChaBa because I thought that a little money wouldn't hurt me, in the end.

"Merciful Monsters Charity Ball," I announced proudly.

"What's that?" said Stary, stabbing a morsel of sushi with one of his chopsticks.

"A costume ball and masquerade. Real fancy. Real stylish. We'll have Ksyusha Sobchak, Zemfira, Renata Litvinova, Zverev, I don't know who else, maybe Fedya Bondarchuk, some red-carpet types, Rublyevka wives, a couple oligarchs, some ministers, I dunno."

"And?"

"And everybody dresses up like monsters. They eat, drink, dance, get high, fuck, and the whole thing will be on TV."

"What's the point?"

"There'll be invitations, which the merciful monsters will get only after making a donation to some charity organization like, I dunno, Destitute Russia. Yeah, Destitute Russia. All profits go to the poor and homeless."

"Homeless . . ." Stary murmured absently.

It was a smart move on my part. Stary always had a soft spot for the poor and the homeless. That is to say, always since the day he hired an underage redheaded whore for five bucks and took her from Kursk station to his place, a humble three-story mansion overlooking the Yauza River. He fucked her, fed her, kept her warm, and decided to keep her for good, like a lost cat. From that day, Stary imagined himself to be the protector of the poor, for they shall inherit the kingdom of heaven.

He often got on my nerves, telling me about their first night together. How she started weeping when he told her she could stay . . .

"Monsters, huh? I like it! There was a movie called *Monster's Ball*. Yeah, a movie . . . with, you know, what's-her-name in it."

. . . And how she couldn't calm down, and kept on sobbing like a baby so that she couldn't even say her name. (Carefully and kindly, Stary first threw away the used condom, then offered the girl shelter, and *then* decided to introduce himself.)

"What's her name, the black one . . ."

"Halle Berry."

"That's right, Halle Berry."

. . . And how she told him through her tears, "M-m-my name is L—L—L—"

"Lee? You must be Foxy Lee with your red hair," Stary suggested, laughing, and when she stopped crying she said, "Foxy, I like that. I'm Lisa, actually."

"Monsters Ball, I like the sound of that. Monsters help the homeless! You've got some smarts, all right! Monsters. I'll get 'em all over here to the Atrium."

"But—"

"I'll rent the Atrium for the night, no problem."

. . . And how they laughed afterward, and how "Lisa" didn't really stick, but that sweet Lee did. That Lee really did stick. Foxy Lee, it almost sounds Chinese.

Foxy Lee, my red-haired little girl.

She said that she liked me from the very beginning. I could never figure out whether she really liked me, or whether I just didn't disgust her. Or maybe she didn't really care one way or the other. On the whole, Foxy acted like a typical female of the species: she didn't get uppity, and she deferred to the strongest male, never forgetting that there were other males around grazing, and that his status as "strongest" was always temporary.

When Stary wasn't looking she never missed a chance to make eyes at me. Although, no, come to think of it, I'm exaggerating. She didn't really make eyes at me. She just looked me right in the eye, staring; but for too long, and her gaze was too moist. The blood from my head rushed to the pit of my stomach and the skin on my back would be covered in goose-bumps. Then I would recall (genetic memory should never be underestimated) how the backs of my ancestors were covered in hair, and that their hair was said to stand on end at the sight of such females.

But Stary was the strongest, the alpha male; and she was afraid of him.

Stary owned millions, and sometimes killed people (although not by his own hand, of course). Stary had gotten the nickname back in kindergarden, because his last name was Starkovsky. He was five years older than me. He was only forty when he died.

And today was the day he died.

Our bus is driving from one train station to the next. By the end of the night it will have been to each one in the city. At each stop the men in masks drag in more half-dead bums, until the bus is totally full, until the smell becomes completely un-bearable, until we come full circle and end up back at Kursk. This is a mission of mercy. This is the route of suffering.

At Three Stations Square there was a whole line of frozen beggars. They all wanted to get a place on the bus, but the merciful took only those who couldn't stand up. Only those who were lying in the dirty snow *outside* the line.

That seems pretty dumb to me. Why pick up only the weakest? If you're going to try to rescue someone, it makes more sense to save the ones who can stand up. They're stron-ger. They have a better chance of survival.

Hey, guys! Save the strongest! You can't save the fallen ones anyway.

* * *

She kissed me for the first time at the Merciful Monsters Charity Ball.

She wasn't wearing a costume. (Stary didn't want his woman looking grotesque.) She was simply wrapped in expensive furs, her red hair down and a fox mask over her face. A simple one like the kind for kids. She was the most beautiful of all—not because everyone else came wearing fangs and bloody or half-decomposed faces, but just objectively. Because she was.

But I had other things on my mind. Her beauty paled in comparison with that of my new bank card.

On that night (as always) Foxy stuck close to Stary, and I (for the first time) tried to remain as far away from him as possible.

On that night Foxy was just a vague red spot, a red spot that was no longer important and that would remain part of the past.

On that night I ignored Foxy. I was busy thinking about my bank card, about its golden sheen, about the fifty grand on it. Everything turned out to be so much simpler than I'd expected. Destitute Russia, the fund that we had started, got good press, and the Merciful Monsters Charity Ball was covered in all the media. Stary was on TV and radio, and the announcers never forgot to announce the charity's bank account number, or else it appeared at the bottom of the screen. Stary's face appeared on huge billboards all over the city. Hey, there's one of them now—by the Belorusskay train station, over by the exit to the bridge!

I designed the ad myself. It's too bad the reeking losers in the bus are sleeping. It's too bad they don't see how well I had everything planned! In the picture, Stary has one arm around a neatly dressed but still unhappy-looking homeless woman, and his other around Philipp Kirkorov, who is dressed up like Freddy Krueger. Instead of a knife, there is a wad of dollars in Freddy's ring-studded hand. He is handing the dollars to the bum, and the bum is leaning toward him—a true idyll. There was another version with Ksyusha Sobchak in a black evening gown with vampire fangs and a stack of dollars again. The slogan reads, *Become a real human, show mercy* (or, *We don't need blah-blah, we need ChaBa!*). And, of course, the account number below.

Not many ordinary citizens wanted to become real humans, even little by little. Anyway, I hadn't exactly been counting on ordinary citizens to begin with.

The most important of the posh guests were sent invitations embossed in (real) gold, and of course the bank account number was written on each one. Those monsters went all out.

Having journeyed through the accounts of various individuals and organizations (those of you who have sent money on such a journey will understand; as for those of you who haven't, tough luck), a sum of half a million dollars ended up in my bank account. As a matter of fact, that is the same amount—$500,000—that Stary spent on the media campaign in preparation for ChaBa. The natural monetary cycle had gone full circle; nothing personal and nothing extra. Nobody knew a thing and everyone was happy. Stary had drawn some good PR, the merciful monsters had gotten their publicity, the television viewers had gotten their circuses, and I had received my bread. The only one who didn't get anything was Destitute Russia; but no matter how much you give *destitute* Russia, it will never be enough. Even the guys in the gauze masks know that. Eh, guys?

Just in case, purely by intuition I stayed away from Stary

at the ball. I also had a ticket in my pocket for a plane that would take me across the planet the very next day. If you were to examine the situation as a whole, then of course Stary had no real reason to be upset with me, even if he were to find out about my golden bank card. But Stary rarely examined a situation from afar. In that respect he was nearsighted. He looked at things close-up, made decisions quickly, and shot unexpectedly (though not himself, of course). Furthermore, I would no longer be working for him; and, well, yes—I had a ticket . . .

"Ladies, choose your partners!"

When the slow dance was announced, Death approached me slowly. She invited me without a word, motioning with her hand. She was not ugly. She was just your average old lady with a scythe, a skull mask, thick white hair, and a mantle that reached down to the floor; but I had no desire to dance with her. Nonetheless, I nodded politely and stepped toward her. The hand that beckoned me was wrapped in a white leather glove covered in little diamond studs. I took one look at that glove and I knew it would be better not to refuse her request. God knows whose spoiled little bitch I might offend in the process. It would be so stupid to get a bullet in the head, not because of my new credit card, shiny and golden like life itself, but because of somebody's bitch dressed up like Death.

I took her by the waist, which was surprisingly slim beneath the shapeless clothing, with a slight feeling of disgust. We began to dance and she leaned close to me with her bony face. The synthetic locks of gray hair tickled my nose, and I prepared myself for the smell of rot, the smell of decomposition and mold, but I sensed none of this. There was only the smell of expensive perfume. Only when she laughed, only when she spoke quietly, only then did I notice the thick red locks peering out from beneath her wig.

"But you weren't wearing a disguise . . ."

"I put one on so Stary wouldn't recognize me."

"Why do you want to hide from him?"

"What do you mean 'why'?" asked Foxy. "So that I can dance with you."

"You took that costume with you just so you could dance with me?"

"Yes," said Foxy. "Yes, yes!"

And then she lifted her mask up, just a little, and she kissed me. Very gently. She tasted of cheap apricot-flavored chewing gum. She made my head spin. I lost my voice.

Stary's guys were nearby. Some of them were even looking at us funny.

"They see us!" I gasped, leading her to the center of the hall.

"Not us. They saw you," said Foxy calmly. "You, dancing with Death. They couldn't have recognized *me*."

And she kissed me again, and I thought it was a good thing I was wearing loose trousers. At first I was thinking of wearing those tight black ones . . .

Then she asked me: "How are you going to spend your five hundred grand?"

And at that moment the size of my pants didn't matter, because all of that blood poured right back to my brain and temples. My head stopped spinning, and for a moment I let go of Foxy, but then hugged her and pulled her toward me again. I shook her to the music and asked her the stupidest question that I could, given the situation. "How do you know? How?"

And Foxy Lee said it was hidden mics. She said there were tapes. She said that Stary recorded all my telephone conversations. "Don't be afraid, no one heard them but me. I took them with me, and Stary doesn't know . . . I was the only one who heard them, only me, only me . . ."

Listening to her hot apricot whisper I understood for the first time in my life that it was possible to kill for money.

But maybe killing her wouldn't be necessary. After all, she is very beautiful, and I'm no stranger to mercy. Besides, killing her wouldn't be that easy, the little snake!

"Is 50 percent enough for you?" I asked, feeling like a gentleman.

She suddenly pulled her hand out of my grasp. She pulled her hand away and shook it as though it had been burned.

"You want more?" I asked, dumbstruck.

She stepped back. Then again. Then she removed her mask.

Her face was pale, so pale that her golden freckles seemed brown. There were tears in her eyes, though maybe they were just shining with anger. Her lips were trembling like a child moments away from wailing out loud.

"I don't need your money," said Foxy Lee. "I just wanted to give you all the tapes. Just in case."

She pulled out a parcel from underneath her gown and handed it to me.

If only I hadn't hurt Foxy Lee's feelings. If only she hadn't taken off that mask.

The merciful in masks are giving the bums grub—instant ramen noodles. I also grab the noodles, so as not to stick out from the rest of them, but I can't eat the stuff. I can't get it down my throat.

Don't ever trying eating ramen noodles in a bus packed full of bums, even if you're really hungry.

To be clear, I hadn't eaten in more than a day. But I gave

away my portion to the guys at the back of the bus (incidentally, no one sat down next to me, which is typical—as though I was the one reeking like a thousand dead rats, not them). Then I went back to my seat.

At Paveletskaya station we pick up three more bums. They stink worse than the seven from Savelovskaya. They are seated in the only remaining free seats, right next to me.

If I hadn't offended Foxy Lee, if she hadn't taken off her mask, everything might have been different. Stary wouldn't have realized that Death, the disgusting old lady with a scythe I'd been feeling up, was his woman, his redheaded little fox. He wouldn't have sicced his bald assholes on me, and I wouldn't have dropped the parcel with the tapes onto the floor when the fuckers bent my hand behind my back. And Stary wouldn't have heard the tapes, and would never have known where the charity money went, and he wouldn't have ripped up my airplane ticket, and he wouldn't have taken my golden bank card, and I wouldn't have ended up tied to a chair in a secret room in his mansion on the bank of the Yauza River . . . if only I hadn't offended Foxy.

Though it must be said that things didn't end so bad after all. Really, everything turned out great, and apart from the stench I have to put up with now, I'm actually happy.

My gold card is with me again, and my half-million is still on it—I checked. Early in the morning I'll get off this shit-wagon and take in a lungful of clean, cold air at Kursk station. One of our guys will meet me there with new documents and tickets for the Moscow-Odessa train in a third-class car. "We can't have the documents done before the morning," said Foxy. "The main thing is that they don't find you during the night, and in the morning you get on the train. No one in his right mind will look for you in a third-class car." In Odessa I'll meet Foxy Lee and we'll board a ferry for Istanbul. ("No one in his right mind will look for us on that lousy raft full of cheap whores and Ukrainian profiteers sleeping on their striped bags.")

"Does the ferry operate in the winter?" I asked.

"Of course it does!" said Foxy

"How do you know?"

"Cause I've been on it."

"With the cheap whores?"

She looked at me sadly, with mild surprise. Like a stray dog being punished for a puddle of urine from yesterday that had already seeped into the floor.

"The cots were hard," Foxy said thoughtfully. "And sometimes the boat tossed and heaved like mad. Do you get seasick?"

I don't get seasick. And no one will spoil the moment for me. We'll be on a Turkish ferry, and I'll be drinking whiskey and Foxy will have liqueur, and we'll walk around on the deck and enjoy the waves. And all night we'll roll around on one of those hard cots, then sleep awhile, and then I'll fuck her again.

I'll fuck her at dawn when we're coming into the Bosphorus.

We'll spend the day in Istanbul and have Turks shine our shoes and fill us up with tea. They'll pour our coffee for us, and stare at Foxy and call her Guzel, and then in the evening we'll fly away to the other side of the world. We'll buy ourselves hats and sunscreen, and we'll eat fruit and play tennis and snort coke. We'll fly on a glider and swim in the ocean every day.

And every day, every single day, I am going to thank her.

Because if it wasn't for Foxy, I would be swimming in the Yauza River right now underneath a layer of ice. I'd be blue, swollen, and dead.

Foxy saved me.

It happened when I no longer had any hope at all. I was sitting naked, tied to the chair in the middle of the room. Stary stood opposite me, looking at me with an expression of boredom in the face.

"You used to work out?" he asked finally, nodding at my six-pack abdomen.

Stary himself was heavy—not too overweight, about twenty pounds, but he hated sports.

"I work out," I said. I didn't want to use the past tense.

"You did," Stary corrected me. "You used to work out."

Again, a pause hung in the air.

"Are you gonna beat me up?" I asked, just to break the silence.

He shook his head. No, he wasn't going to beat me. He was just waiting for the guys to bring him a bucket.

Not only was Stary fascinated with the world of film, he was also interested in literature. His favorite book was *Billy Bathgate* by E.L. Doctorow. He especially liked the scene where Schultz the Mafia boss orders his men to put the "cement slippers" on the traitor, Bo Weinberg, and then throw him into the sea.

An ice hole in the Yauza River was much more effective than the ocean. They could drill a hole in no time. But cement mix and a bucket were harder to come by, even in Stary's mansion. So he had to send his thugs out to buy both. They'd been gone more than thirty minutes, and it was getting late. (They got the bucket right away, at the Atrium, as a matter of fact. They'd hit some snags with the cement mix, though.) They called Stary every few minutes to relate their latest fiasco.

I was shaking.

"I'm cold," I said, but he didn't answer.

Stary's cell phone rang once again, the theme song from the movie *Boomer*, and I gave a start. I began to shudder violently. Not because of the cold; it was just that I didn't want to die.

"What do you mean you still haven't gotten it?"

There are people like that—they look like teddy bears, with button eyes and a button nose. But when they get angry, they look like hawks.

Stary is that kind—when he gets angry, his dull gray eyes take on a noble, mercuric hue, and the earthy shade of his face drains to an aristocratic paleness. His unremarkable nose becomes beaklike, and his bushy brows rise and fall like deathly black wings. In other words, he was handsome when he was angry (and because he was often in such a state, you could say he was handsome most of the time).

"Bastards!" Stary yelled into the phone. "Drive over to Palych's construction site and have him pour some for you!"

That was when Foxy came in. Stary didn't see her; he was standing with his back to her. But I saw everything perfectly. She was barefoot, messy looking, her red hair was tangled, and her right cheek looked swollen. She peered at him with hatred, with absolute hatred—such absolute hatred that I even felt the malicious pleasure of a jealous male, although god knows I had more important things to focus on just then.

"I'm telling you, he's got cement!"

Still keeping her eyes on his back, she took a figurine off the shelf (not even a figurine—it was more like a bronze blob, a piece, as they say, of modern art) and approached him, stepping softly with her bare feet. She waited for him to say, "Okay, see ya," and hang up before she hauled off and slammed that piece of modern art into the back of his head.

Slowly, and somehow picturesquely, he fell.

He died almost immediately. His last words were: "I'm cold."

He really did love the movies, poor guy. A rug spattered in blood, his woman, her hands stained red, "I'm cold"—so Hollywood. Until Foxy Lee untied me and I had checked his pulse, I almost thought he was faking it.

But he died for real.

Naked, shivering, and pathetic, standing over Stary's dead body, I offended Foxy again. I asked her what she wanted—as in, how much I owed her for the favor. I gave the dead body a little kick.

That's when she started to cry. She cried long and hard, like a baby, like an inconsolable child. She was probably crying like that the first day Stary brought her here. She was sobbing and gasping and she couldn't stop. She kept saying, "I don't nee . . . nee . . . nee . . ." I hugged her and stroked her hair. I felt ashamed, really ashamed, even before she managed to say, "I don't need anything. I did it for you. He wanted to kill you!"

I was ashamed. I hid my face in her hair and asked her to forgive me.

Then she whispered: "If you want me, you can have me."

I was already naked, and she undressed quickly. Stary was staring at us out of one bloodied eye. He kept watching silently as I got the answers to my questions.

I found out that Foxy moans.

And that her eyes stay open, but her pupils dilate and become huge and crazed, like two black full moons.

And I found out that she smells like an animal and a child

at the same time, and she tastes salty, like the sea. That her nipples are hard and brown, and that she has freckles, not only on her face but on her shoulders. And that there is a thin line of red hair that stretches from her navel to her pubis.

Then she gave me some clothing, his clothing, because Stary had thrown mine away, and she gave me a stack of dollar bills (his) and she gave me a gun (his) and the gold bank card. My bank card.

As I was leaving, I asked her, "What about you? Are you gonna be okay?"

And she answered: "What about me? They'll be looking for you, not me. I'll stay here and I'll be miserable. I'll say he was lying there when I came into the room." She nodded at Stary.

Apparently, I didn't look too ecstatic.

"All you have to do is make it through the night," said Foxy. "If we both run away, then they'll look for both of us and we won't have any chance at all. If we do it this way, I'll have everything fixed up by morning. Then you'll step off the bus and my guy . . . *our* guy, that is, will give you new documents, tickets, and new clothes. You have to believe me, honey, no one in his right mind would go looking for you in that stinking bus. No one in his right mind will look for you on a third-class train. We'll meet up in Odessa, okay? Is that okay with you?"

I had no objections, because the plan made sense. I had no objections, because I was in love. I had no objections, because Foxy Lee is my guardian angel. Because doubting her would be a sin. She killed him for my sake. And in doing so she harmed herself. That's a fact. It's a paradox. I keep thinking about it, and I never stop being amazed: because Stary was the one guarantee she had in life. In killing him, she lost everything—the mansion on the banks of the Yauza River, money, clothes, perfume, bling, expensive cars, shopping trips to the Atrium—everything.

What would she get in exchange for all that?

Stary was married, but not to Foxy. His wife lived in a modest three-story building on Rublevsky Highway. With the help of a maid, a physical trainer, and two nannies, she took care of their son. Stary came to visit them from time to time. Foxy knew about it. Stary had bequeathed everything to his wife and son. Foxy knew about that too.

So what would she get in exchange for all that?

Me. Just me. And with no guarantees.

It's still dark outside the window, but it's already morning. We're on our way back. We're already close: there's that goddamned Atrium on the other side of Sadovaya. Only five or ten minutes left, no more. All we have to do is turn around at Taganka and drive a little ways to get there, to Kursk.

It's really early, and the Atrium is as depressing as an abandoned medieval castle.

Things are going good, as Stary used to like to say. Soon this will all be over. Things are going good. One of our guys will meet me on the platform. I'll board the Moscow-Odessa train, a third-class car, and, finally, I'll get some sleep. No, first I'll go to the dining car and grab something to eat. Then I'll go to sleep. Things are going good. Except that—

There's one little thing, one small thing that won't let go of me. Like the dull end of a drill, it pierces my brain. Some business I forgot to take care of, or an unanswered e-mail, a mistake in a quarterly financial report, or the last piece of a puzzle that has fallen behind the couch.

I still haven't been able to figure out what that little thing is. Maybe it's just exhaustion, some inconsequential glitch in my nervous system, some whim, and it would probably be best to ignore it. I should just look out the window and not think, not think, not think . . .

I'm just looking out the window—at the road, at the traffic lights, at the Atrium.

The Mercy Bus driver turns on the radio:

". . . record-breaking cold this month, temperatures tonight have plunged down to thirty-eight below! But it's going to heat up today, we have a warm front coming in . . ."

". . . *to understand her you gotta know her deep inside, hear every thought, see every . . .*"

". . . *shhhhhhhhhhhhhh . . .*"

The bus driver turns the dials mercilessly.

". . . regardless of what you say, transformation on that scale is only possible in a democratic society . . ."

". . . *have you ever really really really ever loved a woman?*"

". . . *I'll send you sky-high for a star! . . .*"

"And now for our top news bulletin. A police spokesman has confirmed that the primary suspect in the murder of Nikolai Starkovsky, State Duma deputy and owner of the Star Oil company, is Andrei Kaluzhsky, PR manager for Star Oil and organizer of the Merciful Monsters Charity Ball, which took place in Moscow on the night before the murder. According to police, they have ample evidence implicating Kaluzhsky in the murder. At present, according to investigative authorities, Andrei Kaluzhsky is in hiding somewhere in Moscow. He has not left the city. 'I simply cannot believe that this man would commit premeditated murder,' said Elizabeth 'Foxy' Lesnitskaya, girlfriend of the late deputy, in an interview. 'Andrei was so kind and honest. The whole ChaBa was his idea. It was a lovely charity event, which has already helped hundreds of homeless people!'"

Foxy Lee, my red-haired girl. How kind and foolish you are to protect me. Hold on a little while, soon this will all be over. We're already pulling up. Here we are at the station.

The bus comes to a stop.

No one in his right mind will go looking for me in a third-class car on the Moscow-Odessa train, will they?

". . . police are doing all they can to find . . ."

The merciful in masks are walking down the aisle. Drowning out the blaring radio, they announce: "The Mercy Bus has arrived at Kursk station. Those who can leave the bus by themselves should do so now. Extra medical treatment will be provided for those who are sick or cannot walk. Those of you who are seriously ill can check in at the local hospital."

The swollen, smelly passengers pry their eyes open, hoisting themselves lazily and awkwardly out of their seats.

". . . A photograph and description of the suspect have been sent to all police stations, airports, and trains stations. Police are on high alert . . ."

I stand up and walk slowly down the aisle behind the stooped, stinking zombies.

Through the bus window I see a police car, its lights flashing. Standing next to the car is an officer—that asshole from yesterday—and a herd of other cops.

A photograph and description of the suspect have been sent to all police stations. He'll recognize me. Dammit! He'll recognize me right away. He saw me here yesterday. He'll remember me for sure. I won't be able to get by without being seen!

Stay here. I have to stay in the bus.

". . . The Criminal Investigation Department says that by today . . ."

"You can walk!" a person in a medical mask yells right in my ear. "Please get off the bus!"

". . . Some news just in about the murder . . ."

"I can't," I whisper weakly in response. "Help. I need medical assistance."

I need to stay here, no matter what, I need to be here. I'll give them all the money. They need money too, right? They're merciful guys, I'll give them the whole wad of money. Hey, who in this stinking bus wants a stack of greenbacks for taking me to the hospital?

"I need treatment! I'll pay—"

"Money?" The young man in the mask frowns, looking at my reeking clothes. "What are you talking about? C'mon, c'mon, get off the bus!" he says, giving me a gentle shove in the back.

I fall forward in the aisle and begin to moan quietly.

"Are you all right?" the boy asks in concern.

"It's my heart," I mutter into the floor. "Or blood pressure . . . I have a problem with my blood pressure."

I roll my eyes back. I gasp for breath.

I'm staying here. I am not getting out.

"Lean on me," says the young man in the mask. "It's just a few steps, there you go. The nurse is in the driver's cabin. Here, I'll help you. She'll check your blood pressure. There you go. Now sit down and roll up your shirt sleeve."

They check my blood pressure. By some miracle it's very high. Through the driver's window I watch the herd of hungry cops. They're not going to get me.

The nurse and the boy in the mask are whispering to each other.

"Hypertension," the nurse whispers to him almost inaudibly. "We can't let him go."

". . . Meanwhile, the Star Oil company will go to the wife of the late Andrei Starkovsky who will inherit, quote, only debts and conflicts with it . . ."

"An injection," says the sister of mercy. "A diuretic. And check him into the hospital. That's the only option."

He goes outside. She pulls down my shirt sleeve, wipes my arm with an icy, disinfected cotton swab, and injects the needle. I guess I'm just lucky. I never had high blood pressure in my life, and now all of a sudden—there you go, hypertension!

". . . 'My husband neglected to pay his taxes,' Ms. Starkovsky said in an open statement to members of the press. 'Just a few days before his death, he transferred all the Star Oil shares to the account of a front organization. I have no intention of suffering for the illegal machinations of a person whom I haven't lived with for a number of years' . . ."

Front organization . . . front organization. I have hypertension and my head is swimming and everything is going dark. I am shaking my head and pinching my cheeks and my ears, and I want to crawl out of this darkness. I need to get ahold of myself, because I think I have just found the missing piece of the puzzle.

I watch as the transparent liquid leaves the needle.

". . . These companies are formally owned by Elizabeth Lesnitskaya. 'From a legal perspective, this is absolutely above board,' said Lesnitskaya's lawyer, Gennady Burkalo. 'My client is the owner of the aforementioned companies. These companies were formed in accordance with the law. The funds transferred from Star Oil to the accounts of these firms by Mr. Starkovsky, regardless of his motives, now belong to . . .'"

"One hundred million dollars," says the nurse, and jerks the needle out of my vein.

I feel sick. I can't breathe. It smells so bad in here I think I'm going to die. The gauze mask distorts her voice, but I recognize it anyway. She takes off her nurse's cap and her red hair cascades to her shoulders.

"You thought I needed your shitty card? One hundred million, and it's all mine!"

I feel sick to my stomach. Blood is pulsing in my ears.

My hands are shaking, but still I feel for the gun in my pocket.

"It's not loaded," Foxy whispers gently.

"I'll tell them it was you."

"You won't tell them anything," Foxy says, leaning toward my ear. She smells like perfume and apricot-flavored chewing gum. "You won't tell them anything at all."

"What did you give me?" I yell, crazed. "What did you put into me?"

There is no one but us on the bus. The merciful in masks are helping the bums toward the station.

"WHAT DID YOU GIVE ME!" I scream, and one of them turns at the sound of my cry. He leaves the bum he was walking with and runs toward the bus.

"Everything's fine," says the masked merciful Foxy Lee. "Don't worry, we're all right."

He looks at me. I'm going to be sick. I fall onto the floor.

"She gave me with something . . ." I whisper. "Help me . . ." I can't scream.

"Don' be scared, it won' hurt," and he pulls his mask off. There he is. The leather guy from yesterday.

"Mercy," he says with a smile. "We show mercy."

Another guy in a mask comes up and nods at me. "What happened?"

"Hypertension," Foxy answers. "We gave him a shot."

No! I want to scream. But my tongue won't obey me. I want to scream, *Ambulance!* But instead I just mumble and drool.

I am lying on the floor of the bus.

I think I am dying.

"The shot didn't help," says Foxy Lee sadly.

"Should I call an ambulance?" asks the young man in the mask.

"It's no use, he's already dying."

"Well then, you've suffered your last," says the boy in the mask. "Great is the mercy of God. Blessed are the poor." He snivels juicily and crosses himself.

They pick me up off the floor and prop me in the driver's seat.

It's cold. It's so cold.

I am waiting for mercy. It should be here any minute now.

GOLD AND HEROIN

BY VYACHESLAV KURITSYN

Leningradsky Avenue

Translated by Mary C. Gannon

S he was walking barefoot along Leningradsky Avenue.
The occasional streetlight and moon hung in the puddles on the ground. She jumped from one puddle to the
next, enjoying the warm splash. She held one red high heel
in her hand by the strap. The other shoe she had lost while
crossing the street around the Sovietsky Hotel.

His thoughts were steeped in gold, like the chest of a war
hero buried in medals and crosses. Zemfira was singing about
river ports. The highway was empty. The Sovietskaya Inn had
recently metamorphosed into the Sovietsky Hotel. Prostitutes
had become twice as expensive. Suddenly he saw a kitten on
the road in front of the car. He stepped on the brakes, then
got out. It wasn't a kitten. He picked up a red high heel by
its strap. The shoe was lying just next to the entrance of the
Romany Gypsy theater.

For some reason he brought the red shoe into the car. A
shoe without a girl. The clocked showed 2:55 a.m.

Once again he thought of shipments of Yakutst gold to
jewelry factories in Smolensk. Stalls were scattered along the
street like cheap bijouterie. Occasionally, a fat pearl of a
foreign-made car would swim by.

Cheaper and flatter-chested girls loomed at the intersection with Stepan Suprun Road. They say that Suprun was a test pilot. The whole area was celestial. Across the street at Khodynka Field was the place Chkalov had crashed. The street itself ran all the way to Sheremetyevo Airport.

She's nuts, he thought, nearing Airport subway station, when he saw her jumping along the sidewalk on one leg like she was playing hopscotch. He noticed a red high heel in her hand.

She watched intently as the door of a blue limousine opened on her left. Slowly, as though in a dream, so slowly that she was completely absorbed in it, she remembered her friend's contorted face, a gold tooth in a ring of purple lipstick. Boney fingers shaking a wad of green bills that she had tried to steal from her friend earlier that day. It seemed to her it was a helicopter that had come for her, not a car. She thought she'd have to fly to take the ruby star off the Kremlin spire. She leaned toward the door. A man deep inside the car smiled at her and handed her the other high heel.

She hopped into the car and moved her lips. Inside it was warm, and she realized that she had been cold. She quickly fell asleep.

At home in the bright light he noticed heavy brown knots on her slim bare arms. He looked into her eyes and saw that her pupils were completely dilated, a shiny opaque red, and runny, like broken egg yolk.

"Hot . . . hot!" she yelled. Actually, she yelled the first word; the second she whispered. And fell silent, as though she had lost her voice.

"Hot tea?" he asked.

She shook her head.

"A hot bath, then?" he asked.

She nodded.

He pointed to the door. In one sharp movement she pulled off her short blue dress and was left wearing nothing but white panties adorned with an orange mushroom. And before he could focus his gaze on her small tits, she had already flown past him.

When he was young, he too could wander around the city aimlessly with no memories or money. In the beginning of his career he was a heroin dealer. He was a drug mule, moving bags of the stuff from Warsaw to Moscow. Once he got caught on the Polonez train at Belorussky station. By some miracle he'd been able to escape, fleeing underneath the cars and over the sidings. He'd probably still be in the slammer if they had caught him.

Through making counterfeit Adidas sneakers in an invalids' cooperative, renting pirated videos, and running car dealerships in old movie theaters, he came to gold.

Gold is like heroin. It's simple, homogenous, and omnivorous.

She had been in the bathroom for an alarmingly long time. He knocked at the door to tell her. And to give her a bathrobe. She didn't answer, and he pushed the door open: she was leaning toward the mirror, staring into it, bent and skinny. Heavy black shadows seemed to pass over her face, although he couldn't quite make it out. Maybe they were just reflections cast from the mirror. He called to her. She grabbed some small scissors from the shelf under the mirror and slipped her fragile body out of the bath. Her body was smooth, save for the overgrown shrubbery of her pubis—just the way he liked it.

She threw herself at him. He tried to catch her hand, but she dodged him and sunk the scissors deep into the skin just above his ear. He jumped back, spilling blood on the rug with a picture of a proud eagle on it. He tripped and bumped into the telephone. She waved her arm, the scissors snapped shut, and he was left with the receiver in his hand, its cord dangling uselessly. Okay then, he thought, and felt for the cell phone in his pocket. He took the scissors away from her and pushed her back into the bathroom. He called his friend, the owner of a private drug rehabilitation clinic, waking him up with the insistent ring.

She didn't recognize him at first, but when he came to visit her the third or fourth time, she smiled. A crooked smile, as though her lip had been cut, like a two-way street. He wanted her even more.

They walked around the park on the grounds of the clinic, and she ate two or three berries from the festively ripe pound he had bought for her. She pressed her hand against the bark of a tree for a long time, carefully studying a ladybug. She traced circles and arrows in the sand with great concentration while his phone buzzed and he answered it.

It amazed him how slowly she did everything, how quietly her gaze and her bloodstream glided along. He slowed down too, dug at the bark of the tree, and found a mushroom. After he drove through the gate, leaving the clinic behind, he forced the arrow of the speedometer ahead sharply, to win back the minutes he had lost with her. This sharp change in rhythm shocked and disturbed him.

She asked him to bring her books, and not trusting his assistants, he went to the bookstore himself and bought her Pushkin and Dostoevsky, weighing the heavy volumes in his hand. He estimated how much a piece of gold that size would weigh, and how long it would take someone to read books that heavy. He even tried to read them. But reading was hard; life seemed to get out of sync, and lulls and pauses crept in, as though it had gotten soft and mushy, lost its elasticity. His own life, straight as an arrow, became entangled with his girlfriend's, twisted and confused. During his visits to her he would suddenly find himself rehashing yesterday's business meeting in his mind, searching for weaknesses in his performance.

And during important negotiations he would suddenly go quiet. Closing his eyes, he would see her face before him, and the brown knots on her thin arms. Two weeks later he realized he had an aching in his chest every day. Probably because of the changes in his blood pressure and pace of life.

He did something he had been planning to do for several years: he had an hourglass made for himself with real gold dust in it, and he put it on the desk in his office. He began to disengage from life more often. Suddenly interrupting a dictation or a dressing-down, he would turn the hourglass over, hanging on the steady flow of the dull yellow sand.

They pumped out half of her blood and filled her with many liters of somebody else's. She didn't know that it contained his blood too. She slept for a long time, lost in the drone of the blood of strangers rushing through her veins.

She tried to coax it along in her weak body: to tame it, combine it with her own, to learn to live with it. She prodded, nudged, pleaded, and persuaded. But some of the blood just didn't want to fit in, the way the last fragment of an almost-finished puzzle can go alien and resistant. It was then that she would launch her body against a wall with all her might, or toss a water jug at the window, or throw herself at the feet of the janitor and start chewing the dirty mop. Her blood needed the comfort of a warm fix. Then she begged for the shot, which she was permitted at this stage in her treatment; only she had to wait, and the dose was smaller.

He asked his friend at the clinic whether she could be

cured, and the friend answered that she could—but not right away, and never entirely, because of the quantities of heroin that had traveled through her system. He went on to say that he had an acquaintance with a clinic somewhere in the Alps on a magic mountain, where they slowed down the lives of their patients so much that they needed their fix only once every six months, and they could live like that for a hundred years. His friend said that he wouldn't be able to keep her in his clinic for too long, that according to a new law, private rehabilitation clinics would soon be outlawed and their patients would end up either in basements or in state-run institutions no better than prisons, with beatings and bars on the windows. His friend said that the most important thing now was for her to get off the carousel of misfortune and blood transfusions, to stop spinning around and around in her body and mind. She would have to change her lifestyle, take a trip to the sea or spend time at a resort, reading books and sunning herself on the beach. She must not see her old friends or familiar streets, where every bush would remind her of a dirty needle. She should go somewhere filled with the babbling of an incomprehensible foreign language, where unfamiliar birds sing in the trees. And when he asked for how long, his friend thought for a while, then said: "Very long."

He shut himself up in his office, turned off the phone, set down the gold-dust hourglass in the middle of the table, and counted out all his money in real estate, stocks and bonds, jewels, banks. He had enough to last a lifetime. There would even be some left over for his children. And if the bonds weren't cashed anytime soon, even his grandchildren would have something. He told his partners that he wanted to bail out and disappear forever, that he was ready to hand over his shares on terms advantageous to them. But the important thing was that it had to be done immediately. His partners thought it over and sketched out a business plan on sheets of white paper, illustrating how much of the company was upheld by his own personal connections, which routes of money and gold were dependent solely upon him. "Give us all the connections, and then you can call it a day," his partners said. "That will take six months," he begged. "That's your problem," they said.

He then transferred as much of his money as he could access to an anonymous account in a faraway bank. That money would not be enough for a whole lifetime, and would not be enough to leave something for his children, but it would be enough for half a lifetime. And that, if you think about it, is not such a short time. He deposited the rest of his fortune on an anonymous credit card, bought two false passports and plane tickets, paid a visit to the friend who ran the private clinic to get a note for the guard, and drove off to get her. By the Baku movie theater, where he'd had his first car dealership, there was a traffic jam unlike any he had ever seen in that neighborhood.

Distraught that he had not visited her in three days, and so must have decided to leave her, she decided to commit suicide that night. She had stolen the key to the attic long before, and now crawled to the edge of the roof from which she would throw herself headfirst into the dark green treetops. To fall right through them and end up lying lifeless on the neat gravel walkway. She concentrated, took a deep breath, and sucked in her stomach, calculating the angle of her leap. She mustered all her strength, then fell asleep from the exertion.

At that moment he was standing at the railroad crossing by Grazhdanskaya station, looking at his watch and waiting for a long freight train to pass. It must have had few hundred cars in it.

She stood, eyes closed, on the very edge of the roof, and slept. And she dreamed that she had changed her mind and returned to her room, that she lay down to sleep with a child-like smile on her lips, and that she would live. In fact, she stepped off the roof and out onto the long branch of a tall tree leading to the middle of the park; and she began to walk on it, not opening her eyes, like a tightrope walker. She had never walked on a tightrope before; she had a terrible sense of balance.

He hurried to the clinic, woke up the guard to show him the note, entered the grounds, looked up at her window, and discovered her walking high up above him. Her arms were flapping like the wings of a bird in slow motion. Her white nightgown was fluttering in the sultry night air. Inside his pocket, his beeper, which he had forgotten to turn off, sounded. It was his partners, who had discovered discrepancies in his accounts, as well as his disappearance, and were trying bring him to his senses. The beeper startled her. She opened her eyes, her foot slipped, and she fell down right into his out-stretched arms.

There was an explosion on their airplane as it was landing. First, purple smoke filled the plane's interior for about three minutes; these were the most frightening minutes of their lives. Then there was an explosion that knocked them both unconscious.

The burning plane gave off such unbearable heat that he came to very quickly. She was lying next to him, her neck at a strange angle, a little bird that had been executed. He turned her onto her back and she immediately opened her eyes.

He patted his pockets and pulled out his wallet. The credit card had snapped in half. The electronic notebook where he had saved the number of the bank account was smashed to pieces. The suitcase that contained a written copy of the number had burned, along with the rest of the luggage.

He no longer had any way of getting to his money. It was doomed to move around through the accounts of a distant bank, enriching the bank's owners, just as the gold of Jews murdered during the war underpinned the might of Swiss banks many years later. He told her this, and she nodded.

"I *am* Jewish," she said. "That's great," he said, then added, "We have to get out of here. If I'm seen on TV, they'll find me and kill me." They got up onto their feet and took off. All around them, dying people moaned. A woman mumbled in a foreign language, but more blood than words came out of her mouth. There were body parts strewn about. The head of a dog traveling in a special pet carrier in the next row over had been torn off, but was still trying to yap. It seemed that they were the only ones who had survived. It was a mile to the woods where they could take cover.

The remains of the plane and its passengers were scattered far and wide over the surrounding area. Halfway toward the woods that would shelter them, they came upon the body of a large man in a Versace suit. He had seen this man on the airplane, flying first class. The man's face had been pounded into mush. His suit had not suffered, and looked as though it was draped on a dummy. "Look," he said.

"Look," she said. The lining of the expensive coat was ripped, and a black cellophane package had fallen out of it. She squatted down and took a pinch of the gray powder into the palm of her hand. From out of nowhere, a bright emerald bug landed in her palm and sank into the soft powder. "Is this—?" he asked. "Yes," she answered, "no doubt about it." It was heroin.

It was an offer to begin again, in the very same way. And it was just in the nick of time, since they had turned up in a foreign country without any money or livelihood, and with documents they couldn't use again; since their bodies would be missing at the sight of the crash, they would be put on a watch list. Money, they needed money. She was still sitting on her haunches, and her face turned sharply pink, and then black, as though she'd already had her fix.

She tossed the powder away and rolled up the sleeve of the Versace jacket. "A Rolex," she said. The Rolex was still ticking—a fat gold watchband, and a watch face encrusted with large diamonds.

What do you know, a watch. This time he'll start with a watch.

IN THE NEW DEVELOPMENT

BY LUDMILLA PETRUSHEVSKAYA

Prazhskaya

Translated by Keith Gessen and Anna Summers

T his all happened in a Moscow suburb, in a new development. An engineer who worked at one of the ministries had long been on bad terms with his wife. They had a two-room apartment, with rugs, fine china, a color television, and all of it was in her name, and she would get everything if they divorced. The husband wasn't from Moscow originally, he was from the impoverished provinces, and he'd come to his wife with the clothes he was wearing and nothing more. They'd been at school together, started seeing each other, then she got pregnant and he had no choice but to marry her—he was even threatened with expulsion from school, which was the sort of thing that could happen at the time.

The truth is, he already had a girlfriend. She was a year ahead of him, they were planning to get married and leave the city together, but the way the situation developed, if he refused to marry the pregnant girl his real girlfriend wouldn't even receive her diploma—the pregnant girl's father had put all sorts of pressure on the university, it turned out. So the student-engineer was forced to marry, and not just on paper, not just by signing some forms at city hall, but the whole nine yards. That is to say, for the sake of his beloved's diploma (and she didn't resist, by the way, though she shed hot tears and threatened to jump out the window when he was saying good-bye on his way out of the dormitory to the marriage registrar's; the pregnant girl's father was picking him up in his luxury car, a Volga), he was forced to go and live in that hateful house and remain in effect under surveillance, for two years, until he graduated. In that time his beloved was sent to work in the Caucasus, married a successful Dagestani, and gave birth to a daughter, who was an epileptic, or so they thought: she regularly turned blue and couldn't breathe, so that the doctors told the mother she shouldn't stop breast-feeding, and she didn't, until the girl was practically old enough to go to school. The girl would eat some cereal and then point to her mother's breast.

Vasily learned all this later, after college, when he ran into one of his old classmates at a bar. The classmate worked in the chemical industry and had traveled to Dagestan, where he learned everything about their old classmate and her baby girl. It turned out by then that the apparent epilepsy was actually a form of appendicitis. Once they cut out the appendix the girl's suffering ended. Vasily by this time had forgotten all about his former girlfriend, and one thing he really didn't want to hear about was children: his own wife had had a miscarriage in her sixth month. She lay in the hospital and their little baby was placed in an incubator, where for a month it lived, if it can be called that; the thing was half a pound, a packet of cottage cheese—it died and they weren't even allowed to bury it, it didn't even have a name, they were forced to leave the body at the institute.

Their torture lasted the entire month. His wife's milk came, she went to the hospital four times a day to get her breasts pumped, but they didn't necessarily give it to their little packet of cottage cheese; there were other babies, even better connected, and one of them survived despite being born at five and a half months. His wife couldn't keep an eye on everyone, she wasn't even allowed into the incubator room, she wasn't even allowed to look at their little baby, even when it died, and after that she moaned and shook with tears day and night. The father-in-law also tried, gave gifts to the nurses, but they still couldn't obtain the little corpse. The father-in-law didn't know that he should bribe the boiler-room lady, she would have gladly avoided doing the dirty deed for a half-liter of vodka—she wasn't paid extra for getting rid of corpses, about which she, half-drunk, once raised a stink in the payroll department.

In short, Vasily lived in this family of strangers, alone, his wife aggravated him terribly with all her crying, and he felt sorry for himself too, a child would have been just the thing, there would have been at least one person close to him in this world. But he kept quiet about his wish for a child, that's just how he was. His wife practically burst out of her skin to get pregnant again but Vasily was very careful, he guarded his sperm like the apple of his eye.

Shortly after the wedding, the wife's parents bought an apartment for their daughter and registered it in her name. Should anything happen, Vasily would get nothing—the property was an officially notarized loan to the wife from her parents, and that was that. The wife's parents had covered all the bases; the only thing they didn't understand was that they couldn't keep winding the coil, one day it would spring back with all the pressure they'd put on it.

Finally Vasily's wife got pregnant—in the end her desire for a baby, to wipe out the memory of their little packet of cottage cheese, was just too strong, and in cases like that, no matter how hard you try, the woman will think of something. She'll get you drunk, or drug you, or do it with someone else. And sometimes the husband himself loses control. In short, they had a daughter (that other one, the first, would have been a son); they called her Alyonoshka, their little sunshine, and she grew up before him, all black hair and brown eyes, his very own daughter entirely, because her mother, Tamara, was as white as a moth. Vasily loved his little girl. Even on the night of the murder, on a snowy New Year's Eve, when his wife was almost dead and the girl started crying, he came to her and sang her back to sleep, then returned to the bathroom and finished the hammering, smashed all the bones in her face and cut off her fingers so no one could identify her.

It should be said that Vasily had a big plastic bag at the ready, the kind used for storing furs, but how he got rid of all the blood, no one knows. Maybe he placed Tamara under a cold shower, but somehow or other there was no trace of blood. He wrapped her in a tablecloth—he later explained all this to the police—then stuffed her in the bag and threw it off the balcony into the blizzard (the snowstorm lasted all night). Vasily put his wife's fingers in his overcoat—he'd somehow managed to remove them without making a lot of noise, apparently he just cut them right off. He took his daughter's sled, tiptoed quietly downstairs, loaded the body on the sled, and took it over to the construction site next door, where because of the holiday no one was working. He hid the body in the snow at the site, down in the foundation pit, and stuck the fingers into a pipe, then began waiting for spring, to see if he'd be arrested.

He called the police to report that his wife had gone missing. Of course no one believed him. His father- and mother-in-law told the police all about his life with their daughter, and his coworkers informed them that Vasily was having an affair with an awful witch who kept him on a short leash and squeezed him for money but refused to marry him, because if he left his wife he'd be back in his single suit of clothes and he was thirty-two years old. Even the car that his father-in-law had arranged for him was registered as a loan to his wife. They'd surrounded him from all sides; nothing in the world belonged to him.

But now at least, after his wife's death, he'd have four months of peace until the snow melted—and it was also possible that her body had been buried deep beneath the cement of the new building. Not long after the murder he'd strolled over to the construction site to see if he could find his burial plot, and he couldn't; there were building materials everywhere, and everything was covered in snow.

The wife's parents took their granddaughter to live with them, while Vasily was questioned on multiple occasions by a female police investigator. He kept insisting that he and his wife had gotten along poorly, that they'd had a bad fight on New Year's Eve, that she had dressed and gone to her parents', but that he had forbidden her from waking up their little girl.

At long last the snow melted. Nothing happened; the body of his wife was not found.

But one day in early June, Vasily showed up at the police station to tell the investigator that he'd murdered his wife. The investigator demanded that he prove it, at which point he led her and a team of investigators to the construction site, where workers had almost finished erecting the new buildling. The investigators couldn't find the body, however, and there was no proof of the murder: no one had seen a body or a bag flying from the window on that busy New Year's Eve, nor had they seen a sled, nor anything else Vasily described. He was not taken into custody. People did start saying that his conscience was getting the best of him, which is why he'd confessed, and why he'd abandoned his awful mistress—that is to say, he had changed.

Awhile later, Vasily called his father- and mother-in-law and told them that there was a finger with red nail polish sticking out of the faucet. His father-in-law responded that if Vasily had put Tamara's fingers into a pipe, as he claimed, and this turned out to be part of the plumbing for the new building, then in the month since the building had been finished the finger would have dissolved, or swelled up, and it certainly couldn't have traveled all the way through the water filter, and in any case what does the water system in the new building have to do with their building, which was built long ago? That's what the father-in-law said to him, to calm him down, but this just made Vasily more anxious. Naturally, when the wife's parents came over, they found nothing. Vasily said he was afraid to go into the bathroom; that the finger had probably disappeared down the drain.

And as proof, he showed his parents-in-law a flake of red nail polish that he'd found on the floor. But this didn't prove anything, the parents said: so he found some red nail polish, big deal, many women had probably visited their home. And so Vasily still lives by himself, like an outcast, and still finds strands of hair and other evidence of his crime, and collects it all, as he gradually builds the case against himself.

WAIT

BY ANDREI KHUSNUTDINOV

Babushkinskaya

Translated by Marian Schwartz

He still had the deluxe paid for at the Izmailovo Delta, but he'd decided not to show his face there anymore and in fact to forget all about hotels for the next week or two. They were sure to have searched the registration databases. He circled around on the subway for an hour or so and got out at Babushkinskaya. At the kiosks by the underground crossing, people offered rooms for anyone who needed a cheap place to stay by the day, no papers required. Another half an hour later, armed with an address, he skirted snowbound Rayevsky Cemetery to a twelve-story apartment house on Olonetsky Lane. It was a dank December night. The low sky was blanketed with a floury haze, and it was snowing lightly.

He was met at the lobby door by an old woman who looked like she'd stepped out of a prewar photograph. Wearing a patched pea coat, big felt boots that forced her stance so wide that he was reminded of a hockey goalkeeper, and a fluffy scarf tied at her nape, she took his money and counted it, then asked for his passport. Confidently turning the book back to the right page, she ordered him to stand in the light. Not betraying any irritation, he moved toward the lit window and removed his cap. The old woman studied his face in the picture long and hard. There was obviously something she didn't like about it. She sniffed her fleshy nose, squinted farsightedly, and bit her lower lip. Feeling his ears and crown starting to freeze, Veltsev put his cap back on, fished in his pockets for cigarettes, and watched the old woman examining his visas, not his photograph. He was about to ask her if she was out of her mind, when the old woman forestalled him by returning his passport and motioning for him to follow her into the building.

The lobby walls bore traces of a recent fire. The new doors of the first-floor apartments presented a striking contrast to all the other surfaces, which were either coated in smoke or peeling. With something that looked like a pass key used by a train conductor, the old woman opened a door right off the lobby and looked around before letting Veltsev move ahead of her. He walked in. At one time a fire had had the run of her front hall too. You could tell from the new layer of linoleum on the floor, the new wallpaper, the new paint on the ceiling, and the obvious, albeit blurred line where everything fresh and new jutted into the apartment.

"This is the deal. Don't shit on the floor or piss in the bath. Or smoke in bed," the old woman half-whispered from the door in parting. "Relax. Telephone's in the kitchen. If you need anything, I'm Baba Agafia." Before Veltsev knew what was happening she'd closed the door. The key turned twice in the lock.

He took a step back and, remembering something he wanted to ask, fumbled blindly at the door. There was no handle on the inside—just a loose bolt. In the keyhole he could see a trihedral rod, exactly like the ones in passenger train locks. Veltsev went into the kitchen to call to the old woman through the window, but when he jerked back the curtain he went limp. The grated window, silently ablaze with holiday lights, looked out on the backyard and cemetery wall, which was ringed by garages. Judging from the floor plan, the window of the sole bedroom opened in the same direction. There was no real need to check this, yet Veltsev squeezed between the rug-covered bed and the bureau and peeked behind the brocade curtain. It wasn't that the view thus revealed astounded him—a big photograph of a tropical waterfall had been pasted onto a piece of plywood blocking the view—but this would probably have been the last thing he'd have expected to see behind the curtain.

Looking around, he sat down on the bed and wiggled his ass. The innards responded with the muffled crack of a spring. The room was saturated with tobacco smoke. A little toy man hung on the cord of the cheapo chandelier, which had three different-colored shades.

Unbuttoning his coat and wearily propping his elbows on his legs, he stared vacantly at the floor. In principle, it probably wasn't such a bad thing that he was locked in. He hadn't been able to take the loneliness in the first hours and days after completing his other contracts, and after resting up, he'd probably have headed out to find himself some excitement. Especially since yesterday's bloodbath on Tverskaya hadn't even been a contract but—no getting around it—an act of extreme violence by him, Arkasha Veltsev, his own idea, his own justice, and his own insanity: six corpses, two of whom were—if you don't get bogged down in details about how the scene of the crime was a nightclub closed to mere mortals—"innocent bystanders."

"This is a mouse trap. And I'm the cheese."

Mechanically, Veltsev reached for the gun in his under-

arm holster and turned to face the voice. In a partition behind the door, her legs gathered up into a shabby armchair,
sat a girl of eighteen or twenty wearing a flowered Uzbek robe
and a skullcap tilted over one ear. Her thickly painted mouth
and eyebrows made her look older. She was trying to hide her
smile, tickled she'd been able to hide her presence so simply
all this time, and she rolled an unlit cigarette in her fingers.
Veltsev dropped his arm and straightened his coat hem.

"Who are you?"

Lighting up, the girl released a stream of smoke upward.

"Lana," she answered in a tone that said she was surprised
someone might not know. "I'm telling you—a free offer."

Veltsev pulled off his cap and scratched his head. "That's
why the old woman locked the door. I didn't say that—"

"Remember the tale of Buratino?" the girl interrupted
him. "The one with the cauldron? The cauldron's over there.
Freedom's here."

"What cauldron's that?"

"What do you picture when you feel like a vacation?"

"Nothing."

"That's not true. You picture something." Squinting
dreamily, Lana pushed her skullcap forward and threw her
head back with a jutting chin. "Palm trees. The ocean. Cock-
tails down the hatch. Slut city. Happy now?" She nodded at
the window. "We're not doing so well with sluts, of course.
It's potluck, as they say. But freedom—up the wazoo. What's
your name?"

"Listen," Veltsev sighed, "I just needed a place to crash."

"Ah-hah," Lana answered vaguely. "Just crashing." Tapping
her ash into the saucer under her chair, she played with the
cigarette as if she were finishing telling herself something.

"A place to sleep," Veltsev corrected himself.

"Yesterday"—she smiled—"this old guy, you know what he asked me to do?"

"What?"

"Piss on his privates."

"And?"

"And nothing. I sprayed his balls and that was it. To each his own, as they say."

Veltsev glanced at his watch. "What else do they ask for?"

Lana scratched her sweet knee, which was poking out from under her robe, with her elbow. "Marriage!" She aimed her cigarette at him. "Haven't you heard that prostitutes make the most faithful wives?"

Veltsev lay down. The little man hanging from the chandelier bobbed in front of his face.

"I heard something else."

"What?"

"That wives are faithful prostitutes."

Lana burst out laughing. "Are you married or something?"

"No."

"A virgin?"

He ran the back of his head over the brush-stiff pile of rug. "Listen, lay off."

Lana lowered her voice: "But I am."

"What?"

"Well, a virgin."

Veltsev sighed. "Naturally."

"No, honestly!" The chair creaked under Lana. "Don't believe me? Last month I got sewn back up. I got engaged to an Uzbek, a cotton trader, while he was waiting for the train with his shipment. He fell in love, he said, over the moon. He promised me a car. Only according to our custom, he says, you have to get the bed bloody the first night. To be blunt, he gave me a hundred bucks for plastic surgery."

"So you mean you want to get back at it?" Veltsev picked at the rug with his finger.

"No, why?" Lana seemed genuinely surprised.

"What do you mean, why?" Veltsev didn't understand.

Lana didn't say anything.

"Sorry."

"Basically, my Sharfik didn't wait around for his train. My nice new fiancé got iced. They fished him out over there, from the Yauza, past the cemetery."

"I'm sorry."

"That's all right." She took a long drag. "Everyone's got their own craziness. Sharfik wanted to move his loot here because he got into some shit. But that's like jumping from a train after flies. Can you imagine? You throw away everything you have—every last thing—and get out at the first stop."

"And?" Veltsev propped himself up on one elbow.

"And, well, that's it, all done." Lana crushed her cigarette butt in the saucer, lowered her legs from the chair, went out into the front hall, and came back with a photograph, which she tossed down next to him on the bed.

In the crumpled glossy snapshot Veltsev saw a smiling Southern face with a unibrow. The photo had been taken with a flash, close-up, practically point-blank. The face had come out fuzzy, overlit; but above and behind him the little man hanging from the chandelier was etched down to the last detail. On the back of the photo, carefully, like a monogram, a capital *Ш* had been written with a felt-tip pen. Veltsev spun the photo in his fingers, tossed it aside, sat down on the edge of the bed, and ran his fist across his forehead.

"What's up with you?" Lana asked.

Slowly, not quite realizing what he was doing, he got out his wallet, opened it, and looked at its velvety layered insides.

"What's up with you?" Lana repeated, coming closer.

Veltsev put his wallet away and stared at the floor again. The photograph had reminded him of something important that he'd lost sight of and burned the pit of his stomach, but nothing more specific, so that the next instant he couldn't even say what exactly had made itself felt—a thing, a memory, a presentiment . . . ?

Lana picked up the photo, blew on it, and stuck it in the glass of the sideboard.

"Want some tea?" she asked, standing in the door. "Or maybe . . ."

Veltsev lay down again. "You do your thing there for now. Turn off the light. I have to . . . just . . ."

"Crash, I know," Lana finished for him, slapped the light switch, and shut herself up in the kitchen.

Collapsing on one elbow, Veltsev lit up and stretched out again. He held the cigarette in an outstretched hand, so the ashes would fall on the floor, and with the other fiddled with his lighter. Soon, he heard an amused muffled voice from the kitchen; Lana was talking on the phone. Veltsev tried to remember the girl's clumsily made-up face, but instead he envisioned her sweet knee poking out from her robe.

A long time ago, about three years before, he'd come across an article on the Internet which tried to prove that a man's disposition toward murder and women had their source in the same neurosis—which one exactly, Veltsev never did figure out, though he read the article twice. He was grateful to the author not for his murky verbiage but for the fact that a connection between his inclination for murder and his attraction to women had at least been given some kind of acknowledgment. That is, what he had previously considered something unique to him and had thought of as shameful, like a wet dream, had instantly stopped being either unique or unseemly. After his first contract, he languished a full day, sleepless, and then confessed at the Rozhdestvensky monastery. This act had no consequences for his soul's salvation, but it had plenty of material results. On the way back from the monastery Veltsev fell asleep at the wheel and rolled his car. His first wife was a medical student who happened to be starting her residency that day at the Sklif. More in the dorm than the Sklif ER, she got Veltsev back on his feet. The next morning it was as if he'd woken up in a new world, and just one week later—with a light heart and even, really, a sense of selfless beneficence—he shot the drunk from Tula who'd been pestering her. He and Oksana got on like a house on fire for two and a half years, and Veltsev called what he brought home as his supposed pay as a personnel inspector for a private security agency their "family income." Sex (not with any woman, of course, but with the one he considered *his*) was better than any confession at washing away his sins. When he was with *his* woman, he was restored body and soul, and he saw every embrace as the birth of a wonderful new life, a hundred times better than his own and a thousand times better than the ones he took away. For this reason he thought *Bonnie and Clyde* farfetched. Sexual attraction could not be any great help for heroes in a fight, unless they were homosexuals. And the only justification for a film like *Natural Born Killers* was that toward the end the bloodthirsty characters turned into loving parents, reborn in their children. He imagined himself and Oksana as loving parents just like that—until the Lord God started bothering her with telephone calls (on the basis of her rich ER practice probably). God always called in Veltsev's presence. He talked a lot, didn't answer questions, and before hanging up started wheezing into the receiver. "It's awful," his wife admitted guiltily. "I can hear perfectly but can't make heads or tails of it." In the six months that passed between the first call and that memorable (for Veltsev) night when the Lord decided to speak through Oksana and she was carted off with seizures to the Kanatchikovaya psych ward, she was able to get the full gist of only two divine revelations: "Everything will be jaga-jaga" and "Boys bloody in the eyes."

His second marriage, the marriage of Veltsev and Dasha, who did not love him, lasted longer, strangely enough, nearly four years, but fell apart overnight—flew apart in sprays of blood yesterday, at dawn, when, tipped off by an anonymous text message, Veltsev shot the traitor, her lover and his "employer," Mityai, both of Mityai's gorillas, Repa and Jack, and the couple sitting on the far side of the screen behind their table. Veltsev had had a bad feeling about this in the fall when he came back from a business trip to St. Petersburg. Dasha, previously willful and hot-tempered, had suddenly softened and become compliant and pleasant. The change in her behavior could have been considered a good sign had it not been simultaneously a sign of infidelity, which destroyed the only thing that tied Veltsev to his wife—the all-renewing and all-forgiving quality of their intimacy. It was amazing, but up until yesterday's disaster he had laid the blame for the fact that he had ceased to perceive Dasha as *his* woman not on her but on himself, and had even contemplated, cravenly, divorce. More than twenty-four hours had passed since the slaughter at the club, and he still couldn't shake the feeling that he'd started to breathe an empty air that was ripping him up inside, like a deepwater fish tossed on shore.

"Don't hide. I can see you," he sighed, crushing out his butt on the windowsill. "Come on out."

The kitchen door, which had been opened just a crack so she could peek through, was flung open, and Lana walked right up to Veltsev. She wasn't wearing the skullcap anymore and the clown makeup had been wiped clean, and in the thick shadow between the freely swinging sides of her untied robe he saw white, not of her clinging panties but her naked body. Slipping his hand under the robe, Veltsev felt her warm skin, which his touch covered in goose bumps. Lana leaned into him.

"Have you decided to tempt me?" Veltsev asked.

"I misled you," she said.

"About what?"

"I . . . well, I'm not, I didn't have plastic surgery."

"So?"

Her belly tensed under his fingers. "You won't laugh?"

Veltsev coughed thoughtfully. "Wait . . . You, that is, you mean you really are a virgin?"

Lana covered his hand with hers.

"Would you like to check?"

He didn't say anything but neither did he take his hand away. Lana froze and stared at him, as if waiting for him to blink. Veltsev held her gaze, but the second the girl touched his zipper, he grabbed her wrist. Lana's arm was so thin and frail he figured he was hurting her, though she didn't think to stop him, let alone take offense. So, with one hand, she opened his fly, jerked his pants down over his hips, pulled down his underpants, took his prick, and stroked it, spellbound. For a minute, maybe more, they didn't move, coalesced in a silent scene. Lana studied and fingered his quickly swelling manhood, and Veltsev, not thinking anything, kept holding her arm. Then she climbed on the bed and kneeled so that she was squeezing him between her thighs. The movements of her fingers, up until now cautious and even fearful, became brusquer by increments. Carried away, she began entertaining herself with the sensitivity of his flesh, as if it were a toy, and didn't seem to notice when she scratched the tip with her nail. Gasping from pain, Veltsev crushed her small breast. "Now you . . ." she said, and let him go. Squeezing the burning spot with one hand, Veltsev caressed Lana with the other—just to distract her. "Not like that," she sighed with annoyance. She hopped down and went to the sideboard and started digging around. Taking advantage of the break, Veltsev took his gun out of his holster, put it into his coat pocket, and slipped out of his heavy shirt. Lana came back with a jar of a fragrant ointment and mounted him again. With the cordiality of a hostess, generously, she rubbed it on his prick, as if it were a sandwich, guided it between her legs, and peered at Veltsev. He lingered a moment and didn't press hard. Lana shrugged off her robe and tossed it aside. Seeing she was hurt and scared, Veltsev kept pressing—not leaning into her but pulling her toward him by the hips—softly, slowly, with the feeling that something awful was about to happen. But it didn't, and Lana made no sound. It took a moment for Veltsev to realize he was completely inside her. Lana lifted and dropped back down, tilting her pelvis, either bracing herself or getting used to the pain, after which she renewed her cautious vertical movements. She came three times with convulsive shudders; each time Veltsev thought that was the end of it, but then Lana would start moving again.

At last she dug both hands into Veltsev, grabbed a fistful of undershirt and skin on his chest, and, as if making up for something she'd missed, began moving erratically, speeding up with each thrust, so powerfully and boldly the glass in the sideboard started rattling and dust rose from the rug. Holding her by the waist, Veltsev looked stupidly at her swinging breasts, the tips of her braids sticking to her clavicles, and her flushed face. The little man hanging from the chandelier was revolving slowly over her head. Gasping, Lana would grab Veltsev's shoulders and then, as if trying to get away from him, retreat a little. To each of her exhales, which coincided with a dull, squelching thrust to his groin, a moan was now added, and she nearly broke into sobs. Veltsev felt like he was starting to suffocate, like a shivering heat was rising from his knees to his belly. Under the rug the bedsprings sang and creaked, and the metallic scream for some reason made him think of the couple who took the bullets in the club. "Damn, damn, damn," he started intoning in time with Lana's furious galloping, and he tried to move too, as much as he could. They came almost simultaneously: Veltsev with a quiet moan, crushing her hips; Lana absolutely silently, shuddering finely and collapsing on him facedown, as if she'd been shot.

After catching his breath he kissed her burning temple, moved her closer to the head of the bed, grabbed his crumpled coat, and locked himself in the bathroom. His bruised groin was copiously stained with blood and gave off the stunning aroma of a blooming flowerbed. The instant Veltsev approached the mirror it fogged up. He leaned his forehead against the foggy glass. Somewhere in the wall, a water pipe was rattling. There was a child's toothbrush in the drinking glass on the shelf under the mirror. Veltsev glanced at his watch but stopped being able to see it before he could figure out what time it was. Like his opened wallet, the dial seemed to offer itself as a reminder of something important and forgotten. He ran his hand hard across his head, looked up and from side to side, and couldn't remember anything. Thinking he might yet find some hint, he rummaged through his coat pockets, took out his gun, ejected the magazine into his hand, and put it back in the grip. That after yesterday there were just three cartridges left, he already knew. "Bang bang," he said to his emerging reflection, set the Beretta where he could easily reach it from the bathtub, and crawled into the shower.

Lana maybe? it occurred to him as he was soaping up his groin.

Standing stock-still, he looked up at the ceiling again, shrugged, and kept washing. Whether or not Lana was *his* woman he couldn't yet say, of course. Just as he couldn't say whether she'd been a virgin. On the other hand, as soon as he had washed off her blood, he realized something he hadn't been able to put in words before: in his preferences he was guided less by the obvious pluses of his partners' youth—if they couldn't be his daughters, they were still a lot younger than he was—than by the fact that their age gave him—childless in deference to his profession—the illusion of a full-fledged family. His women were also his children. Not daring to acquire any real descendants, he acquired them in his imagination, which lent their bodily intimacy the characteristics of both conception and birth. His woman was like an improved Eve, not simply a resident but the guardian of paradise, holding the forbidden fruit in one hand and in the other the serpent tempter—by the throat.

Veltsev moved his head out from under the shower stream and listened: through the wall he heard a rumbling, first soft, then louder. He'd been hearing this rumbling for a while and hadn't paid it any mind, thinking it was the pipe rattling, but once he turned off the water he realized the din was coming from the apartment and it was a fight, not the plumbing. Muffled blows and shuffling were interspersed with Lana's cries and a man's voice choking from fury. While Veltsev was drying off and putting his clothes back on, the point of the tussle became clear to him in general outline. The man, who spoke with a strong Asian accent, was demanding information from Lana about Sharfik (doubtless the smiling guy in the photograph) and about some major debt. "If he doesn't come up with it, I'm coming for him!" the man yelled hoarsely. "He's a dead man! Understand? A dead man! And that guy in the bathroom—does he know? Ask him."

"Idiot!" Lana replied, sobbing. "That's the renter. I told you."

Dressed now, Veltsev attached the silencer to his Beretta, slipped a cartridge into its chamber, carefully, held his thumb down on the safety, touched the trigger, stuck the gun in his holster, flung the door open, and came out of the bathroom.

Lana, wrapped in her robe, was sitting on the bed holding her broken nose. Not only her face but her arms above her wrists and her neck as well were splattered with blood. The imprint of a slap burned on her cheek. Opposite her, his arms akimbo and legs spread, stood her attacker, a strapping, athletically built Uzbek wearing a sheepskin coat sprinkled with melting snow and a large Kalmyk fur cap, earflaps down. A small scar crossed the uninvited guest's mouth on a slant from nose to chin, beads dangled from his fist, and the merest edge of his knife's carved hilt stuck out of his fur-trimmed right boot top. *Birds of a feather*, Veltsev thought. Then: *Who the hell let this guy in?*

"Who are you?" the Uzbek breathed out at Veltsev, turning toward him slowly, as if he were going to kick him.

Veltsev peered at a very still Lana.

"Go get washed, please," he told her.

She rose silently; splashing him with the scent of her floral cream, she proceeded to the bathroom. The bolt clicked in the door. Veltsev collected the photograph from the sideboard glass and held it out to the Uzbek.

"I'm here because of him too."

"What?" The Uzbek grabbed the snapshot and stared at it vacantly, as if it were blank. "Because of what?"

"I know where the money is," Veltsev explained. "You came for the money, right? So did I. Let's go."

The Uzbek threw the photograph at his feet and swung his beads. "Where?"

Veltsev backed up and glanced into the front hall: a key with electrical tape wrapped around the handle was jutting out of the keyhole. "To get the money. I'm telling you. It's close by."

The area around the front of the house was spectral, tinted by the light from the windows. Big fat snowflakes were falling from the sky. The trees, the cars, the garages—everything with the exception of the Land Cruiser blocking the alley—was covered in a layer of white. The newly fallen snow creaked underfoot. Veltsev lit up, peered around as he was walking, and nodded at the Uzbek waiting in the lobby. Passing down the ravine between the cemetery fences and the business center, they descended to the Yauza. Not wide, ten meters or so, the channel appeared narrower than it actually was because of the ice frozen along its banks. Veltsev touched the thin crust with his boot tip, as if he were searching for something, took a few steps up and downstream. Saying not a word, the Uzbek shone the flashlight for him. "Here," Veltsev said at last, pointing at random at the black water. "Only we need something to retrieve it with." The Uzbek had come closer to the water too, and was regarding it warily. He was holding the light in his left hand, and the end of his knife hilt peeked out of his closed right hand. "We need something to retrieve it with," Veltsev repeated, and walked over to the reeds on the riverbank. Pulling his gun out of the holster, he took a quick look around. Not far away, on the river, outside the circle of light, he heard the quacking of ducks, and down the opposite bank fireworks were chirring and exploding.

In the air, thick with snow, the shot clanged softly, as if getting stuck in it. The bullet hit the Uzbek at the very base of his neck, knocking out of his cap a puff of what was either steam or dust. The Uzbek dropped the flashlight, sat down briefly, and fell face-first into the water. After rifling the dead man's pockets, Veltsev took his car keys and shoved the body with his feet farther into the water, where the current would quickly bear him away. The earflaps of his fur cap, which was still smoking from the shot, floated in the water. A double ribbon of blood danced on the bottom in the flashlight's tiny glow.

The snowfall had been heavy enough that Veltsev didn't find his own tracks on the way back. On the other hand, he did find a handprint on the driver's door of the SUV, which was parked in the middle of the road. "Asshole." Veltsev made quick work of searching the hash- and sheepskin-impregnated glove compartment, drove the car to the cemetery gate, and abandoned it there on the shoulder of the road. On the way the car phone rang twice, and both times he could barely restrain himself from answering with some graveyard humor.

When Lana found out what had happened, she clutched her head with both hands, dropped into the armchair feet first, and said, "That's it. I'm a dead man too. "

"Why's that?" Veltsev asked.

"He'd been on the phone arranging . . . a meet-up with his pals near the front door."

"A meet-up—for when?"

Lana looked at the cuckoo clock. "Eleven-thirty. In an hour, I guess." Still holding her head she turned toward Veltsev. "Listen, couldn't you have asked me what was going on? Before you—"

"Do you have the 300,000 he was talking about?" Veltsev interrupted her.

"Where would I get that?" Lana's eyebrows shot up. "I've got five hundred rubles till Wednesday."

"And this Sharfik of yours—do you know where he is?"

"I told you where."

Veltsev pulled his sleeve back over his watch. "In that case, calm down. They didn't come for the money today."

Lana dropped her arms. "What did they come for?"

"You."

"Why?"

"He was going to have himself a horror flick. Do you have somewhere to go?"

"No."

"I can put you up in a hotel for a little while."

"I can't."

"Why not?"

"I don't have my passport."

"Why not?"

"Baba Agafia has it."

"So?"

"So she won't give it back."

Veltsev wiped his face, which was still wet from snow. "Damn. I can't stay here long."

Lana sniffed her swollen nose. "I'm not keeping you."

Grinning, he gave her a close, appraising look. "That's not likely to win you a star for heroism."

Hugging her knees, Lana looked blindly ahead and fiddled with her toes. "Fine with me. We've got a whole cemetery full of heroes right here."

Veltsev took the magazine out of the gun, brought it up to his eyes like a thermometer, and jammed the weapon back in the holster. "I'm asking you for the last time. Will you come with me?"

She didn't answer, in fact she seemed to have stopped hearing him altogether. Veltsev took his wet cap off the shelf in the front hall, replaced it with three thousand-ruble bills, took one more look at Lana, and pushed the door open with his fist.

It was snowing a little less, but the wind had picked up. In the courtyard the wind beat only at the treetops, but as soon as Veltsev came out in the open it took his breath away. He was walking back to the subway, heading toward Menzhinsky Street, following the same route he'd taken an hour and ten minutes before—down the shoulder of the road between river and cemetery. "Pigheaded fool," he said aloud through clenched teeth, squinting at the cutting snow. He raged less at Lana than at himself for imagining god knows what about her. Waiting for the Uzbek's buddies to show up was sure suicide, and Veltsev had no idea where to get ahold of more rounds now. He'd cut off access to his home arsenal yesterday, and there was too much risk involved in going to his old suppliers. There was still one other Mityai gunman left, of course, Kirila the Kalmyk. Veltsev had beaten off a band of skinheads for him the year before last and ever since had been practically a second father to him. After what happened yesterday, however, when Kirila was left completely out of the loop, even his filial feelings might have changed; furthermore, contacting him now presented a purely technical problem. Veltsev had smashed the SIM card from his own telephone and thrown it out the day before as he left the club, and a call from Lana's apartment could easily be traced. After taking a few shaky steps, Veltsev stood up and brushed the snow from his eyelashes. The thought of the phone in the Uzbek's Land Cruiser came to him the second before he noticed the SUV there in front of him, right where he'd abandoned it.

Kirila the Kalmyk answered the moment the call went through.

"Yeah."

"Got the number?" Veltsev said instead of a greeting.

"Yeah," Kirila replied after a slight hesitation.

"Call back from a pay phone. Only not from your building or wherever you are." Veltsev hung up, started the engine, adjusted the rearview mirror with a finger, and examined himself carefully. *Weirdo psycho.*

A transparent sticker with Arabic lettering bubbled up in the corner of the mirror. Veltsev was about to scratch it off when the phone rang. He picked up.

"Hello."

The acute, spacious silence of the ether pulsed in the receiver. Veltsev called the incoming number—they were calling from a cell phone. Calling the Uzbek, that is.

"Hell on the line," Veltsev said and he waited a little, ended the call, and looked in the mirror again. "Warm already."

When Kirila called, his voice was cracking from strain. "Everyone got blown away. What were you thinking? The committee's mopping up both the crooks and the cops. You know who Mityai was working for. They've got three mil on you."

"Already know how you'll spend it?" Veltsev asked.

Kirila said nothing, breathing loudly through his nose.

"Sorry," Veltsev sighed. "Here's what's up. I need a couple of clips for my Beretta—bad. Forty minutes tops. Bring them?"

"Where?"

"Babushkinskaya. When you turn off Menzhinsky onto Olonetsky, there's this business center. Right behind the cemetery. Can you make it?"

"I'll try."

Veltsev tossed the phone on the seat, turned the wheel from side to side, and, without putting the vehicle in gear, hit the pedal a few times, so abruptly and hard that the heavy vehicle rocked.

Half an hour later, Kirila's Cayenne, plastered with snow, rolled into the vacant parking lot in front of the business center fence. Veltsev, who had left the Land Cruiser in back of the apartment building, was waiting behind the trees between the road and the river. Once he was convinced that Kirila had come alone and hadn't brought a tail, he got in the car with him. The smell of alcohol struck him immediately.

"Batya"—the Kalmyk called him "Father" even though he was just ten years younger—"I respect you!" The man broke out in a smile, holding out his right hand to Veltsev and three full magazines in his left.

Veltsev shook the fighter's rock-hard hand, took the magazines, and reloaded his gun. "What do you respect me for, Kila-Kirila?"

"Oh, just in general." Kalmyk shook his shoulders. "If Mityai had done the same to me, with my Svetka . . . I don't know. I wouldn't have had the nerve. Maybe if I was high."

Veltsev holstered his gun, distributed the extra magazines in his pockets, straightened his clothes, and stared into Kirila's eyes. "Well, how's it going? Many gunning for the three mil?"

"I don't know." Kirila sobered up instantly. "I haven't seen anybody today. Everyone's crazy angry, of course—at you and at Mityai. The committee's after him for treason. You know all about it."

"Right." Veltsev glanced at his watch and reached for the door. "Gotta go."

"Listen!" Kalmyk barked. "Maybe I should come along."

"No, Kila." Veltsev jumped down into the snow. "You've helped enough as it is." Slamming the door, he headed for the alley behind the parking lot.

"Well, I'll hang out here another five minutes anyway!" Kirila shouted after him.

Veltsev waved him off in silence.

The storm was picking up. Snow was eddying in the lane and from time to time the wind gusted so hard it made his ears ring. A few meters before the corner, between the rear and front façades of the apartment building, Veltsev heard a woman's anguished cries coming from the courtyard. He could make out the blue glow of a flashing light. His gun at the ready, Veltsev peeked around the wall. Where the Uzbek's Land Cruiser had recently been parked, Mityai's empty Geländewagen sat idling in exhaust. The flashing light was poking up off the top of the armored car's roof. Next to the car, on the narrow patch of ground between the alley and the door of the scorched lobby, Baba Agafia was trying to beat off Kostik, Mityai's chief bodyguard, who was attempting to strong-arm her. "I'm not letting you in! I'm not letting you the hell in! Get out! Get out!" Baba Agafia rasped as if it were her last breath, and she tried to hit Kostik, windmilling like a swimmer. Mishanya Ryazanets was marking time behind Kostik. A little farther off, in a side alley, wiping his frozen mustache with his wrist, a thug Veltsev didn't know wearing a cashmere coat and a tall fur cap was pacing back and forth, a lit cigarette in one hand and a walkie-talkie crackling in the other. Veltsev stepped back behind the corner and pressed himself to the wall.

Thank you so much, Kila-Kirila.

He had to make a decision, but before he could think of anything he saw Double Dima—the identical twin of Jack, who had died yesterday with Mityai—coming around the opposite corner of the building, from around back. Cursing, Dima was zipping his fly as he walked and stamping his feet from the cold. A walkie-talkie antenna was poking out of the pocket of his sport coat, and his legs were caked with snow up to the knees. Veltsev ran toward him with his gun in his outstretched arm, so that by the time Dima finished with his fly and looked up, his forehead nearly ran into the Beretta's silencer.

"Back," Veltsev commanded, advancing. "Nice and easy."

Dima, dumbstruck, started backing up submissively. Around the corner, in the front garden, Veltsev made him kneel in the snow and noticed a line of tracks near the wall.

"Have you been peeking in windows, you bad boy?"

Dima vaguely waved his raised hands. His bulletproof vest bulged out between the lapels of his open jacket.

"Give me the walkie-talkie," Veltsev said.

Dima fumbled in his pocket and handed it over.

"Easy," Veltsev said, "nice and easy. Tell them you see me and can take me out through the window. Repeat it."

"I can see . . . him through the window, I can take him out."

"Do it."

Dima spoke the words into the walkie-talkie, and as soon as he heard the reply—"One sec, we're there"—Veltsev shot him right between the eyes. Shuddering as if gripped by a powerful chill, Dima collapsed onto his side and stretched out his legs. The snow under his head sank quickly and turned dark. Riveted by the sight of blood, Veltsev recalled how he'd shot Jack yesterday the same way, in the head; he spat and made a cross over his numb chest. Double Jack, who you could only distinguish from his brother by the mole over his eyebrow, was lying in front of him. Dima had been guarding Mityai yesterday. "If he twitches, whack him, don't wait," cooed the walkie-talkie, which had fallen into the snow. Veltsev picked it up and was about to say something but turned it off instead and dropped it by the body. Kneading his numb fingers, he stole a glance around the corner. First to appear on the path along the rear wall was Kostik, followed by Mishanya wielding his gun, and then the guy in the cashmere coat, hanging back like a coward. "Bang bang bang," Veltsev whispered.

They dropped, one after the other, no sound, just like that, all three, like a row of dominoes. Kostik and Mishanya died before they hit the ground—the former got a bullet in the eye and the latter bcv fb's nose was obliterated—but the thug in the coat, after he crashed forward, suddenly answered fire. Stumbling, Veltsev dropped back around the corner. He tried to count the shots, but immediately realized that was impossible. He probably wasn't firing an ordinary silenced piece but a gun with noiseless ammo, which meant you could only distinguish a shot after the bullets had ricocheted off something. Regardless, there was no time to waste. The thug could call in reinforcements over his walkie-talkie at any second. Veltsev caught his breath, emerged from his cover again, and, moving along the wall, started shooting at the mustached man's twitching back. He held the trigger down until he'd emptied what was left in his magazine, all eleven cartridges.

Even though his face had blossomed like an onion and was smoking like a pot, the thug nonetheless kept squeezing his gun, which had its safety engaged. Propping one elbow on the ground, he aimed up at someone in front of him. When his arm dropped, sapped, Veltsev picked the gun up delicately with two fingers.

It was a silent, six-round Vul, a special make for special agents like this. Before this Veltsev had only seen one in pictures. You couldn't get the gun or ammo for it on the black market for any amount of money. Now, after firing, the open chamber didn't even smell of powder. Actually, examining his trophy, Veltsev wasn't thinking about its unique characteristics anymore but about how he no longer needed to search the dead man for documents because his identity was obvious. An agent of the special services—whether GRU or FSB was irrelevant—had just given up the ghost.

After dragging the bodies around the corner and stacking them next to Double Jack, he drove the Geländewagen on, into the rear yard, and parked it next to the Land Cruiser. The blizzard was not abating. Veltsev tried to warm himself for a couple of minutes behind the wheel. Even though he was soaked with sweat from dealing with the bodies, he was still chilled to the bone. "We're rolling, rolling, rolling," he intoned, holding his palms over the humming heating vents. He stared at the thug's loaded gun in front of him.

The Uzbek's gang showed up at Lana's entrance like clockwork, at exactly 11:30. Three men came out of their SUV, which differed from the Land Cruiser parked out back only by its license number. Veltsev was waiting for them to go through the door, but after conferencing at the lobby threshold, the trio returned to the car. Veltsev blinked away his frost-induced tears. There was a weak crimson glow spreading behind the Land Cruiser—probably from the taillights, but broad enough that it lit up the whole section of the apartment building spread out behind the car, as well as the buildings in the rear of the courtyard, about 150 meters away.

When it became clear to him that the SUV was headed down the track blazed by the Geländewagen around the building, the Land Cruiser had already driven into the rear courtyard, rocking over the potholes. Veltsev removed his gun from its holster. "Rolling, rolling, rolling . . ."

After hurrying to the abandoned cars, the trio moved around them in single file, and then—obviously following Veltsev's tracks—came upon the bodies heaped in the front garden. Veltsev, whose teeth were now chattering from the cold, leaned his shoulder into the edge of the back wall. The blizzard was seething all around, but a silence fell over the front garden such that when mustache guy's walkie-talkie started talking in the snowdrift behind it—"Five, where'd you go? Over"—Veltsev nearly pulled the trigger. Disjointedly, reluctantly almost, the trio turned toward the sound. Seeing their vacant young faces animated by death, he shot them calmly and methodically, like targets at a shooting range. Only the gunman at the far right had time to throw up his arm before falling onto the powdered bodies. "Five, are you asleep?" he heard behind him.

Veltsev rested his hands on his straight legs as he bent over. He was struck by a chill. "I think that's enough for today," he muttered, glancing at the front garden. The trio's car was parked with the engine running and its bulk lit up, and once again he caught a glimpse of a reddish glow behind the SUV, only now its source definitely wasn't the taillights but something beyond the cemetery fence. The trees and flying snow on that side were tinted by a hazy crimson. Puzzled, he walked over to the Land Cruiser, opened the door, and looked inside. Nothing special. The same smell as in the Uzbek's car, half sheepskin, half hash. A sticker with Arab lettering on the rearview mirror. A phone. A cigarette burn on the driver's seat. Veltsev was about to slam the door shut, but he froze when he noticed a fresh drop of blood next to the melted hole in the seat. Stepping back, he peered down at his feet and saw something tiny break off into the snow from the Beretta's silencer. He raised the weapon in front of him: the left side of the gun, and the tips of his right fingers as well, had obviously been dragged through blood. Frosted oily traces had caked across his coat's lower lapel. On the upper lapel, to the side of the lower button loop, gaped a small hole. Veltsev opened his coat. The silk lining on the left side, some of his sweater below his chest, the edge of the holster that touched his shirt, and his pants down to the knees—all of it was wet and steaming with blood. The bullet had penetrated his waistband and entered his belly above his pelvis, a little lower and to the left of his navel; judging from the fact that his waist was still dry, it had landed in his abdominal cavity. "The Vul," Veltsev whispered, and then closed his coat. "Nice and easy . . ."

He used the sterile wipes from the car's first aid kit to plug the wound, but he didn't try to treat it with iodine for fear of passing out from the pain. He chewed a few painkillers and tried to calculate how much time had passed since he'd taken the bullet; in any event he was sure to go into shock soon and wasn't going to last long on the capsule he'd just swallowed. He thought a moment and then dialed the Kalmyk's number.

"Hello!" Kirila shouted, turning down his loud music.

"Where are you?" Veltsev asked.

The music stopped. "Still here. Why?"

"Do you have Promedol with you?"

"As usual. Why?"

"Wait. I'll be right there. "

If you're not a fool, Veltsev thought as he made his way through the deep snow to the alley, *you'll drive away. Or shoot first. If you* are *a fool . . . Actually, the human heart is always a mystery. Everyone saves himself in his own way.*

The Cayenne was parked in the same place by the business center fence. Using his gun to press the plug to his wound, Veltsev climbed into the backseat. Kirila half-turned and looked silently at his bloody clothes. When Veltsev held out his hand between the seats, Kirila quickly opened the army first aid kit in front of him.

Removing the cap with his teeth, Veltsev jabbed a needle into his belly through his pants, slowly pressed on the plunger, and spat the cap on the floor.

"Where'd you get that?" Kirila asked.

Panting, Veltsev set the empty syringe aside. "It's nothing. I'll live to see my wedding day."

"The butcher's going to weep over you." Half-rising, Kirila picked up the syringe and put it back in the kit. The handle of a Walther flashed between the lapels of his jacket. "Let's go, eh?"

"Not just yet." Veltsev shook his head. "I have something else . . . I thought you wanted to help."

"Yeah." Kirila straightened up. "Sure. What?"

"I shot a guy here on the Yauza. I have to go clean it up. Will you help?"

"Let's go, Batya. You should've said so first."

"Godspeed then." Veltsev nodded.

The current had not taken the Uzbek's body far at all, a couple of meters, to a bend in the river where it must have caught on an underwater snag. Whistling, the Kalmyk stood on the bank and tested the ice with the tips of his boots. Veltsev pressed the plug over his coat with his left hand and cautiously freed his gun.

"We need something to retrieve him with," Kirila said without turning around.

"No we don't," Veltsev answered, firing twice.

The bullets struck the Kalmyk with a *boff* right below the shoulder blade. Shaking his sloping, bearlike shoulders as if chilled, and shifting from one foot to the other, Kirila calmly peered back at Veltsev, lowered himself without hurrying, reached toward the water, and then just as smoothly lay down in it head first, as if it were a bed. Through all this the water didn't so much as splash. "The butcher did cry," Veltsev said, breathing heavily, and then he spat. "Three hundred thousand cried."

Scooting behind the wheel of the Cayenne, he changed the sodden towels on his groin, wiped his fingers, and, looking at the dirty gun lying between the seats, remembered who he could go to for help. All his old working options connected with Mityai were obviously out. That left only two: head to the Sklif, or to the guy who was kicked out of the Sklif for drugs—Oksana's classmate—who lived on Trubnaya. *Let's try the last first*, Veltsev decided, and he started the engine. *Trubnaya.*

On the ice-packed road, the powerful SUV swerved from shoulder to shoulder; right in front of the exit onto Menzhinsky it took a turn that swung him around onto the median. Veltsev lifted his hand over the wheel and a tremendous shudder ran through it. His belly and left hip were numb, and a fever was rising from his groin to his chest that made his head swim. Veltsev tapped the SUV's wheel with his nail. "Okay. Correction . . ."

Driving up to the apartment building at a snail's pace, at the last minute he confused the gas pedal and brakes and slammed into the Geländewagen's rear fender. Halfway between the front garden and the piled up cars, at the end of a bloodied rut, lay one of the trio's gunmen, facedown. Veltsev had to step over him. He ran right into Lana by the lobby door. Gasping from fright, she backed off with her key extended like a weapon. Veltsev reached out his trembling open palm to her.

"It's me."

In the apartment she carefully sat him down on the bed, squatted next to him, peeked under his coat, buried her head in the sleeve of her pea coat, and started crying bitterly. "God, I . . . you . . . me . . ."

"I'm asking you for the last time," Veltsev said, smiling in pain, "will you go away with me?" He freed his gun from under his coat and set it on the rug. "Or rather, will you drive?"

Lana looked at him skeptically. "Where? In what?"

"To see Dr. Doolittle. Can you drive?"

"Listen . . ." Swallowing her tears, she hugged him below the knees and gave him a gentle shake. "A medic lives right here in the next courtyard. He did an abortion at our house for Baba Agafia's niece. Should we go see him?"

"Are you serious?" Veltsev frowned.

"Wait." Jumping lightly to her feet, Lana kissed him on the lips and hurried into the kitchen, where Veltsev immediately heard the clicking of telephone buttons.

He took out his lighter and flicked it idly. Lana hung up with a clatter, came back, and sat down by him again.

"No answer." Worried, she blew hard on the fist she'd brought to her mouth. "Let's do this then. I'll run over to his place, and if he's home I'll set it all up. If he's not, we'll go see your Doolittle. Can you hold on for a couple of minutes?"

Veltsev kept flicking the lighter and watching her silently. He heard but wasn't listening to her. He was listening to himself, to the sensation that for some reason felt like a memory: right now he wanted to be with her more than any other women he'd ever been with. It seemed strange and at the same time simple, like the strawberry flavor of her lipstick.

She was saying something else, then she kissed him again, turned off the light, and ran into the front hall.

"Where are you going?" he asked with difficulty.

Lana spun around and turned the key over in her fist. "I told you."

"Wait." Veltsev tried to stand. "I'll tag along."

"Right," she hedged, opening the door. "And if you check out, should I call an EMT? Or a hearse? Wait." The door banged shut behind her and the lock clicked twice.

Veltsev lit up, leaned back on his elbows, put a cushion under his head, and lay down across the full length of the bed. The little man hanging from the chandelier swung in the smoke streams.

He woke himself up coughing.

A cobweb danced on the ceiling. Smoke from burning wool ate into his eyes and singed his throat. The cigarette had fallen from his fingers and set the rug pile on fire. Rubbing out the smoldering fibers with his sleeve, Veltsev glanced at his watch and shook his wrist, perplexed. He'd slept more than fifteen minutes. The plug had pulled away from the wound so that blood was seeping through not only his sweater but also the rug under his spread-out coat. Veltsev rose cautiously from the bed.

"Lana," he called.

The reply was a ringing, rugged silence. Thinking his ears

might be stopped up, he opened and closed his mouth. The floor rose and fell under his feet in big even waves. Propping himself up on the wall with one hand, Veltsev made his way out into the front hall. The door was still locked. He looked through the peephole, tugged at the bolt, opened and closed his mouth again, and listened. Somewhere far away, almost out of hearing range, in that rugged silence, he heard the gasping siren of an ambulance or the police. Suddenly the phone rang in the kitchen. Veltsev pushed away from the door but stopped half a step away. There was no second ring; the rugged silence had swallowed that up too.

He returned to the room and was about to lie down when the phone started wailing again, and again broke off after the first ring. Veltsev smeared the wallpaper with his blood as he hobbled to the kitchen. He could barely feel anything between his chest and knees, and it seemed like his legs were moving independently of his body, first lagging behind, then rushing ahead, which made it quite a trick to maintain his balance. The light was off in the kitchen, but the small room was illuminated by garlands of colored lights framing the window on the inside. The red light on the old telephone, below the dial, was shining. Sitting at the table, Veltsev picked up the receiver, brought it to his right ear, and held it with his shoulder. His left hand, stretching toward the dial, rested on the table. In the receiver he heard the nervous voices of Lana and Baba Agafia interrupting each other—the telephone was on an extension.

". . . when I saw him I nearly pissed myself," Lana rattled on, short of breath. "I thought, that's it, he's going to shoot me. My Phuket's fucked. Can you imagine?"

"Oh, and about that card of his," Baba Agafia chimed in, barely listening to her. "It fell out of his passport, but he didn't notice. After I locked you in I found it in the snow, and when I got home I couldn't believe it. Why go to a hotel, I thought, if you have a residency permit, and then, if you've already paid for the hotel, come all the way out here? Well, I'm no fool, so I went and turned on the television. And there—saints alive!—I saw his photograph and his name. And a number to call." Baba Agafia sneezed loudly, with a chesty wheeze. "I nearly died."

"And nice Farid, when he came over"—Lana spouted laughter—"after I called you I gave him a buzz right away and figured out about Sharfik's debt . . . He was in the bathroom then . . . so I let that little fool Farid know"—she whispered wickedly—"and an hour and a half later he and Sharfik shoot it out."

"You could have done it earlier, dummy," Baba Agafia said reproachfully. "He and those downtown characters nearly fell into each others arms out there. Where are your brains?"

"Well, you shouldn't have told such a massive lie then," Lana snarled.

"Well, who knew they'd show up so fast, and in this blizzard?"

"Well, you just shouldn't have. This guy wasn't going anywhere."

"How do you know?"

"Because he fell for me, that's how. I don't know why. But I can always sense what these lechers are up to. More than likely—it's not all that complicated—it was my latest sew-up. Even I didn't expect that this time. There was even a little blood." Lana paused. "Yeah, by the way, what did you tell them, the ones who came in the Mercedes?"

"Oh, I don't know." Baba Agafia sniffed. "They didn't just not have three hundred thousand, they didn't have a kopek. I said I wouldn't let them in. Over my dead body. Well, I could see they realized they were barking up the wrong tree. They walked away, whispered their secrets, and drove off. And now, just before you, they called again. They said they'd be right over. With the money. What about yours?"

"Who?"

"Oh, little Farid's mujahideen."

"That's why I'm calling. This guy fixed everything, looks like, finished them off. Amazing."

"How do you know?"

"None of their cells answer."

"That means you're free. And you have the money. You got away from me and little Farid." Baba Agafia cackled, tickled. "Where are you hightailing it to?"

"Thailand, like I told you. Tomorrow there'll be last-minute tickets on sale at this office I know. We think we can pull it off. Hey, dead man," Lana said away from the phone, "what do you think, are we going to get those tickets?" Baba Agafia could hear a muffled male voice. "The dead man says we are."

"All right, then," Baba Agafia sighed. "You and I have talked too long. They might still call and the phone will be busy. Are you sure you locked that guy in?"

"You want me to go over and check to see if he's already broken out?"

"Oh, I'm just afraid of him, the murderer. That look of his . . . makes my skin crawl."

"Don't be afraid," Lana chuckled. "He's the one whose soul is hanging by a thread. If he has one, of course."

"Listen"—Baba Agafia's voice dropped to a whisper—"what if he's listening on the extension right now? Ugh, I didn't think of that."

"Not likely." Lana chuckled again. "That's the least of his problems. And even if he *is* listening . . . Hello," she said in lower voice. "Hell on the line. I've got your number. God will call when—"

"Curse that tongue of yours, fool!" Baba Agafia shot back. "Fear God, you shameless girl!" There was a staccato chattering, after which short beeps started leaping in the ether.

As if expecting to hear something more, Veltsev held the receiver to his ear for a while longer, and then, sitting up straight, he lowered it carefully on the hook.

Rattling the chair, which he pushed in front of him like a walker, he headed over to the still smoking bed, took his passport out of his pocket, leafed through it, shook it out upside down, and tossed it aside. The rug seemed to be tilting to the left with the whole bed. *It's going to break where it's weak*, he thought, remembering how yesterday at the registration desk he'd slipped his hotel card between the pages of his passport and how today he'd searched for it in his wallet without knowing what he was looking for. A hot sea seemed to be overflowing its shores inside him. Smiling distractedly, like someone dangling his last cigarette in his fingers, he pictured Lana's tear-stained face as she sat in front of him, and wondered at this image, at how it already existed on its own, as if it were something outside of him, which meant that the laughing voice he'd just heard in the ether no longer belonged to him. The cuckoo clock on the wall shuddered. A moment later, its chilled steel struck half past 12. The bird's door didn't open, it just shook; however, behind the toy mechanism Veltsev heard heavenly thunder. Someone was fiddling with the lock in the front door very carefully. Without looking he picked up his gun, cocked the trigger, and chuckled at the little man on the string: no one had called.

PART II

DEAD SOULS

PART II

FIELD OF A THOUSAND CORPSES

BY ALEXANDER ANUCHKIN
Elk Island

Translated by Marian Schwartz

Bogorodskoe Municipality,
Eastern Administrative District, 1996

When Nikolai Petrovich Voronov is sitting there like that and looking like that, expect trouble. Actually, if he's looking some other way, you should still expect it. Nikolai Petrovich and trouble are twin brothers. Behind his back they call him Banderas, after the Spanish actor who conquered the world with his incredible muscularity and crazy machismo. When you look at the Hollywood Banderas, you can't believe he actually exists. No one's really like that. At least, that's what they say. Me, I haven't been to the movies for a long time. It's expensive and pointless. Especially since a real homegrown Banderas is directly in front of me right now and I'm sitting here looking at him.

I realize that meeting a man like this on one's life journey is tremendous good fortune. Don't think I've got some alternative orientation or I don't like women. God forbid. It's just that Nikolai Petrovich is truly magnificent.

He's forty or so, his hair's the color of a crow's wing (as they write in books), he combs it with a side part, but it's too long. He's been on duty for more than twenty-four hours but he's wearing a snow-white shirt without a single wrinkle in it, and his collar, my god, his collar.

He has piercing eyes. Right now, as I write this, I can come up with only one comparison: a movie about sin city. The movies again, damnit, but that's how it goes. Agent Voronov is top dog in the district of sin, the region of sin, the administrative division of sin. Strictly speaking, he's sin and its nemesis all rolled into one.

He also has a mustache that droops down to the middle of his chin, deep wrinkles from his temples to the middle of his cheeks, and few teeth. Just the front ones, and those are smoked out, boozed out, brown. When he smiles—no more questions. A cop but an alcoholic. An alcoholic but he can stop. Can but won't. He'll kill. Without a second thought.

He lights up his third cigarette—he chain-smokes—in ten minutes, and through the poisonous haze of his Java Gold looks me right in the eye. His eyes are brown, but his look is icy, colder than the ocean. Our staring match has been going on for more than two months, ever since I came to work for him. That is, became the junior agent in the property crimes department of the Bogorodskoe Internal Affairs Department of the Eastern District Internal Affairs Department of the Moscow Main Internal Affairs Department. It all happened so suddenly, it wasn't my doing, but that's beside the point today, the subject of a whole separate novel. I've been a bad boy. I'm twenty-four and my very smallest tattoo, a huge kraken devouring the world, starts at my right ankle and ends at my left ear. I spent all the money I made seven years ago—when me and the boys drowned this drug dealer, a guy in our class, holding him by the leg in the Yauza—on this tat. That was when I suddenly developed my acute sense of righteousness: I was able to convince everyone that selling drugs was very bad. We forced that monster to promise not to do it anymore and then took his money before finishing him off. To teach him a lesson. Then there were the ladies. We swept the district clean of pimps, small-time profiteers, and fences, but at some point the guys stopped me. Actually, it was too late. I'd turned myself into one big walking sign, a yakuza out of a Takeshi Kitano nightmare. Twigs, leaves, branches, Celtic knot, and Japanese dragons—all the world's evil spirits battled it out on my body for the right to a free millimeter of skin. What was going on a little bit deeper inside me—well, best not to even try to understand that.

I had only two options left, and I chose the wrong one. Now I'm an agent, a puny sergeant with a regulation cannon, in puny Bogorodskoe Internal Affairs, where druggies steal drills from construction sites, and druggies rape druggies, sometimes without even being clear about their victim's gender, and druggies kill druggies to get themselves a little heroin—drugs aren't just born under tram tracks after all. And tracks are the only thing (if you don't count druggies, of course) we have an abundance of in our district.

Nikolai Petrovich is sitting in his white shirt across from me smoking his fourth cigarette. Today's kind of like a holiday for him. After the obligatory five years, they made him a major. He's on duty, but there hasn't been anyone at all on Boitsovaya Street, where our department is, for the last few hours. Even the lunatics are lying low. Pretty soon we'll go out and celebrate his stars. Fuck every living thing.

I light up my second and look at Voronov. He's relaxing. A meter and a half from us, behind the door, the perps and vics—all jumbled together—await their fate on the sagging vinyl bench in the corridor. Soon Nikolai Petrovich, a king in

his white shirt, with two nonregulation guns in his tan under-
arm holster, will start seeing them. He'll punish and pardon.

But for now he's sprinkling some nasty Nescafé some broken Hindu brought him from the market early this morning
into his cup. Voronov sprinkles in one spoonful. Two. Three.
He pauses for a moment over the fourth and then throws that
in too, with the decisiveness of Alexander the Great. Oh, and
seven lumps of sugar. A stream of boiling water, a dirty spoon,
the first noisy swallow. The agent lights up again and leans
back in his chair, which is worn down to the veneer. He closes
his eyes, takes a drag, and releases the smoke. Then—with
just his eyelids—he gives me the order: Go. I open the door
for the first time that night.

I cautiously slap the first petitioner on the cheeks. He's
been sitting there for a long time. Neighbors relieved him of
the nice new TV in his room in a communal apartment on
Otkrytoe Highway. Voronov has already warned me we'd be
rejecting his appeal. This vic will never see a criminal case.
He was born to suffer, to be a vic. I'm learning to be like Nikolai Petrovich. Why do you think the street our department's
located on is called Boitsovaya—Fight Street? Pretty strong
people live and work here on Boitsovaya. To be blunt, they
don't have much choice.

Here's another. They just brought her out of a jail cell. She
threw her newborn in the garbage. She reeks of sweet cheap
alcohol that makes me sick. In the time we spend questioning
her I run out four times to our filthy two-holer—one for the
cops and one for the crooks—and puke. I must be puking my
stomach out. Voronov's as calm as a sphinx. His ironed white
shirt gets whiter and stiffer all the time. He says, "You'll be
going to that garbage heap soon. Believe me. There, in the
garbage, you're going to find the corpse of another newborn

infant who had a couple of gulps of air and then got stupidly fucked up. You're going to feel awful. You're going to search for his damned mama furiously, you'll find her, you'll put her in that chair where you're sitting now. You'll sit where I am and look into her eyes in hopes of seeing hell. But what you'll see is emptiness. Emptiness, my young friend. Emptiness is hell. And vice versa. I want you to lose your illusions as fast as you can and understand all about where, how, and why we are the way we are. Believe me. I'm one of the better ones."

I get queasy again and dash off. Voronov waits patiently; today he has no intention of stopping.

"By the way, they're going to give this mama two years' probation. You'll be very lucky if this story doesn't repeat itself on your watch. But if it does, that's bad. It could break you, even though by then you'll be pretty tough."

He hands me a vile cigarette. I try to strike a match and on the fifth try manage to light it. I see the various back alleys through the window. Every day I walk these alleys, but I don't remember exactly what the streets are called. I'll admit, I don't want to either. As far as I'm concerned, it's just endless emptiness. The whole Eastern District. Not too far from here you get to the school I went to. A little farther and there it is, the tram stop where, in a frenzy, I battered the painted iron kiosk with my fist, trying to take away the pain of love. And there's the courtyard where I had my first dead body, a dead body whose name and murderer I found. I found him quickly, in the next entryway. At the time I was given a commendation—as the youngest detective. Only Voronov didn't join in the general rejoicing at my success. He said, "One day everyone's going to die. Absolutely. Then other people will come, either cops or doctors. They'll come and tell you the cause of death. You just have to understand, student, that no one in my memory has ever been resurrected by that. Don't take pride in it or you'll start wanting to be a little like God."

Later I cursed him all night long and couldn't sleep. I think I cried. But in the morning he was standing on Boitsovaya, just like a monument to a poet. Smoking, blowing off the ashes. Waiting for me. He was always waiting for me. He liked working with kids like me.

"Life is a lot of things. And it takes crazy shapes. You don't mind that I'm like a biology teacher, do you? Love your neighbors and your family. Everyone else deserves death. You think I'm wrong?"

He found a way of instilling all this wisdom of the ages in my head in the three minutes it took us to walk back to the department. I couldn't remember school or the institute anymore. It was stupid, in fact, to remember those chalk-stained wusses. I had a real man walking on my left. Someone who had known life and then fucked it doggy-style. He always liked to be on top and couldn't stand lying down. Or sitting down facing you. Or standing. Impressive.

His shift's over and it's time for us to go. We leave the department, slipping on the chipped steps, which are coated with a thick layer of ice. Today there hasn't been a short-timer or drunk in jail—no one to hack the ice off—and the fat guard would never get off his fat ass. All he does is dream of somebody installing a bedpan in his chair so he'll never have to get up again. We slip and curse and light up. Voronov starts the engine of his Moskvich, which he bought with his fifth wife's money. His spouse never seemed to begrudge him anything. The most powerful mass-produced engine with the most affordable afterburner. On the highway this battered heap hits as high as 250 kilometers an hour. When they hear that sound, the sound of the engine on Voronov's heap, young skinheads move to the shoulder out of respect. Right now we're driving to the Field of a Thousand Corpses. It's a special kind of place.

I have a little time now, while the car is warming up, while we're driving. The whole trip takes about fifteen minutes. Let me tell you about this field.

Once, a very long time ago, after God created the earth and people divided it up into pieces, one particular town chopped up its own territory. Each ragged piece was attached to a specific district. Only somewhere, in the very rear end of the Eastern District where several boundaries come together, in Elk Island National Park, the police chiefs messed something up. They ended up with an odd piece of land that wasn't anyone's at all. A kilometer by a kilometer. No one lost any sleep over this. What kind of crimes could you commit on that pathetic patch of ground? But those who thought like that were wrong. When all the cops in the vicinity realized exactly what their lands bordered on, that patch of ground turned into a living hell. Unidentified corpses were ferried here, and here they rotted away. Local thugs and uniformed officers both came to settle their disputes. They set up meets here, and once, before my very eyes, there was a very real duel. Two young lieutenants fired at each other over a female expert from the district CSI. I was the second for one of them, and I had to stuff my new jacket into the gaping hole in the wounded guy's belly. He turned white, then gray, and honestly, never before or after have I seen someone's face change color that fast.

For those who know anything about life and death, the field is a cult location. That's where we're going. Actually, we're nearly there. Coming toward us through the night, through the black branches, reflecting off the thin crust of ice, are the headlights of someone's car zapping us in the eyes. They're waiting for us. Voronov has a lot of friends.

"A guy died here once," Voronov says, addressing no one in particular, and he kills the engine. But I know—he's continuing my education. He's teaching me how to live. We get out of the car and look both ways. A junior agent, Khmarin, takes the alcohol and snacks out of the trunk. "It probably took a few days," Banderas continues. "His car broke down on the parkway and he crawled here. He lay here, rasping, calling for help. All kinds of vermin ate him up."

"What kind of vermin?"

"All kinds. It's a national park. They have wild animals here." He spits a yellow gob long into the snow.

The oncoming car switches its beams to low. Men get out, shivering in their summerweight leather jackets. I know them only vaguely. District criminal investigations. All friends of my new boss. They're scary, but I'm getting used to them. For them the field is a known quantity. For me it's still wild and exotic. We shake hands. The men break up into groups while Khmarin and I serve up an improvised meal on the hood of a long American automobile. There are lots of cars, ten or so. They pull up one after the other, forming a lopsided circle. Each on his own side of the field. I'm cutting sausage with fingers stiff from the cold, and I realize that here today they're going to solve a dozen crimes ranging from serious to very, just like that, easily, plastic cup in hand. One pours for another, the other for a third. They're cutting deals, and first thing tomorrow morning they'll start writing reports.

"Does everyone have some?" Voronov asks, lifting a ribbed white cup.

"Aaaaoooo!" the agents respond.

"Down the hatch," my boss sums up, sending 120 grams of pepper Kristall down his throat in a single motion. We're lucky. The Kristall factory is the Eastern District agents' patrimony. At least we drink high-quality vodka.

Adam's apples are bobbing. Up and down. The cops are getting a buzz on. Stealthily I pour myself a half at the hip. It's comfy here sitting on this mossy piece of concrete. Slippery but comfy.

The picnic drags on. It's looking to be dawn soon. I examine the faces of the men surrounding me. They're stinking drunk but not repulsive. They're just talking a little louder, and more and more often their hands, with their thick short fingers, slice the air dangerously close to whoever they're talking to. Yes, the word "danger" right now couldn't be more accurate. These men, unpredictable and invested with almost limitless power, could do something terrible stone sober, but now . . .

Another bottle makes the rounds. And another. I've stopped counting and stopped being amazed at the foresight of those gathered. How much did they bring? Their business discussions are drawing to a close. Here and there—bursts of laughter. The cops are in a great mood today.

"Banderas!" a cop shouts from the other end of the field. "Listen, they told me that after a liter you can hit nine out of ten with either hand! They were lying, right?"

"No way." Nikolai Petrovich throws back his heavy head. "They only lied about one thing: it's ten out of ten. Even after two."

The field laughs. This slippery topic ought to be shut down, it seems to me, and I even open my mouth, but they get ahead of me. I think things over too long to say anything original.

"Well now, let's see if it's true." A man of about fifty totters out to the middle of the field. I know him. He's the deputy chief detective from the next department over. A colonel. He was in line for a promotion to Moscow homicide, but something didn't work out. They say it was the vodka again. The colonel takes an apple from the pocket of his pretentious leather jacket, blows tobacco flakes off it, and places it on his own head. The field bursts into laughter again.

"Watch," the young agent Khmarin elbows me in the side. "Something's about to happen."

To be honest, I'm scared, but Khmarin is perfectly calm and smiling his big gap-toothed smile.

"Two years ago Banderas stood three Tajiks here, rapists. They didn't want to write confessions. He put an apple on top of each head, and took out two barrels. They say it stank of shit, but nothing bad happened."

"Did they write them?"

"Sure did. You'd write anything if a bullet grazed your head." Khmarin sniffs. "True, I didn't actually see it. But that's what people say."

I don't doubt that's exactly how it all went down, but my alarm doesn't abate. I'm looking at Voronov. He's very, very drunk. Catching my look, he smiles and the tips of his mustache go up. He comes closer, leans toward my face, bathing me in a haze of vodka, and whispers, "If you get together with an old friend and buy a case of pepper vodka, you can have a pretty decent time of it. You just have to leave your guns at home. Someone told me that too, but I forgot. Just so you remember, student."

I'm gripped by panic, but changing anything—that's out of my hands. The colonel stands in the middle of the field and keeps smiling idiotically. The apple is shaking on his head, looking to fall. Voronov marks off twenty-five paces and stands facing him. The cops fall silent. You can touch the silence now, you can cut it with a knife and spread it on bread. Snow crunches under someone's feet; the officers are freezing in the winter woods, and warm boots are not their style. Voronov gets his nonregulation TT out of his left holster, examines it carefully, and closes his eyes for a second. Right now I can feel him as if I've entered into his mind. He aims with eyes closed, without raising the barrel. The next instant something terrible happens. Chilled from standing there in one place, the colonel sneezes. We still haven't heard the sound and don't realize what's happening. All we see is his face suddenly crumple. His mouth opens wide, the apple falls off his shaven head, and the night silence is shredded by gunshot. He sneezes and drops like a sack into the snow. His legs bend, his arms fling awkwardly to the side, and the 7.62 caliber bullet pierces his head like it's a ripe melon—straight through. Now his left leg twitches spasmodically—the tiniest bit. Once, twice, three times. All his muscles tense and his chest rises and falls. The thousand and first corpse on the field.

No one seems surprised. The agents collect the remains of their feasting silently and efficiently and toss the bottles and snacks into their trunks. One after another the engines start up and the dry snow creaks under their wheels. Another three minutes or so probably pass, or maybe it's an eternity. And here we are. The two of us on the field. Voronov nervously squeezes the TT in his hand, and I'm frozen in an awkward pose on the mossy concrete.

The colonel's corpse.

Our eyes meet. Banderas walks over to me and looks me up and down. He throws the gun at my feet.

"Keep it. It's a present." He turns on his heel and walks toward his car. "Boy, cops don't go to prison. They die fast there. Or stop being cops. Or stop being at all."

"And so?"

"You still don't understand."

"Aha."

"Aha. Idiot. You're a cop. That's all. God help you. And if
he does—you'll understand real fast. Bye for now."

He starts his engine and leaves. I'm alone. I sit like that for
another hour, until my drunk is completely passed. My brain is
now amazingly clear, and I know what I have to do.

I put on my gloves and pick the TT up by the barrel. I
painstakingly wipe the whole gun with my handkerchief and
walk over to the corpse. I try desperately to remember whether
our colonel was a lefty or not. No, I don't think so. His fingers
have already started to stiffen, but all is not lost. I put the gun
in his right hand and carefully survey the field. Yes, all's well.
The apple is lying a meter from the corpse—yellow with a
red blush. I pick it up and take a big bite. I like slightly frozen
apples. What can I say?

There's nothing more to do here. Crunching on the apple,
I quickly take the path toward Rostokinsky Road. I still have
some money. I have to grab a passing car and make my way
home. And be at work at 8 a.m. tomorrow.

I know what'll happen in the morning. Banderas will look
me in the eye and I'll nod silently. He'll nod in reply and shake
my hand. Just like that. Two men shaking hands. He won't
ask questions, since he never asked me to do anything the
day before. Everything I did, I did myself, of my own free will.
Any one of us in the smoke-filled two-by-three offices at 12
Boitsovaya Street would have done the same.

The months and years will pass, and Nikolai Petrovich
and I will share the same two-man office.

We'll catch, solve, and punish or tell the pesky vics to fuck
off.

Old man, you shouldn't have put your valuable property where everyone could see it. Even on the surveillance cameras in stores they write: *The management is not responsible for your valuables.* What the hell are we supposed to do?

As it is, we have a heightened sense of fairness, and the next Internal Affairs office over, by the way, has an excellent deputy chief detective now. A young muzhik, smart. A recovering alcoholic, they say; doesn't drink at all. I should stop by and say hello someday. First we'll repair the Moskvich since it's not respectable to go to a first meeting with a colleague with these rusty fins.

I remember everything and know everything, and everyone else knows it too. And I have absolutely nothing to fear. For the last five months I've either been staying home or going to the prosecutor's office. I'm lucky they kept me under house arrest and didn't send me to Lefortovo because it's close. Such a stupid thing, you know? It was really dark there, and scary, I admit it. None of us knew what would be there behind the door, and I was standing in front. I haven't been junior or a student or a probationer for a long time, but I was in front again. My whole life I've been in front. When the muscle took out the door and jumped aside, I went in and fired at the sound. Now in my statements—however many there've been—I write: *She thrust something out toward me.* It was a syringe, just a syringe. But at the time I nearly shat myself, word of honor, and fired four times. I shoot well, though not as well as Voronov. When they take us out to the range once a year, he still hits ten out of ten, and my best record is eight. The officer there says that's actually pretty good. But this time I was like a different person: all four bullets went in side by side, and after that the girl had no chest left.

She was nineteen or so, I don't remember anymore. My

investigator is a good guy, my age. I know before any arrest he'll let me go home. I call Nikolai Petrovich, we go to our field, and I suggest a game. He can't refuse me. But he shoots better. This is how it has to be. They can't put me in prison. I'll die there. Cops don't go to prison. They stop being cops there or they die. And it doesn't make a rat's ass bit of difference which.

PURE PONDS, DIRTY SEX OR TWO ARMY BUDDIES MEET

BY VLADIMIR TUCHKOV

Pure Ponds

Translated by Amy Pieterse

As usual, Maxim walked at full speed coming out of the Pure Ponds metro station, throwing his muscular legs out in front of him as though they were the cranks of an engine. Actually, an engine—lacking vision, hearing, and a sense of smell—would have had a much easier time in this "heavenly" corner of Moscow. Maxim had to squeeze through two chains of sweaty people, human sandwiches who were handing out poorly printed leaflets with the addresses of a translation agency. Past the piss-stinking bums draped nonchalantly all over the Griboedov Memorial. Past the crazy, long-haired old man with a loud amp who sang psalms accompanied by Arabic music. Past a dozen dogs that took turns drilling the same lascivious bitch. Past the foul creek that our shortsighted forefathers had, for some reason, chosen to call *Pure*.

Maxim recalled a song that Igor Talkov had sung in his time. Sung until he caught a bullet at a showman's showdown. A bullet straight out of a handgun that sent him to his final resting place. The mawkish lyrics were a parody of the present situation: *Pure Ponds and shy willow trees/Resemble maidens who've fallen silent at the water's edge/Pure Ponds, timeless dream of green/My childhood shore, where the accordion sounds.*

Willows? What willows? More like disgusting benches with morons lounging around on them. What accordion? Only the monotonous thumping of electronic music blaring from the windows of cars stuck in a traffic jam.

And maidens? Sluts, all of them!

Maxim hated places like this, places that were once steeped in an aura of history or cultural tradition. Now that Moscow had stuffed itself with oil dollars to the point that it was about to explode and send pus flying in all directions, places like this were identified in his mind with unwashed, stinky socks.

Of course, he could have pretended to be a machine and slipped off to his base, which long ago had been the Jatarang Indian restaurant. He might have moved on by, blind, deaf, and paying no attention to anything. But he was another type of machine entirely. And his capabilities and functions were very different. He had survived to the age of forty thanks only to his capacity to observe the details of his surroundings, any of which might prove a lethal threat to him.

Before, in the mountains of Afghanistan, death could lurk in the swaying movement of a twig, or the suspiciously smooth (not by the hand of the wind, but the hand of a minelayer) dust on the road.

Later, after he'd finished his service and killing became both his trade and his boss, with a big fat wallet, a lawyer, and a manager, the bony face of death could be hiding behind the dark tinted windows of a jeep, in a crowd, around the corner . . . anywhere. There was no front line anymore, no rear guard, no fortified base. The front line was wherever Max happened to be.

Now that he had chosen to play big time—which he did not so much for the money (he had enough already), but rather to prove to himself and to others that at the age of forty he could still be a match for any little twenty-year-old chump—he was surrounded by death on all sides. Theoretically, guns with silencers could be aimed at his forehead, and at the back of his skull, at his temples, right side, and left, simultaneously. It couldn't be ruled out that at that very moment someone was aiming an infrared beam at the top of his head. Despite the enviable virtuosity of his five human senses, honed to perfection, he remained vulnerable. He needed his animal instinct. And it had not once betrayed him. Although just once would be enough.

Three weeks ago, Maxim had accepted an invitation to play an amusing game. The jackpot was ten million. The last player (out of twelve) left alive would be declared the winner. The rules were simple. The game board was the Moscow area, within the limits of the beltway. Each player chose his own weapon. You could hook a howitzer to the back of your jeep and drive around town with it, or carrry a sharpened nail file in your pocket. Players were to kill competitors in any way possible, filming the process on a webcam that was connected to an online server. The game's powerful organizers refused assistance to contestants taken into police custody during play. Such individuals would be put on trial, hence disqualified from the game. They were allotted one month. If there was more than one player left alive when the time was up, the referee would draw lots and the unfortunates would be shot in the head.

The contenders were told that a group of around twenty millionaires were behind the game. They were the ones at the bottom of the *Forbes* list, the ones with only a sorry twenty or thirty million to their names, which they had come by in the drug trade or illegal gambling. Maxim didn't really give a damn about who, what, or where. There's a lot of money sloshing around in this sweepstakes, where folks bet on people, not on horses, cutting each other up with great expertise. As long as they coughed up the prize money at the end of it.

There were only six days left, but he was already bone-tired. He had killed not only five of his opponents, but nine others as well. Collateral damage, it's called. Three of them were merely the victims of a misunderstanding. A case of mistaken identity. But they had acted suspicious too. And it wasn't like he had a lot of time to make sure. In that situation, it's just a matter of who pulls the trigger first. None of them pointed a gun at him, but then, not one of those poor suckers had even had a gun on him to shoot with. Tough luck.

Six of them deserved to die. One of the players had hired them as informers for next to nothing. They shadowed his opponents and kept him notified of their whereabouts. Maxim didn't feel sorry for them at all. Nope. He recalled how one of them, a nervous guy of around thirty, begged him to spare his life. Said he needed the cash because his five-year-old daughter had sarcoma and needed expensive treatment, or she'd die. And if he died, she wouldn't make it. Maxim almost let him go, in exchange for the telephone number of the player who hired him. But when he found out it was the same guy who had killed Arkady, his old army buddy, he couldn't restrain himself. He broke the kid's neck so quick the guy didn't even notice his own death. It's different if you're nailed to a hospital bed, but not many healthy people see it coming. Death is especially quick at the hands of people who make it their profession. Fast as a bullet that has already found a home inside a lifeless body by the time the shot rings out.

Maxim sure hadn't expected to find Arkady's name among the players. They had been close friends back in Kandahar, with ghosts firing mortars at their marine company. And there was Nikita too. They had been the only ones left alive in their platoon. They made a vow of eternal friendship. But a lot had changed since then. Things were different now. And they weren't the same guys they had been either. Life's a bitch.

"I really need the cash," said Arkady, staring at Maxim over the bridge of his nose. "I don't have a choice."

"I have no choice either," Maxim replied. "Although I could do without the cash. In fact, I could even help you out, I've got some savings. But it's too late now to call it quits."

It was true, the players were already in the game. They'd signed a contract with the devil in blood. Refusal to continue with the game carried a risk of the secret being leaked, so any such player would be liquidated. Everything was absolutely fair. And gentlemanly.

Obviously, Maxim and Arkady agreed that they would not kill each other under any circumstances. If, by the end of the month, only the two of them were left, then lots would be drawn to decide the answer of "to be or not to be," a bullet shot out of the barrel of a gun in a game of Russian roulette. After all, they were army buddies and not some pussy bastards off the street.

The agonizing problem solved itself, really.

He walked on, scanning everything up ahead—to the left, to the right, behind him—calculating all the possibilities for how the present situation might develop. Two clerks, a mother and daughter, three rough-looking losers, a wino, a student, a bum, a prostitute, an old man, WHO'S THAT? An athlete? Yes, definitely an athlete. Three teenagers with snowboards, a spaced-out druggie, WHO IS HE? HE'S GOT HIS RIGHT HAND IN HIS POCKET! No, his wrist is straight, and the pocket's too small, yeah, he's just a jerk. And old woman try-ing to look younger than her age, a suicide case definitely a suicide, a workaholic, a cop, a guy looking down at the grou— NIKITA!

Yes, it was him. It wasn't easy to recognize the handsome and easygoing buddy he had known from his army days in this unkempt person, slumped over on a bench with a one-liter plastic bottle of extrastrong Ohota beer. Ripped sneakers, his big toes nearly poking out of them, threadbare jeans, a filthy coat. Gray hair speckled his five-day-old stubble and made its way up to his temples and into his once black hair. But most horrifying of all was the expression in his eyes: dull and lonely like an autumn swamp. His gaze wasn't staring inward. It wasn't staring outward either. It was unfocused and wander-ing somewhere in the direction of nonexistence.

Maxim paused, although in the present situation this wasn't very safe. But he couldn't just walk past a friend who looked like he needed help.

"Nikita!"

"Oh, it's you," Nikita said, as though he hardly recognized the person he was speaking to.

"What's all that?" asked Maxim, nodding at the plastic bottle that seemed to be a primary attribute of all the down-trodden and hopeless.

"You sure got this life thing all figured out. Looks like you got it made," Nikita said, his voice so shrill he was almost shouting.

"Hey, what's wrong with you?" Maxim scanned the hostile territory around him.

"What's wrong with *me*? Where were you three years ago? I wrote to you from St. Pete. Tried to get hold of you. And where were you a year ago, when I was all alone, up to my neck in shit? What's wrong with *me*?"

"Give me a break! I moved into a new place and got a new number. And I'm not in Moscow much anyway. Come on. What can I do to help you now? I mean it, right now."

It was obvious the guy was in bad shape. He was angry at the whole world, and appeared comfortable that way. His body language was saying, *Forgot about me, the bastards, stabbed me in the back! Not one single son of a bitch came around when I needed help. Well, I don't need you assholes anymore. Scram!* Guys like that never admit that it is they, and not the "bastards," "sons of bitches," or "assholes," who are to blame for their misfortunes. Backed up by such sentiments, they enjoy not shaving and going for weeks without changing their underwear; guzzling Ohota or Baltika 9 as they go under, until they stop somewhere about six feet beneath the earth's surface and worms start gnawing at what's left of them. Even worse, Maxim once heard about a dog breeding company where bull terriers were fed a diet of homeless people, live homeless people, to turn the dogs into killers and cannibals.

"You should have helped me out back then when I needed it, before I ended up in Moscow," said Nikita.

When, at last, he ran out of excuses to prop up his ego, Nikita told his story. It turned out that three years before, in St. Petersburg, he had made some big money and decided to move to Moscow. What's the big deal, everybody's going! It's the city of unlimited possibilities. So he sold his Petersburg apartment and added that money to the bundle he'd received from Valya Matvienko for working on her election campaign, and bought a three-bedroom apartment at Pure Ponds, one that was big enough to house their whole damn platoon back in Kandahar. He partied for a month, spending dollars like they were five-kopek coins. After that, he settled in. Turned out that the easiest part was finding a mate. Or something like that. Whatever. She was beautiful, smart, sexy, and devoted. Or she seemed devoted back then. That was why, three months later, he awarded her the official status of wife, and a note was made of this both in his passport and in an official registry book.

Making a living in Moscow proved much more difficult. He tried opening a souvenir shop on Taganka. They wouldn't let him. He set up a snack shop at Kitai-Gorod. It was burned down two weeks later. He signed a contract to deliver a small consignment of Polish perfume. He got cheated, cost him fifty grand. Well, after that he gave up on having his own business and got a job as a security guard at the Reutov casino. His salary, plus the interest he received on the Petersburg money he'd put in the bank, was enough to live on quite comfortably.

Fate, however, decided to play a trick on the Afghan war hero. The bank went bust. With great difficulty, Nikita managed to get a tenth of his savings back. But he lost even that at the very same casino where he worked. He went in one weekend just to try his luck. Just about hit the jackpot too. His wife's devotion, like snow in April, began to melt steadily. She soon turned into a terrible fury. Even so, her three other good qualities remained. She was sexy (though she stopped sharing that particular quality with her husband). Beautiful. And smart. In fact, she was smart enough to kick Nikita out of the apartment three days ago.

"What are you, some kind of wuss?" said Maxim. "Show her who's boss! You've got fists, don't you? Tell her to get the hell out."

"She reregistered the apartment in her own name. I'm like the heir or something."

"Then kill her! Have you forgotten how it's done? Make it look like an accident."

"I can't. I just got baptized. I made a vow, for the rest of my life. Besides, look." Nikita stuck his arms out in front of him, palms facing downward. His fingers shook visibly, like those of an alcoholic.

"Ouch," said Maxim, shaking his head. "I'd head for a monastery, bro. And how about your vow never to touch the drink again?"

They were both silent for a moment, puffing on their cigarettes.

"How about this," Maxim said, interrupting the silence. "I'll kick her out myself. Then you'll be off the hook. Where's your place?"

Nikita gave him an address. It was nearby, 12 Pure Ponds Boulevard.

Maxim waited around until someone opened the door at the main entrance and then held it open for the young mother pushing a stroller. He went up to the third floor and turned off the switch in the fuse box he found in the hallway. Behind the door, where Nikita's wife Zhanna lived, the television set fell silent.

Maxim went up one more flight of stairs. He waited, giving her time to call the electric company, who would tell her that everything was working down at the station and that she should check her fuse box.

Of course, Zhanna peered through the peephole, but not seeing even the smallest sign of danger she opened the door. Before she had time to realize what was happening, she was back inside the apartment, a hand pressed over her mouth and her arms clamped to her sides.

Maxim turned the key in the lock twice and carried Zhanna deeper into the apartment.

She tried to resist.

"Don't make any noise," he said in a whisper. "If you keep quiet, I'll let you live. Got it? Whisper." Slowly, he uncovered her mouth and relaxed his grip. Zhanna was silent as she studied the intruder.

"Money?" she asked softly.

"No."

"Oh, I get it. My jackass sent you over to say hi. My ex-jackass, that is."

"He said you were smart, and he wasn't lying."

It was then that Maxim noticed that she was also beautiful. Beautiful, as in sexy. The thought occurred to him that there was no real difference between one rape or two. Nikita would understand.

So he changed the character of his grasp: from clenched, to imploring.

He noticed with surprise that she did not try to resist. On the contrary, she seemed to press her body toward him (and she smelled so deliciously female!). She gasped with excitement.

Maxim had an instant hard-on.

But he didn't lose his head. He took off his coat with the webcam that was always hooked up to the game server, and hung it up in the hall so that the camera was facing the wall. There was no reason for them to watch this.

Zhanna moaned. She squeaked. It was unbelievable. You only come across this kind of girl once every six months, Maxim thought to himself.

He drilled her in her cornhole like a wild animal. Like a baboon. Like an orangutan. And she enjoyed it.

That crazy bitch couldn't get enough. "More!" she howled,

cursing like a Shanghai whore giving herself to a platoon of sailors.

They peeled themselves apart. He listened without interrupting as she praised him. He listened as she cursed her impotent husband. As she begged him to stay. Forever. How happy they would be together. Fucking amazing. Those were the exact words she used: *Fucking amazing*. But she didn't just say them. She sang the words, which lost their foulness and gained a certain eloquence. Maxim listened quietly, nodding his head. Dream on, baby, he thought. Dream on.

And then he drilled her some more, with the same ferocity.

He came.

Then he noticed she had an Adam's apple.

Fuck!

A transvestite!

It was a dirty and dangerous game that Nikita had gotten him into.

He stayed cool, not letting on that he had noticed.

"Let me get us some drinks," said the transvestite. "Okay?"

"Sure."

The transvestite brought in two glasses of wine from the next room. And Maxim realized that he wouldn't drink it even at gunpoint.

He took the glass.

"What's wrong?"

"I want to watch you drink. You're so beautiful, I'm sure you drink beautifully too. My cock is ready for action just watching you."

The transvestite laughed, and took two sips. His Adam's apple went up and down two times and then stilled. It wasn't that big. But it was obviously a man's.

Maxim set his glass down.

"Why don't we start off with the usual question," he said, his fingers locking around the transvestite's throat. Not too tight, but probing. "Who are you working for? Tell me quietly."

In all likelihood, at that very moment Nikita was glued to his own transmitter, which connected to an opponent's webcam and mic, and it was extremely important that he not hear a thing. Each player had a transmitter that allowed him to hook up to his opponent's channels and receive picture and sound from their webcams, broadcast nonstop. The pictures helped players track each other down if they recognized their opponent's location.

"I don't understand."

"Yes, you do. Now listen carefully: this is your one chance to stay alive. Tell me the truth. Everything, and in great detail. Who hired you and why? And what do they want from me?"

The transvestite shrank back. And spilled the beans. About how they sometimes sent people to him who he didn't know. And he "served" them, the same way he had served Maxim. Then he would put clonidine into their wine. And when his client fell asleep, he would call a certain Artyom, who would finish them off while they were still knocked out. Then, at night, the body would be taken away by two bald guys in a jeep. The transvestite knew nothing more. The answer why seemed pretty clear, but who was behind this? That was the question.

Another question was how had Nikita turned into such a cunt? The traitor! But Maxim tried not to think about that.

"You don't kill?"

"No," answered the transvestite, blanching.

"So you guys have a division of labor and everything. You got one son of a bitch working as a decoy, another giving sexual favors, and the third does the killing. Four and five get rid of the body. You guys are a goddamn hockey team!"

"Please don't kill me," whispered the transvestite.

"Did you tell me the truth?"

"Yeah, honest. In the beginning I didn't know what was going on. I just wanted to make a little dough. But then, after that first time, I couldn't refuse. They'd get me too."

"All right, you can live. Call him."

"Who?"

"The killer, Artyom."

When the door opened, Artyom got a blow on the head with the handle of a gun. As he was collapsing, Maxim saw that it was Nikita.

What a fucking world, Maxim thought. What a goddamn fucking world.

He even spat on the floor. Rather, he spat on Nikita's stained jacket, which was his uniform.

"All right, holy man, start talking," said Maxim when Nikita came to.

Nikita was quiet.

"Do you realize you're not getting out of here alive, you Judas?"

Nikita nodded.

"Did you kill Arkady?"

Nikita nodded his head again, staring at the floor.

"Talk."

"I had to."

"What, does your five-year-old daughter have leukemia?" asked Maxim, recalling the thirty-year-old whose neck he'd broken, snapped just like a chicken's.

"No, I owe big money. They took my wife. Gave me three months to pay."

"How much?"

"Five hundred grand."

"Holy shit!" Maxim roared. "What are you doing? I have the money. I have a million! I could have—"

"How was I supposed to know that? It's like everybody just kind of up and left. Life fuckin' pulled us apart in all different directions."

"Okay. I give you my word that I'll get your wife out of there. Now talk."

So Nikita started talking again. He told Maxim how the program manager had decided to play under the table. Of course, he kept that secret from the organizers, who paid the prize money. Player number four was supposed to get ten million. No risks on his part, because the manager had put together an unofficial team. That was where Nikita was working. The unofficial team had two functions: guarding number four, and not letting opponents get near him. Also, they got rid of "extra" players using any means possible, including what they had tried on Maxim. The payoff for the mongrel team was supposed to come from the prize money that number four would receive. Nikita agreed. How much the others were getting he didn't know; naturally, the manager would be taking the largest cut.

When Nikita finished, Maxim handed him a gun with one shot in it.

"Don't worry about your wife, I'll get her out. But don't try any funny stuff, cause you know my response time was always better than yours. Do I make myself clear?"

Nikita nodded and moved into the far room.

Time slowed down to almost a standstill. It got as thick

as ketchup that doesn't want to come out of the bottle in the freezing cold.

Outside, a baby started crying.

Water rumbled in the pipes.

Then it got quiet.

Then a shot rang out.

"That's it," said Maxim. "Get dressed."

The transvestite, chalk-white with fear, started.

"No!"

"Idiot. You're going with me. You'll be a witness."

"Why?!"

"You're not on trial, darling. But I have to explain to the investors why I crushed all those snakes and cut the manager's balls off before I killed him."

Maxim crossed the streetcar tracks and jumped the low barrier dividing the fetid boulevard from the street stinking of exhaust fumes. He strode toward the house with columns, digging the heels of his massive lace-up boots into the road. The manager had twenty minutes left to live. His moronic bodyguards, with earphone wires sticking out from underneath their jacket collars, had even less time.

The transvestite hurried along, sticking close by, in a tight English skirt, his face crumpled in fear. From an outsider's perspective, it might have looked like a stately middle-aged man walking an exotic, purebred dog.

A bum sitting on a park bench took a sip from the bottle of extrastrong Ohota he had just found—miraculously, almost full. What a wonderful evening, he thought to himself.

DECAMERON

BY IGOR ZOTOV

Silver Pine Forest

Translated by Marian Schwartz

Facewise, Ryabets resembles a skull: gaunt, with a deep-set, chalk-white gaze and lips slightly parted—a permanent grin of large yellowed teeth. At school they called him Skull behind his back but didn't dare to his face, so they gave him a nickname from his last name: Ryaba.

Now that he's on the wrong side of fifty, the skull resemblance applies to his whole frame: shriveled and bony.

At breakfast Ryabets is reading the *Moskovskii Komsomolets* police blotter. While he's tapping around the butt end of his egg with a spoon, while he's peeling off the shell, he skims through the second-grade girl lost in the taiga outside Krasnoyarsk—takes a bite of buttered bread and chews—the drunk officer who shot a soldier—takes a sip of ersatz coffee—the . . .

Under "Private Prison with Torture Chamber in Silver Pine Forest," it says that the cops picked up a naked vagrant wearing handcuffs, right there on the street in broad daylight, with a cracked skull and evidence of beatings to his body. The vagrant called himself Andryukha and managed to say he'd been tortured in a cellar with "electricity and tongs." He whispered the address, 43 Second Line, then fell silent. They didn't get

Andryukha to No. 67 Hospital in time. He died in a traffic jam without regaining consciousness. The cops went to the address but the jailers were gone and the trail was cold. But the prison was remarkable: three cells with a stun gun, tongs, a rack, a Spanish boot, and all kinds of other things. The two corpses were also Silver Pine Forest vagrants. *An investigation is under way.*

Ryabets sets the newspaper aside and looks out the window. July. Hazy, hot, and stuffy. When he's finished with breakfast, he puts his Marlboros, towel, swimsuit, three big sausage sandwiches (carefully wrapped in that same newspaper so they wouldn't go bad), a bottle of water, a bottle of 777 port, and a plastic cup into a paper bag.

He tucks his short-sleeved shirt into his pants and slips on his sandals. Two trolley stops to Kaluzhskaya and then the subway to Kitai-Gorod. The route remembers itself, even though the last time he took it was back in the early 1970s, when Kitai-Gorod was called Nogin Square. Transfer to the purple line to Polezhaevskaya. He'll ask from there.

Not much out the trolley window has changed in all those years: dust, buildings, poplar trees. Here's the arched bridge and to the left another bridge—red cables, looks new. Beyond that the river and the Krylatskie Hills. The trolley dives down a slope and stops at a square. Ryabets gets out.

A few streets fanning away, fences, and behind the fences pines and high dacha roofs. Ryabets glances around—should be here somewhere. There used to be a beer stand here, but not anymore. They'd gone from the beer stand to the dacha last time. Not him. His feelings were hurt so he went home. Bolt took his book away from him. A word clicked in his memory: *Decameron.* Oh yeah—a stinging sleet slashing at the burn site, his heel making little holes in the black muck—the cover was charred, with dark blue, intricate twisting letters, Bolt's book . . . He came here in the fall, before the army. How could he not? No, later.

It's too hot for port . . . He then bought beer at a stand and took a sharp left turn into the woods.

Ryabets sleeps briefly. Right here under this willow. The beer-sun has taken it out of him. More like dozing, with quick dreams involving water splashing, children squealing, and a female mocking whisper directly above him. He opens his eyes but no one's there and it's quiet. Close them and all over again—a squeal, a splash, a whisper. And a rustling—are they stealing his bag? No one, a total haze. He sits up, gazing blearily at the river and at the white church on the opposite bank, cockeyed.

Below—stretch his legs out—the evening water lightly laps-spills over. Music, laughter, a shashlik smell coming from beyond the fence on the private beach. A volleyball thumps. A little closer, in a chaise longue, a woman with a book. The view from behind: short haircut, folds in her neck, the edge of her glasses, her ass. Ryabets reaches into his swimsuit and tugs and tugs—nothing doing. A languid spite sours inside him. He did drag himself all the way out here! Halfway—no, all the way—across Moscow!

The woman is approached by another, younger, who leans over and says something as her white breasts rise lusciously from her blue swimsuit. Ryabets is back in his trunks, kneading away furiously. Nothing. The cupola radiates an officious sneer. He gives the church a dirty look and kneads and kneads. Out of the corner of his eye he notices Luscious observing him, a combination of revulsion and curiosity on her face. He pulls out his hand. Just scratching. He stands up—his trunks sag in back—scrambles down the bank, and swims noisily. The water isn't refreshing; it's too warm.

Ryabets slowly plies the shoreline, watching Luscious. You'd think he wouldn't care, but imagine, he's horny; he feels dumb too, old goat.

Once Luscious leaves, Ryabets moves ashore. He towels off and gets out the 777: to drink or not to drink? No, first go *there*. He eats his sandwich, takes one last look at the address in the paper, gets dressed, and leaves.

First he follows the shore and edges around the beach fence, but immediately, in a young pine grove, he runs across some naked men lying there, privates exposed. Ryabets sidesteps them but the farther he goes, the more naked men there are catching some rays, arms spread wide. "Cocksuckers," he mutters, veering more to the left. He tries not to look but can't help it. The bushes along the river are filled with naked men's bodies. He spits. Right in the middle of Moscow!

He fantasizes TNT exploding and scraps of genitalia in the bushes—too many to collect! The bloody image calms him, and Ryabets moves deeper into the woods, emerging on paths that lead to Lake Bezdonka. Evening is falling and the crowds stretch from the riverbank to the park entrance. Ryabets has nearly changed his mind about going to the address in the newspaper. He's tired. He wants to go home. He's walking down Tamanskaya when across the street on the left he notices a street sign: *Second Line*. He stands there a second and turns. Did I make the trip for nothing?

The street is suddenly quiet. The dachas are behind a fence. Turrets, porticos, balconies. As if they weren't right next to that half-naked, heat-wasted mob. No. 43. In back of them, a new red-brick, three-story house. The kind ministers of state and oligarchs live in, Ryabets thinks. Actually, the house gives the impression of being uninhabited. Ryabets "accidentally" pushes the gate, which yields with a light creak. The house is standing where the dacha burned; Ryabets recognizes the lawn behind it and the semicircle of tall pines. But a prison? Construction debris, doorframes in their original packing, the porch unfinished. On the door, yellow police tape—looks like this was indeed the prison.

Cautiously he unsticks the tape and opens the door. Inside it's half-dark, and he senses the staircase on the right. He gropes for the light switch on the wall and heads downstairs. Exactly: three cells fabricated out of thick sticks. In front of him a table, two chairs, and a mechanism that looks like a welding apparatus. Were the cops too lazy to pull it out? On the floor, reddish-brown spots and broken glass. Torture—and why not? Hah! Vagrants, human matter. Hah!

Ryabets doesn't linger. It's all just like the paper said. He goes upstairs, turns off the light, walks out, and puts the tape back. Not a trace of the other dacha, as if it were never there. He wants to go home.

But before he moves out to the street he decides to take a look, refresh his memory, see where he kept watch once upon a time. Over there, over there . . . Wait, wait . . .

In the lilac bushes past the pines, in the exact same place, he notices a figure on the ground. The instinct to flee subsides instantly. No cop would sit squatting in the bushes! On top of everything else, it's a female. She waves. He's walking, glancing from side to side to make sure no one else is there. But there is. The female has a dog at her feet. It raises its head to Ryabets.

"Got anything to drink?" she asks. "Who are you?"

Definitely a woman. And drunk. Two leathery folds are slipping down her belly from her unbuttoned pink top.

Cellulite legs in white ankle socks spread wide. Bezdonka, hah!

While Ryabets is considering her, the woman takes out of her bag (just like his with his Marlboros) a bottle (just like him with his 777), tosses her head back, and glugs down the last of the liquid. She kicks an empty bottle aside.

"Commander, fill my glass! See? Not a drop! I won't fucking say anything to your wife."

A flat face, dark, slit eyes, no neck, formless all over. *Like a steak!* Ryabets thinks culinarily. *But something very familiar I can't put my finger on. What?*

"Ryaba? Ryaba! Ryabets! Is that you? Yes, it is!" The woman scrambles onto all fours, straightens up, and starts hobbling toward him, as if she were wearing prostheses. The dog, too, yawns and wags its tail.

Buratina! Fucking amazing. Burataeva! he shouts in his mind.

This clumsy creature had been Ryabets's erotic dream. Nadya Burataeva—Buratina, as they'd called her in school. The nickname was a jibe at her flat, half-Kalmyk, but definitely not Buryat, nose.

"And you're just the same, Ryaba, just the same. Maybe a little shrunken, hee hee hee! Still jerking off?" Burataeva's a meter away and Ryabets can smell her sour stench. "What are you standing there for? Pour! To our meeting! You wouldn't begrudge Nadya Burataeva a drink, would you? How many years has it been? Eh? Gotta be thirty."

Ryabets reaches into his bag, removes the bottle and cup, pulls the cork out with his teeth, pours, and offers it to Buratina. He drinks from the bottle.

"So tell me, how have you been? What's up?"

* * *

Ryabets is sitting under a pine facing Buratina. Echoes of her fate surface right away. She was burning up in the fire so she jumped, broke her foot and back, spent a long time in recovery, and after all that discovered she was pregnant. It was born dead, actually. She went quickly downhill. Her parents supported her but she drank, then her lover (a recidivist) did and she drank, they put him in jail and she drank, her parents died and she drank, another pregnancy and she drank, a miscarriage and she drank, she sold everything and drank, her apartment too and drank, disappeared and drank.

"This is Polkan," she introduces.

Ryabets nods but the dog isn't taking to him.

"Don't wet your pants, Ryaba, he won't touch you. He's been with me since he was born. Andryukha brought him when he was just a puppy, thi-i-is little. You can't imagine how glad I am to see you, Ryaba!" Buratina hiccups. And in a gleeful non sequitur: "They shut down the beer stand a long time ago, back under Gorbachev. And all the stores too. We go over the bridge, to Priboy. I've been living here ten years, Ryaba, across Bezdonka. I'm moving to Kazan station now. They say it's a rich place—you can take melons off the trains from the Chuchmeks. You won't die of hunger near a train station. I'm not staying here, no way."

"Why?" Ryabets recalls the morning paper.

"Hell if I know!" Buratina shrugs. "Everyone's run off. Even Andryukha. He promised me. 'You and me, Nadya, we'll go to Kazan station, I won't abandon you.' So where's Andryukha now? Kaput. Hee hee hee."

"Why are you limping?"

"I'm limping? What do you mean I'm limping? What do you mean? I know why I'm limping, I know. But I won't tell you. Never!" Then she mutters under her breath, "Maybe I'm

Madame de La Vallière! Listen, Ryaba, I'm limping because I'm Madame de La Vallière!"

If Ryabets had known how to put his emotions into words, it would have come out something like this: *Did I really lust after this woman once? Her? Me? Incredible!* Ryabets crinkles his nose.

". . . How I've lived this long I don't remember, Ryaba. I took a leap from the second floor! Broke both my little legs. I could've suffocated. All the others did: my Alik, and Lidukha, and those other two, I don't remember who they were. And that fat one who carried around the pictures of women."

"Boltyansky?"

"That's it, Ryaba, exactly! He suffocated." And suddenly she winks. "Should I tell you?"

"What?"

"This! Remember how you used to moon over me, Ryaba? Remember? Hee hee hee! You did, I know you did! But I wouldn't give it up for you! I would for anyone else, but not you." She falls silent and starts rocking from side to side.

"Is it true there was a prison here?"

"Definitely. Yes!" And now he can't tell whether it's the drink talking or she's serious. "I won't let you have any now either, so don't get any ideas! Don't you look at how old I am . . . You're no stud yourself. All skin and bones. They used to call you Skull, remember?" She fell silent for several moments, then suddenly: "Andryukha died here. Kirei died and Sabel died. We were four in this pipe—I mean the four of us lived together . . . I'm all alone now . . . Andryukha left a week ago, said he'd grab me some booze . . . He didn't . . . It's scary here, Ryaba. Where can I take Polkan? Huh? They won't let him into the train station. Will you take him?"

"That's all I need."

"Yeah, right. You like a little port now and then too, I see! Like when we were kids. Don't you make enough for a little brandy, Ryaba? What's your job these days?"

"Cook."

Buratina whistles. "In a restaurant?"

"A cafeteria. I feed the black-assed negroes at the university. Fortunately, it's only ten minutes from home."

"What do you cook for them?"

"Oh, everything: goulash, groats, cabbage soup."

"Did you ever try foie gras?"

"That's only a name: it's goose liver. What's there to try? Put it in rassolnik, potroshki—just the ticket. And the cucumbers have to be thickly sliced, preferably marinated." Ryabets pauses to pour for Buratina. "Here's to our meeting!" He takes a swig.

"Ryaba, you know why I wouldn't let you have any? You look all cold, but on the inside—phooey! One of those. Us girls didn't like you; you had this look, like you wanted to maul us. Maul us with your eyes and go down there with your nose. Hee hee hee! Our dear departed Bolt was like that too, but I felt sorry for him. Who was going to give that fatso any? He carried those dirty pictures around, but you mooned, you just egged me on. Oh, poor Bolt! And poor Mesropych, even if he was a stinker."

"Why be sorry? They're gone."

"Who would have thought? Not one gray hair," Buratina mutters.

"How'd you see me?" They're sitting in total darkness now and can't even make out each other's faces anymore. Buratina's smoking, a cheap bitter smell.

Ryabets stands up to pee. He's not shy.

"Don't piss on the grave!" Buratina cries.

Ryabets says nothing.

"Listen, Ryaba, here's what I'm thinking. Maybe I could come to your place? With Polkan . . . ?" The dog growls huskily. "I'll wash up. Do you live alone? Are your mother and father dead?"

"Yeah."

"I can't even remember the last time I slept anywhere clean. What's there for me here? They killed Andryukha! And Kirei . . . and Sabel . . . What about you, Ryaba, not married?"

"No."

"Why not? Waiting for a princess? Or for me? Hee hee hee! Maybe I'll give you some today, but Ryabets . . ." Buratina babbles.

Sometimes he can't tell whether she's really drunk or just pretending.

"You didn't answer me, Ryaba. Why haven't you gotten married?"

"I've been waiting for my dick to grow up."

"Hee hee hee! You? I don't believe that! Why did you jerk off outside my window? I remember . . ."

"My first little darling is lying over there." She nods toward the fence and a night-black honeysuckle. "Do you think his little bones are still there?"

Ryabets imagines the child's half-decayed bones. "Of course not, after all those years. Maybe a skull . . . or the tibias, they're thick."

"You're a chef, you should know. And the second one next to him. I buried them at night, the snow was coming down; I remember, it was November."

142 // Moscow Noir

"You got the first from Mesropych?"

Buratina nodded and hiccupped.

"Whose was the second?"

"I don't know. I was sleeping with everyone. I'd go to sleep under one and wake up and another's going at it. Let the dogs have their way! And my baby girl. She's lying right over there. She'd be nine . . . Pour me a little, why don't you."

Ryabets splashes some in the cup and Buratina drinks greedily.

"My baby girl was Andryukha's. We lived over there, where you see the gazebo now. We had a concrete pipe, like this." Buratina tries to show him how big with her hands. "We lived there a good five years. Or more. With Andryukha and Sabel, and Kirei came later."

"You mean you gave birth there?"

"Where else, I'd like to know! Andryukha sterilized the knife in the fire and cut the cord. I wanted to leave my little girl, my baby daughter, with *them*, the people with the fanciest house. I thought at least then she'd have a life. Only she died a week later. Right when I was about to give her up. Andryukha would bring her food, he knew the cashier at the store on Zhivopisnaya, a good woman, and she gave it to him for free. Milk, Ryaba, and cereal. You can imagine what my milk was like. My little girl . . ."

Buratina strokes the ground and weeps silently, only her sniffling gives her away.

The noises on the other side of the fence have died down completely. Only occasionally does a car whoosh by, unseen.

"It was nice when we lived in the pipe, Ryaba. Even in the winter, it was a palace! We'd fill up the opening on one end and hang a towel over the other. A foursome makes it cozy—terrific! Tchaikovsky Hall! There weren't any windows, but what good would they do? And the other cops left us alone. They'd come, take a look, and leave. There was this one, Lieutenant Bessonov, he was old and had a red nose, a lush. He'd come have a smoke at our fire. He used to say that when he retired he'd move in with us. Hee hee hee! He'd just grab his fishing rod from home, he didn't need anything else. That's what he used to say. He was joking, that cop. Later he disappeared. And the cops turned mean! They set all my stuff on fire twice, Ryaba, they burned it! Oh, what good stuff . . . mattresses! We moved over under the bridge, then to the church—you know the one, past the bridge? But now, Ryaba, that's it, it's time to stop!"

Buratina stirs, and Ryabets listens.

"Pour me some more. I'm going to drink my fill today, as if it were the last time, Ryaba! My life's been bitter. And now I have to go to Kazan. They must have their own ways there, those station whores must be on top there!"

"Did you think I didn't know? Hee hee hee! It was you who burned down the dacha, Ryaba. You! You! Damn it all."

"Cut the crap."

"You always wanted me. I remember the way you used to look at me, the way you hung around outside my window, peeping! Hee hee hee!" Buratina's voice is so raspy he can hardly make it out. "You still had your beret, the brown one. Ryaba in his beret!"

Ryabets remembers those fall evenings well. He did walk around under Buratina's windows, since she lived on the second floor, and he would keep an eye out—in the window just a fine veil of tulle, and Buratina prancing around her room in her panties, tight white panties. Before she went to bed she'd examine herself in her window reflection. She really didn't have a mirror? She'd touch her breasts, belly, hips. Those brief minutes were the ones Ryabets lived for. He never suspected that Buratina was doing that for him, the spy in the night.

She was telling the truth. In school Ryabets couldn't take his eyes off her. Everyone knew it. He'd sneak up behind her after class, staring at her strong, curvy legs, and fantasize. Knowing this, she'd tease him. First she'd stick her foot out in the aisle between their desks, then *happen* to clasp her breasts, then *happen* to touch herself *down there*. She was teasing him, and in his erotic visions every night, he tortured her ingeniously as only a youthful imagination can. None of his classmates digested the porn Boltyansky unfailingly brought to school as avidly as Ryabets. He'd arrive at school in the morning listless and gray from lack of sleep.

After the fire he found out that Buratina had survived and was in the hospital, pregnant. He was afraid to visit her. But he did visit the burn site right before he went into the army. His three years' service were pretty cushy, stationed at a garrison kitchen in Baltiisk. He was eventually discharged and went back to those windows, but Buratina was gone. Her Kalmyk father was watching television in the next window; her mother was bustling around the kitchen. He kept going back there for two weeks. After dark. He started culinary school, graduated, and wound up at the cafeteria where he'd worked to this day. He'd lived unsociably, especially after his hard-drinking parents both died. He never married. He gratified his urges (occasionally, on days he got an advance or a paycheck) with train station prostitutes, whom he threw out after coitus. Had they known that he could barely stop himself from strangling them as he was ejaculating, they would have thanked their lucky stars.

Later he moved on to self-service, thanks to progress:

there probably wasn't a better collection of porn films in Moscow.

"Bolt was better than you, just fat. He didn't jerk off under my window. He came to me honestly and said, 'Give me some, Buratinachka, just once. What's it to you?' Hee hee hee! He'd come down to my place. We lived near each other, remember? Like he had a question about biology." (Buratina was good at biology; she'd wanted to go to medical school.) "He'd come and sit down and breathe hard, like a sperm whale . . . He'd bring me that book . . . what was it? About the Italians who told stories."

"*The Decameron.*"

"That's it! He said he'd taken it from his parents. He's reading it out loud and squeezing his thigh . . . And he stinks to high heaven, Ryaba, from cologne. He must have poured half a bottle on himself so I'd give him some. I even thought maybe I should. Why let the guy suffer? But I decided—first Mesropych . . . I wanted him to pop my cherry, hee hee hee! Then we'd see! I had some real studs, didn't I, Polkan boy?" Buratina scratches the dog's scruff again. "I'm a whore! I'd give some to Polkan, but the animal gets me all scratched up. What do you expect? Hee hee hee!"

Ryabets remembers. He remembers very well. He remembers Buratina being the only girl in their class—to the envy of the other girls and the greater dissatisfaction of Pichuga, their homeroom teacher—to wear lacy stockings, which made Ryaba's heart race.

"Remember, Ryaba, the story in that book when one woman arranges to meet him at her house? He comes, and the maid says, 'Wait a little, her husband's there . . .' And she—the maid, that is—gets it on with the man. That guy was out in the cold all night! Just like you! Hee hee hee. But later he had his revenge, he drove her out on the roof, I think . . . Right?"

Buratina takes the bottle and finishes it off in one swig.

"Whoo! All right, Ryaba, what the hell. You can't bring 'em back. Not Bolt, not Mesropych, not Lidukha. I don't remember the others." She suddenly falls over, first on her side, then facedown. "But you, Ryaba, you're not getting any. I was going to give you some, but I'm not. Sleep, my beloved children."

Her hands stroke the rough grass and fall still.

Ryabets has a headache. He shuts his eyes. He should be getting up. It's late. He's not going to spend the night here, on her children's bones. Or is this crazy woman lying? Though no, she said some sensible things too. Such a strange day. But there's still the newspaper. His mother didn't give him up when that detective came poking around. He'd asked, *Could someone have fought with Mesropych, or Boltyansky, or even Burataeva? From their class, maybe someone was getting back at them? Or was it just the drinking and carousing?* The detective questioned everyone. With some, he went to their houses; others he called in. Eventually he decided it was an accident, a cigarette butt. Besides, it was so dry there. Like now. Drier even. The peat burned, definitely. There was smoke. People were coughing.

Crackle, pain, heat. Ryabets opens his eyes and sees Buratina, her arm raised, holding the bottle—the moon's predatory reflection on its jagged edges. She's going to kill me! He moves to the side, Buratina falls—crack!—a red rose plunges into the sand.

"Bitch," he whistles, clutching her shoulders and pressing her to the ground. "You wanted to kill me?"

Buratina is silent, and for a moment her back is tense under Ryabets's hands, but then it goes slack. He holds her down with his knees and moves his hands to her neck. Blood drips black on her hair. He smells fresh urine. Finding the thyroid cartilage, he presses and presses on it from both sides, vividly imagining her anatomy. A quiet whistle like from a bicycle tire, and then silence. Off to the side Polkan's shadow is wagging its tail, baring its teeth. "Nadya, Nadya!"

"You never read *The Decameron?*" Boltyansky exclaims.

Ryabets doesn't like Boltyansky. That he's fat is bad enough, but he has those sticky little hands and those manicured nails, damnit. On top of it all, Boltyansky keeps bringing porn to school, photos blurry from being copied so many times. Girls with big tits and grayish bodies (the result of the copying) straddling muscle-bound guys. Or offering up their cushiony asses. Or spreading their lips. One look is all it takes and then there is strawberry jam all over the floor.

Boltyansky shows the photos in his hand, gripping them with his little pink fingers. If for the others the viewings are a standard diversion, it's different for Ryabets. The sticky feeling has degenerated into horror at a female's touch, be it a hand, elbow, accidental breast, or innocent hair. Even his mother's touch—extremely rare, fortunately—repulses him. If Praskovya Fyodorovna so much as strokes his head when she's tipsy, it turns his stomach and make his insides clench up.

"*Droll Stories* too. That's Balzac," Boltyansky preaches. They're walking home from school.

"Can I read it?"

"I'll bring it tomorrow. I'll bring *The Decameron*, not Balzac. Balzac's in a series. My parents would notice. They don't let me lend books. *The Decameron*'s better than Balzac anyway. Balzac just has one weird story, about how he disguised himself as a woman so he could fuck her. Well, I mean, first he'd make friends and all that, you know, and then he'd fuck her. The rest is just boring. *The Decameron*'s more interesting."

Boltyansky does bring *The Decameron*, a fat blue volume with an elegantly lettered title, and gives Ryabets a two-week deadline. Ryabets skims the yellowed pages and sets it aside. Final exams are starting soon.

"Wouldn't you know? The minute I climb off her, the bell! She goes to the door and wipes off the blood, all scared. 'Who's there?' Boltyansky: 'It's me, Nadya.' Her: 'Damn! What do you want?' Him: 'Want to go for a walk?' Ha ha ha!" Mesropov nearly falls down laughing. "Just imagine. A walk!"

"What did she say?" Ryabets's lips are dry. He and Mesropov are standing in the schoolyard. The graduation party is starting in half an hour. Everyone's already been drinking and they're sharing the news half-soused.

"She's practically rolling in laughter. Well, I sneak up from behind while she's talking to him through the door and give it to her good! If only Bolt could have seen what we were doing four inches away!"

Six months before, Mesropov had vowed that before graduation night he was going to pop the cherry of one of their classmates. Fiercely handsome and ox-eyed, he drove the girl crazy.

"I just came and he says again, 'Nadya, Nadya'"—Mesropov mimicked Boltyansky's squeaky voice—"'Let's go for a walk . . .' Well, I yanked the door open! Just as I was, no underpants, only a T-shirt! And a rubber flapping in my hand. Catch! Bolt's eyes bug out and he runs! Ha ha ha!"

"What about her?" Ryabets is breathing fast.

"Who? Nadya? Nadya's fine, Ryaba, just fine. She plays along! We fucked like bunnies for hours. Whoo! I can barely stand up. So we're going to Silver Pine Forest tomorrow, right, Ryaba? Nadya's got this friend, Lidukha. She's little but she's got titties out the wazoo! I'd rather have Lidukha, but Nadya . . . It's nice there, in the forest. Never been? Tons of bushes! 'Under every bush she kept a table set and a home!' Ha ha ha!"

Some other classmates come up and Mesropov starts recounting his adventure.

"Bolt gave me *The Decameron* to read," Ryabets says when he's finished.

"What? *The De-cam-er-on*? Give me a break! That *Decameron*'s kid stuff. Ever heard 'Luka Mudischev'? The actor Vesnik does it. 'The Mudischev clan was ancient, it had a patrimony, villages, and giant firs!' Come over, I'll play it! *The Decameron*. Hah! Kid stuff, Ryaba, kid stuff!"

"It all depends on your imagination," Tregubov the intellectual interposes weightily. "Some guys can get off on a keyhole. I don't think *The Decameron*'s half bad. Quattrocento, feast during the plague . . . Italy! It's not ancient Russia. Signorine, not girls! Pinos, not pines!"

Tregubov knows what he's talking about. In his not quite seventeen years he's the only one in class who's been abroad, he even lived in Italy. His father worked at the Soviet consulate in Rome.

"Pinos? Is that like a blowjob?" Mesropov.

"No, amico mio, it's a Mediterranean pine tree. A sky of purest blue! The sea! The sun! *O sole mio/ sta 'nfronte a te!/ O sole, o sole mio/ sta 'nfronte a te!/ sta 'nfro-o-o-onte a te-e-e-e!*" Tregubov sings, breaking into a falsetto.

"A goddamn Caruso!" Mesropov says with respect.

Boltyansky enters the yard wearing a black suit and a skinny black tie. His black hair is combed back and slicked so it shines. Seeing Mesropov, he nearly stumbles and his cheeks break out in red spots.

"Hey, pino," someone shouts, "want to go for a walk?"

Friendly laughter.

Ryabets doesn't stick around for the party. He takes his diploma and leaves. As he's walking down the stairs from the auditorium, Boltyansky catches up to him.

"You're taking off?"

"What do you care?"

"You're not staying for the dance?"

"I don't give a damn about that."

"When are you going to return the book? My parents have been asking. Did you read it?"

"Not all of it. Exams. I'll finish tomorrow. I'm fast."

Buratina passes them on the stairs. Powdered cheeks, high heels, short little skirt, lacy stockings, and looking slightly sloshed—she's giggling oddly. Boltyansky licks his lips. Three more steps up and she stops.

"Ryaba, want a drink? The kids are in the gym. They still have some left."

"No, I'm going home. I have a headache."

Ryabets can't tear his eyes away from Buratina's legs. She smiles.

"Home, home, home," she teases. "To his mama . . . Why don't you come to Silver Pine Forest tomorrow? Third beach. Know it? We'll go swimming at 5 or 6, when we wake up. My girlfriend Lida has a dacha there, her parents are taking off, so . . ."

"Fine," Ryabets rasps, and heads downstairs.

"What's with you?" he hears the teasing directed at Boltyansky. "Want to go for a walk? Hee hee hee!"

Boltyansky calls at 4 or so.

"Are you going to Silver Pine Forest? Did you forget?"

"Too far."

"That's okay, you can stay over. Nadya's friend has a da-cha there."

"I don't know, maybe I will."

"And grab *The Decameron*. My parents are pestering me."

"All right." Ryabets hangs up.

Followed by a surprise: Buratina. She's calling! In the whole ten years they've been in the same class, this is the first time.

"Ryaba, hi." A depressed voice, as if she's holding back tears. "Are you going to Silver Pine Forest? Take me."

Ryaba's heart is pounding. Joy! But fear too. Picturing Nadya in a swimsuit, he can't imagine what he'll do with himself. His swimsuit's going to bristle!

"All right."

"Should I come by then? In an hour?"

Ryabets hangs up and runs to the bathroom. He decides that if he does *it* a few times he might get by . . . He twirls in front of the mirror—uses his mama's powder on his zits, combs his hair back, then parts it; changes his shirt, rolls up his sleeves, rolls them down. What else? What if she walks in, he kisses her, she responds, and—

A ring. Not the door, the phone. It's her.

"Listen, Ryaba, I'll wait for you at the bus stop. If I come over, you'll rape me. You gave me such a look yesterday! Hee hee hee!"

Oof!

Ryabets grabs his bag and towel, throws *The Decameron* in—he suddenly remembered—and runs outside.

Nadya's wearing a yellow shirt with the top buttons undone, and there are her breasts. And a miniskirt too. Her face is creased; she drank and partied all night long. She's got a mark on the back of her neck. A hickey? Her eyes, half-Kalmyk to start with, are swollen; the abundant mascara highlights this. Her perfume—from a long way off. Ryabets stares and joy bubbles up inside him alternately with horror.

It's a long trip: trolley, subway, transfer, subway, trolley. Ryabets notices glances at his companion—men's leers, women's frowns.

Ryabets can't for the life of him figure out why she isn't with Mesropov. It's a puzzle. Going with Mesropov makes sense. Mesropov would take her in a taxi. All the way to the beach. His parents are really rich.

The trolley crosses the bridge toward pines, pines, and more pines. Pinos.

"Lidukha lives way over there," Nadya points out the window. Tall green and blue dachas with turrets amid century pines. "We'll go to her place after the beach, tonight. Her parents are off traveling somewhere. Will you go?"

"Maybe," Ryabets mumbles.

They get out. Ryabets is holding his bag in front for obvious reasons.

They're walking down the road next to a very high fence. "Who lives here? Artists?" he asks.

"Big shots, diplomats, and artists too. Did you see the Japanese flag behind the fence at the stop?"

"Lucky dogs . . . In Moscow, but like being in a forest."

Nadya shrugs.

They leave the road and walk among the pines across the

sand. Nadya takes off her platform shoes. Ryabets lags behind a little. *Make up your mind!* is knocking in his brain. *She went into the forest on purpose, on purpose!*

He puts his hand on Nadya's shoulder. The girl stops.

"What are you doing?" She removes his hand.

"I . . . I—" He drops his bag and tries to put his arms around her.

She dodges him. "That'd be just great. This place is full of people!"

"I . . . I . . . just . . . wanted . . . to kiss you."

"Kiss me?" She gives him a quick kiss on the lips. "There! Later, later . . ."

"When?" Ryabets rasps.

"Tonight, maybe. Who makes love in the afternoon?"

Mesropov and the gang are already at the beach. Boltyansky's there too. The others are strangers, dark-haired and guttural, Mesropov's fellow tribesmen. They greet the appearance of Ryabets and Burataeva cheerfully, by pouring the Armenian brandy. Ryabets doesn't drink. He takes a whiff and sets it aside. First of all, he's never tried anything stronger than New Year's champagne, and second, he's angry. Nadya's the only girl in the group. She goes for a swim. She swims for a long time and he watches her. She's already squealing and giggling, and they're already pawing at her. Mesropov and his friends. "Bastards! Bastards!" he shouts with his head under water so no one can hear.

They play ball, jump around, roughhouse. Ryabets sits on a lounge and rages. Then they wander over to a beer stand on Krug. Mesropov and Burataeva take up the rear with their arms around each other. Ryabets looks back. He doesn't go near Buratina at the beer stand or later when they finally show up at the dacha of Lidukha, a little brunette with small, intense eyes. She greets her guests on the porch. Mesropov kisses her hand, and at that moment Buratina remembers Ryabets and glances around. He's standing at the gate.

"Are you coming or what?"

"No, I'm going home."

He'll kill her, the bitch, he will.

Ryabets squeezes his dry fists.

Laughter from a second-story window: "Ha ha ha ha! Ho ho ho ho! Hee hee hee hee!"

That last is hers.

Ryabets feels the rough wall. It's dry, it's going to burn, so don't cry, mama!

First, gasoline. No problem. There's a car by the gate.

Second, a hose. Where's the hose? There—the dead snake on the dry grass. Everything's very dry. Laughter and more laughter. Drunken and insolent. And music. Someone's puking.

Third, a bottle. Here's a jar under the porch. Two of them. Liter bottles. Great!

Ryabets uses his teeth to rip off a piece—about a meter long—of the snake-hose's black flesh. There we go, there. He twists off the gas cap. Now suck—ha ha—suck! Acrid fumes, more, more . . . till you feel like puking. More, more . . . *E-ro-tic!* Boltyansky would say. He wouldn't have to listen to his, Boltyansky's, laughing, fearless, or him jerking off in the hall . . . Not a damn thing was going to be left of him either.

It's flowing! First down the throat, then into the jar. A liter. Let's pour. Another liter. That's it, no more sucks out. That's enough. It's so dry it could catch without gasoline.

Now to wait. Cover the jar with a towel at least, so it doesn't evaporate off, and wait-wait-wait.

Ryabets moves away from the dacha and sits leaning up against a sticky pine trunk. Wait. It's a good thing there's no dog. No dog.

Ryabets's hand slithers into his pants. No, he shouldn't. If I come I'll back down. It's wrong. For three years she's all I've been thinking of. Hands off!

Her short haircut in the window. She's smoking, tapping the ashes right where he was just standing. Oops! The butt flies like a drunken star and drops next to his invisible feet. And smolders. But it could catch fire. It could. Excellent. She's gone. Yesterday Mesropov said he wanted her girlfriend. But who wants *her*? These guys? The Chuchmeks? Bitch.

It's not jealousy, it's justice. Like in *The Decameron*. She keeps him waiting in the yard in winter while she consoles herself with someone else. Italy. And the wife forced her husband to climb into a barrel to caulk it up from the inside. She's standing there and showing him where . . . while another guy fucks her from behind. Cheerful folks. And there's the one who pretended to be deaf and dumb in a convent. That's the life!

Ha ha ha ha! Ho ho ho ho! Hee hee hee hee!

When are they going to settle down? First brandy, then beer, then brandy. How will he get home? How? The trolleys will stop running. So will the subway. I'll call my mother. Or maybe I shouldn't. Evidence. They'll ask his mother, *When did your son come home?*

Phooey! He's in trouble again. Don't do that. Go home. Jerk off as much as you can. Until you can't, ha ha.

Shhh. They've turned off the lights. Gone to bed? Bolt

too? With who? *Quietly by myself* . . . Super! The terrace door creaks. Ryabets presses up against the trunk and tucks his feet in. The shadow from a nearby bush hides him. A rustle. Lidukha with the big tits. Mesropov. They stop and whisper.

"I won't without them. Where did she throw them, the fool?"

"Over here somewhere. It's dark, where should I look? I'll be careful, I promise."

"You promise but it's my ass!"

"Lighten up, will you? I swear, I'll be careful!"

"Uh-huh, and then it's you and Nadya?"

"What's with you? I didn't invite her, you did. You and I have all day tomorrow, don't we? When are your parents coming back?"

And he paws at her, the Chuchmek, he paws at Lidukha. He pulls her to the ground and lifts her skirt, goddamn decameron!

Ryabets goggles at the silhouettes fornicating. He feels like coming out and . . . kicking, kicking! Just be patient. Wait and be patient. Lidukha gives a faint cry. And Ryabets notices *her* look out the window. Her profile is sweet, but her eyes are harsh. That means she sees everything and isn't going away. Why? Why? Mesropych rolls off the girl. Like a tick. Nadya spins around and vanishes.

They stand up, shake off, and leave. They close the door. Lock it. Very good. Wait.

Ryabets, crouching, moves toward the house, right where the couple was. There's something kind of white in the grass— condoms! Two packets held together by a rubber band. Why did they leave them here?

Ryabets is standing behind the bridge pylon watching. The

flashes he could barely make out a minute ago are visible now, and furious. The pinos are burning, the pinos! Like candles!

He stands and watches. Another ten minutes and it'll be dawn. Two fire engines speed past. And an ambulance. Too late.

He descends to Novikov-Priboy Street, finds a telephone booth, drops in a two-kopek coin, and dials. His mother doesn't answer right away, she mumbles incoherently, and Ryabets is relieved. She's drunk. If she's drunk, that means his father's been asleep for a long time too. No need to hurry.

Last man standing. How powerful is that? Like Mesropych. Boltyansky once asked Zinaida Leonidovna, the lit teacher, about *The Decameron*. Had she read it? That idiot four-eyes exploded. "Who gave you permission to read books like that?" And Boltyansky said to her, "But it's a classic. It says so in the preface." "A classic?" Zinaida Leonidovna hollered. "I'll give you a classic, Boltyansky! I worry *that's* all you think about! It's never occurred to you that *The Decameron* is primarily an anti-clerical book. Go to the board, Boltyansky. Tell me about the images of Communists in Mikhail Aleksandrovich Sholokhov's *Quiet Flows the Don* and *Virgin Soil Upturned*. Or should I fail you immediately? Tell your parents to come see me tomorrow!"

"You mean we shouldn't read Balzac either, Zinaida Leonidovna?" This was Tregubov, a top student. She wouldn't dare yell at him. "What Balzac?" She was buying time. "*Droll Stories*, Zinaida Leonidovna!" She blushed deeply, removed her glasses, and put them back on. "Today we will continue our study of *Virgin Soil*. Open your notebooks . . ."

Ryabets finds an open doorway and hides under the stairs. He can wait here a few hours, in the corner, and then the trolleys will start running. And the subway. Don't cry, you'll wake people up. Don't cry.

THE DOPPELGÄNGER

BY GLEB SHULPYAKOV
Zamoskvorechye

Translated by Sylvia Maizell

Once there lived an actor in Moscow. For many years he performed in a celebrated theater and appeared fleetingly in TV serials. He was considered famous although he never made it as a popular icon. And this didn't bother him in the least. It happened long ago, about twenty years or so—he had the good fortune to play a small but impressive role in a famous film about the Revolution. Eventually he settled down, having decided he'd made his mark, that he'd already been inscribed in the history of cinematography.

After that film they recognized him for many years on the streets. But without any frenzy, without their eyes popping out. *Hey, look who's coming, uh, what's his name . . .* And there followed the name of the character he played, since no one remembered the actor's real name.

He lived many years alone in a tiny bachelor apartment the theater provided for him, in a Stalin-era building by the Paveletskaya station, in the Zamoskvorechye neighborhood. The theater administration had offered several times to move him to a new place on the other side of the river, closer to work. But each time the actor refused. He liked living here. Over time he had grown fond of the mysterious silence of the streets on Sundays; more and more often he imagined another life that was long gone in its sagging mansions; in the evenings, when he strolled the narrow streets, it seemed to him that this life hadn't ended one hundred years before but still flickered—there, behind the dusty panes, behind the chipped wooden shutters. He was fond of the amusing and naïve residents of these streets, who were on a first-name basis with each other, who at the streetcar stops exchanged rumors about a maniac from the chocolate factory; about a sect that met in the abandoned church by the metro and devoured ancient ecclesiastical texts; about the corner house with the rotunda that housed a secret brothel.

And so on.

His daughter used to come from Germany to visit him here in Zamoskvoreche. She'd clean the room and stuff the refrigerator with provisions. She'd bring medicine for his chronic cold. Photos of his twin grandchildren. And then she'd be gone for a year.

He kept a photo of the twins with a stack of fan letters in a desk drawer. He'd study the identical faces with amazement and disdain, making out, through their German imprint, the features of his ancestors.

His hobby, his passion, was telescopes. Spyglasses in particular. He assembled them, with his own hands—after shows or in the morning if there were no rehearsals. He calculated angles and radii from magazines and handbooks. And distances. He'd send a list to his daughter and she'd bring him first-class German lenses. He'd fit them in a tube made by the theater metal workers (for some reasons these workers loved him). Thus a telescope on a tripod made an appearance. And he'd pull heavenly objects somewhat closer to Moscow.

What can you see in the blurry Moscow sky, where only

the moon—and that with difficulty—makes its way to the viewer? Nonetheless, right after a performance, he'd rush to Paveletskaya. If the night was more or less clear, he'd sit down on the wide windowsill and sharpen the focus. Or he'd spread maps out on the floor and make calculations. He'd determine the favorable days and segments of the sky in which a constellation would appear.

And so he lived this way from year to year. He went on film shoots and tours, to festivals in Sochi and Vyborg. He took on a lover from the theater orchestra. He'd call on her at the dormitory on Gruzinskaya Street. But mostly he spent his time between the theater and the stars. Until, ultimately, this thing happened.

One March morning he set out for the laundromat, as he did every other Saturday, to drop off his underwear and shirts. The establishment was close by, two stops on the streetcar. Since on the weekends you can wait forever for Moscow's public transportation, and since it was sunny, he decided to go on foot. He had just set off when suddenly, ringing and rumbling, a streetcar came bounding down the street.

It simply emerged from the flow of traffic and flung its doors open.

There was nothing to be done. It was fate. He was in luck. He made his way to the end of the car and set his laundry bag down. He looked around. The car was empty, except for a man in a sheepskin coat and an old woman with her grandchild sitting up front. The car started off; the mansions, like rickety old wardrobes, drifting by. Somewhere church bells were sounding—the Saturday chimes had begun. The actor closed his eyes and imagined they were riding through old, prerevolutionary Moscow, as in some Ivan Shmelev tale or a play by Ostrovsky. *A hundred years ago the bells probably rang exactly the same way*, he thought. When he opened his eyes, he saw that the man in the sheepskin coat was standing near the front, about to get off.

His profile seemed familiar and the actor was touched with the thought that earlier, two centuries ago, everyone here would have known each other.

Moving down the steps, the man turned around and their eyes met. The actor gasped. He saw that this man resembled him; they were like two peas in a pod.

And that, in essence, before him stood he himself—only in different clothes.

Amazed, the actor dropped his bag and a towel fell out onto the dirty floor. When he managed to stuff it back, the doors had already slammed shut. His double had disappeared. The actor rushed to the window but the pane was covered over with glossy paper. Nothing was visible through the face of an advertisement diva.

He pulled the window open and leaned out. An enormous billboard, *Gold*, and a yellow church fence caught his eye. That one, the other one, was standing on a corner looking right back at the actor. And again, with frightening clarity, he saw himself. His own face—familiar to the point of disgust from all the films and posters.

Well, so what? Anything can happen in Moscow. But still, thoughts of a double made him anxious. At first he drove them away, annoyed at his stupidity. He tried to make fun of himself. He laughed. He recalled many films with just such a plot. But nothing helped. The image of his double was haunting and tenacious.

What if it's my twin brother? After all, it was postwar times. Total confusion. We were returning to Moscow from the evacua-

tion . . . Mother remembered she was holding a little baby, and that
he didn't make it, that he had died . . . Maybe he simply got lost?

My daughter too gave birth to twins.

No, this just can't be true.

He'd sit down on the bed and drink a glass of water from
a decanter. He'd nervously stare at the hair on his bare legs.
Then he'd take out the photo of his grandchildren and scruti-
nize it once more. With each night it seemed they resembled
him less and less—because they looked more and more like
the man in the sheepskin coat. From the empty streetcar.

That means people recognize him on the streets. Of course they
do! They want to know how things are. They ask for an autograph.
Maybe he's an honest fellow and tells them they are mistaken. But
what if he isn't?

He imagined clearly how that one, the other one, arrives
instead of him at the theater, pays visits to the flutist. And
he'd throw himself on the bed, snarling into the pillow from
rage. But soon another feeling began to penetrate his impotent fury—of emptiness, total emasculation, of indifference.
He had only ever experienced something similar after difficult
performances. When he played a role he didn't fully understand. One he hadn't quite entered. He felt like a coat shoved
onto a hanger; it just hangs there, dangling in the darkness,
completely forgotten by everyone. Dead. He'd pinch himself
and pull at his hair. He'd grab the phone. But who could he
call?

Not the police.

His life gradually began to take a new turn. He shifted
the telescope from the sky to the streetcar stop. For hours
he'd track the people clustered there in hopes of seeing the
one in the sheepskin coat. For no particular reason he kept
going downstairs to the store. He hung around the counter

a lot so they'd recognize and greet him. If they didn't, he'd begin to panic. He'd loiter around the neighborhood, peering into faces, and his feet would inevitably take him back to that corner with the yellow church fence and the *Gold* billboard where his twin, the stranger, had disappeared.

But the twin was nowhere to be found.

What's more, they stopped phoning him from the theater to remind him of performances and rehearsals. As if they had forgotten or fired him. Once he made the call himself, but an unfamiliar voice didn't recognize him. He got frightened and hung up. So he stopped calling. He was afraid.

A week later, he simply got in his car one evening and drove downtown.

Under the notice *Today* on the poster in front of the theater, his performance was announced.

So, the impostor has already taken my place.

Relieved, the actor sat down in a café and began to drink, although he had given up alcohol after a heart attack ten years earlier. Cognac, beer, vodka—he ordered them indiscriminately. He drank greedily, without a snack, gazing between glasses at the ad behind the dusty window. *Your blood will save a life*, a girl urged from the poster, smiling her celluloid smile.

He couldn't remember how he got home. The smoke-filled cellar at Novokuznetskaya station and the patchy shadows, in whose company he'd swigged down vodka and belted out songs, flashed in his memory.

He collapsed in his clothes but couldn't fall asleep because he was sick at heart. Pulling his knees to his chin, he lay there and listened to the very same sentence that kept echoing in his head. *Your blood will save a life*, someone's quiet, velvety voice kept repeating.

Your blood will save a life.

He had finally begun to doze off when a thick, enveloping nausea overtook his body. It rose up like sludge and flooded his consciousness. His heart became a big balloon about to burst into pieces. *So that's how one dies*, he thought, starting to lose consciousness, vanishing slowly into an airless well and resurfacing later in the darkness of a sleepless night. At dawn, coming to on sweat-soaked sheets, he moved to an armchair. Hunched over from the pain in his heart, he sat there until daylight.

Around 11 he was jolted by the ringing telephone. It was a call from the theater; the troupe, it turned out, had just returned the day before from a short tour. The director's assistant was reminding him there was a performance that evening. "In your honor," she flirted.

"But how can . . . ?" he mumbled into the receiver.

"The new cloakroom attendant got it mixed up," the woman nattered on. "Instead of *Tomorrow*, he put up the sign that said *Today*. We'll rehearse the dance an hour before curtain, as usual." And she hung up.

Standing under the shower, he came to his senses. He was amazed how quickly, with one single phone call, the nightmare vanished. It simply came unglued like a plastic advertising sticker and flew away in the wind. Sobered up, cheerful, he set about tidying the whole apartment. He washed the floor and windows. He dropped off his underwear, which had been lying in the corner since that day, at the laundromat. He for the first time ever phoned his daughter.

"Imagine, such nonsense!" he said, chuckling into the receiver. "I knew they were supposed to go on tour, but I simply forgot."

"Everyone's so nervous!" The daughter gave a Chekhovian sigh, and it was obvious she was thinking of someone else as well.

"The Irish call one's double his fetch," she said in parting. "I'll send you some pills. That should help."

That evening they gave the performance. And they say he played Caesar as never before, fiercely, implacably, desperately. In such a way that before the ovation, when the emperor exits into eternity, a pause hung in the air for a few seconds—as in olden times, when the spectator truly believed what was happening on stage.

Returning home, the actor didn't feel his usual fatigue. On the contrary, blood was racing through his veins, his energy was overflowing. He even got out of the cab and walked home on foot, swinging his arms widely. *A new life*, he thought, *will definitely begin from this night forward. It will be wonderful and serene. Unpredictable and clear.*

Not like the one which he had lived.

He entered his apartment. Without taking off his coat, he began to wander around the room. *How about going back again on the street?* he thought. *How about a breath of fresh air? To hell with it, how about meeting some woman, maybe even from the railroad station? Maybe go to a café, or a movie.*

He stood looking out the window, watching how persistently and interminably the cars moved around the ring. Then his gaze fell on the telescope. It was pointing to the streetcar stop, as before. And rubbing his palms, he triumphantly sharpened the focus.

In the lens, two round-shouldered teenagers stood shifting their feet and spitting noiselessly. He moved the tube forward a millimeter and saw next to them a man with a briefcase.

His twin, his double. That very one.

When he ran out onto the street, the kids were trying to snatch the briefcase out of the man's hands. An empty jar was rolling along the asphalt. A hand flashed, the sound of a dull, crunching blow. The double clutched at his face.

"Hey!" shouted the actor across the street. "What do you think you're doing!"

And he stepped out into the road.

The impact of a car flipped him around several times in the air. He fell, and tumbling along the asphalt, he came to a stop, his arms flung wide.

Through the dark sludge that was flooding his consciousness, he was able to see his double take off down a side street. Then someone's hands ran along his body, and he thought about the flutist, how she would undress him, caress him. But these were other hands. Fast and clumsy, a man's hands. They dug into his pockets and grabbed his watch. Then wiped it off with disgust on the sleeves of his raincoat.

"Look at this weirdo, he's a copy," sounded over his ear. "Same face."

There was some spitting and a swish of fabric. The last things he saw were two pairs of tattered sneakers retreating swiftly down the street.

PART III

FATHERS AND SONS

DADDY LOVES ME

BY MAXIM MAXIMOV
Perovo

Translated by Matvei Yankelevich

Her students hated her. For not being young, pretty, or fun. For not being different from who she was. Or they loathed her for something altogether different. Who knows what reasons people find to hate each other . . .

Although she was, like her colleagues in humanity, made up of 90 percent water, that water was not potable, which in a different circumstance may have, at least partially, influenced the formation of sympathy toward her in her students as well as others around her.

Dad had called her Danaë. According to her passport she was Danaë. For her students and colleagues she was Dana Innokentievna, a teacher of Russian language and literature.

She had mutual feelings for her students, not because she thought it necessary to answer loathing with loathing, but just because it happened to be so: she was hated and she also hated. A pure coincidence of feelings directed toward one another (if it is allowed that hate is a feeling).

And so, she hated her students—just as in childhood she'd hated lumps in her cereal. In essence, they were indeed lumps in the undigestible cereal of existence. And Danaë imagined herself a lump as well—big, flabby, stale. In fact, Danaë loathed the directress Gavriushkina like she loathed fish oil or boiled onions. Yet she tried to act nice. And the more she pretended, the more she loathed—her students, her colleagues, the scantily clad woman standing in front of her in line at the supermarket—yes, that very woman with the cart full of ad-emblazoned frozen dinners.

Sometimes Danaë thought with bitterness: *Why don't the terrorists take all these vermin hostage? Why don't they get blown up? Why do serial killers pass over the directress Gavriushkina and that lady with the frozen dinners?*

Danaë Karakleva was forty-seven years old. She knew that there was nothing more to come. It was all over. All the gifts she could have received had already been received. She was simply brought into this remarkable thrift store with the breath of a violated cosmos wafting through it, and they said to her, "Pick something out," and then they locked her in, in this thrift store where everything had already been picked over. And in this thrift store with the breath of a violated cosmos wafting through it, she had spent forty-seven years.

As regards this existence's amorous propositions, Danaë Karakleva could say the following: "I was never certain that I loved any of those not numerous men who—each in his own time—shook their fatty deposits over my trembling bosom. If Cupid ever shot at my heart, he must have been shooting blanks."

This thesis which she had invented herself resembled fact, much more so than the rumors about her inevitable old-maid-hood. Among the large-horned herd of her students, it was commonly said in such cases: "Oh yeah? Suck *this*."

She liked looking at the shower of pills, especially the round ones, that resembled squashed pearls. She liked to ride the tram past the hospital and look at the sapphire windows of the operating rooms and imagine the surgeon making a fatal error . . .

Danaë and her dad lived in a five-story building, erected under Nikita Khrushchev in the time of the artificial, government-approved destruction of the ark of communal living. There were more than enough such buildings in the neighborhood of Perovo, as there were in many of Moscow's outlying quarters. They were built out of either panels the color of tubercular spit or gray-pink brick. Each of these residential buildings lacked an elevator. Outward attractiveness and interior comfort—all this was also lacking. It might be easier to list what was present in these buildings: the metastases of all varieties of cancer; staircases by which one might climb to the heights of despair, and if one were to descend it would be into pits of madness; guitar chords of underworld ditties oft performed by green-horns fated to disappear in the sands of Afghanistan or the ravines of Chechnya. Also present in these buildings were walls that had been viciously fooled by promises of becoming supplementary scrolls for God's commandments . . .

Every day, Danaë returned to this building, having first stopped at the market or grocery store; she returned with a feeling of a hole, a nagging pain, in the very center of her being . . .

From the Karaklev family's kitchen window one could see the subway entrance. In the morning rush hour, before heading out to work in the nearby school, Danaë slowly downed a cup of instant coffee while examining the dark human mass. The mass penetrated the underground, shuffling from one leg to another in penguin fashion. The sleepy faces of those people—especially in the dusk of winter mornings—looked ominously similar to one another, lacking features, something like the heads of nails when viewed face on.

Danaë's manner of speaking was as bizarre as her vision. Her speech was understood only by the portraits of the classics that hung on the classroom walls, and not even by all of them. She doubted Maxim Gorky, for one. As regards her pupils— they simply whimpered. Or cursed. Some quietly, others with full voice—depending on how much nerve they had. Danaë was kept employed by the school because she seemed rather like an animal that had been listed in the little red book. A wide-faced, warty roe deer, for example.

"As recently as the beginning of the twentieth century, the Perovo neighborhood in the south-east of Moscow consisted of a treasure trove of toxic swamps, the kingdom of poisonous mycelium, and randomly intersecting paths along which it was dangerous to walk alone . . ." In this manner began the oral dictation, concocted by Danaë in order to test the literacy of her pupils, who had come back from their summer vacations with their heads well aired out. It ended thusly: "And now, fuckity-suckity, here you dwell, young sluts and indefatigable jerk-offs . . ."

Having spoken these words in her mind, Danaë stretched her pale lips into an ambiguous smile and began dictating another text—a fake one—that had been approved by the pederasts from the Ministry of Education: "In the spring the forest is awoken by trills, drills, spills, trolls, and various other junk . . ."

Her daddy, who had schooled her in the art of complex linguistic expression, was dying of cancer . . . Yes, Innokentii Karaklev adored phrases that produced an effect. And he had taught his own daughter to adore such turns of phrase. As a result, the speech of both the Karaklevs was as out of place in the neighborhood of Perovo as a fugue for organ would be in a shawarma shack in a resort town.

Watching over her daddy's demise was crushing. Danaë thought it unbearable to have to live and suffer watching such a thing. But damn it if she thought her life worse than death. She was convinced that she could live on, even without a future. Somehow. She wished for her daddy to disappear. Yes, to disappear, like a bout of hiccups, which, having come from god knows where, torments you for a while and then *snap!* it's gone just like that, no one knows how or where. Daddy—she had thought since childhood—wasn't fated for the grave. She rejected the idea of his decomposition in that stuffy heat and darkness. Her daddy couldn't become a skeleton. That's what Danaë had thought previously. And her daddy could not be turned into an urn of gray powder. But Innokentii Karaklev was dying—he emitted the smell of decomposition and his daily caprices were driving his daughter closer to the brink.

The salary of a Russian schoolteacher permits one to purchase three of the most inexpensive urns, then dismember Daddy and shove him into the urns in equal parts, and transport the urns to three different polling stations, pretending that one has simply mistaken the place to somewhere else. But the salary of a Russian schoolteacher can only nurse Daddy back to health if he has been afflicted with a foot fungus. By purchasing the appropriate ointment. Yet Innokentii Karaklev was dying not from a foot fungus, but from cancer of the innards. The chemo had made him look even more cancerlike: his eyes bulged, his back had lost its layer of fat, and touching it brought to mind the shell of a shrimp. Soon he'll learn to walk backward, thought Danaë.

At school, many knew of Danaë's misfortune, which went on without end. The directress Gavriushkina, with all of her predatory, livid, gloating heart, sympathized with Danaë. Gavriushkina would say to her: "Danochka Innokentievna, you should get a good night's sleep. I'll think of someone to substitute for you, Danochka Innokentievna . . ."

Danaë couldn't bear expressions of pity directed at herself. In her mind she quickly but carefully rolled up the velvety paths of pity—embroidered with gristle and spread out before her—and having rolled up each and every one of them, shoved the scrolls deep inside Gavriushkina's cyclopean ass.

"Thanks for your concern, Maria Petrovna," Danaë would reply to the woman, "but I think I can manage just fine . . ."

"It's clearer to one looking at you from the outside," Gavriushkina parried. "Your beautiful eyes have lost their shine."

I'll show you some shine, thought Danaë, and following right behind the scrolls of velvety paths, into the back end of the directress, she stuck a metaphysical myriad of wrinkled sheets, recently soiled by Daddy's excretions.

Sometimes Daddy liked to frighten his daughter. When she was six years old, Innokentii Karaklev told her the story of a Chinese governor who had two pupils in each eyeball. It was because of these four eyes that he had received his political appointment; Dad said that the Chinese guy lacked any other talents. Six-year-old Danaë was unable to sleep without having nightmares for a whole month. The Chinese guy visited her in her dreams and made eyes at her relentlessly.

Innokentii Karaklev had been an archeologist. Unfortunately, he'd never dug up anything worthwhile, anything for which one might win an award. All the Troys had been excavated before him. In his youth, he had planned to search out the tomb of Abel Adamovich Yahweh-ev, but somehow it just never panned out.

What's wrong with me? Danaë was indignant with herself. *He must have dug something up, I've just forgotten.*

"Listen, Daddy, what was it you dug up?" asked Danaë as she changed his sheets.

"Cancer."

"Yeah, but what else?"

"You . . ."

"I think it was something related to the burial mounds of the Scythians."

"Yeah, well, the burial mounds . . ."

"You don't want to talk about it?"

"Why would I want to talk about it? Soon I'll be a Scythian myself . . ."

Once Danaë got a call from the bank and was offered a line of credit. What the bank needed with Danaë in particular even the bank didn't know. The one who called had a hissy voice of unidentifiable gender.

"I don't need any credit," said Danaë into the receiver. "My dad's dying of cancer."

"Forgive me, for god's sake. Forgive me. Accept my condolences. All the best to you," the voice poured out like a frightened fizz.

"No, wait!" shouted Danaë. "Don't hang up!"

"Yes, yes?"

"What kind of condolences? What made you say that?"

The voice was silent.

"I don't believe it's possible, do you hear me? It's just impossible!" Danaë yelled. "I don't believe you! You cannot offer condolences, do you hear? You are just a petty, greedy maggot! I don't even know your name, or your age, not even your gender, you son of a bitch! How dare you offer me your condolences? And where did you get my number?"

But the fizz wasn't listening anymore. It had gone flat. Danaë hung up the phone and lit a cigarette, looking out the window at the other side of the street, where a tram rumbled past a plaza recently torn up by excavators. The plaza—pockmarked with ditches in which lay naked sewer pipes gazing at the ashen sky with their tired, rusty eyes—was empty. It was empty, if one were to ignore the statue of three orthodox nuns hanging their heads in mourning over that which could not be seen from the window, and that which Danaë could not recall, even though she walked past these nuns-in-ditches every day on her way to school.

It was cheaper to go to the market. Although daddy hadn't taught her how to bargain. It was all for the better, taking into accent Dad's slow demise, that double-mouthed Karaklev family had begun to consume less food.

"One Karaklev mouth is foaming," said Danaë unconsciously to the lady attempting to sell some pig's feet that would never know flat-footedness.

A month ago Danaë went to see a certain bastard who had been referred to her by another bastard. Both of them were medical professionals who considered themselves transmitters of veritable mercy. They rallied for euthanasia, adding that if she were to tell anyone about it, they would make her into a visual aid to Vesalius's anatomy. The pill that would spare Dad an agonizing death would cost Danaë eight-ninths of a teacher's savings. She remembered that day well. She was walking home from the train station, down 2nd Vladimir-skaya Street. The sky was the color of boiled pork. The traffic lights were doing what they always did—preparing to break down. Flattened cigarette butts lay strewn about the asphalt like pharaohs whose sarcophagi had been jacked. Stray cats dashed away from short-order cooks dealing shish kabab on the street.

Danaë poisoned her daddy. Innokentii Karaklev felt drowsy. Danaë tucked him into bed and went to the kitchen to wait for him not to wake up. But Innokentii Karaklev did wake up. He even drank a little chicken broth. When he went to sleep for a second time and, after a short while, woke up once again. And the third time was the same. The fourth and fifth times too. So passed three days, and Daddy was still not dying. The poison didn't tarry in his sick body: it left with the urine or the shit, she didn't quite know which. Then Danaë telephoned the bastards.

"What did you give me?" she asked them.

"What you asked for," was their answer.

"But it didn't work! Three days have already passed!"

"Don't shout. Wait awhile, it'll work. And don't call here again."

Danaë began to wait. A week went by. Innokentii Karaklev was dying, but not all the way. Every day the same. He was dying, but not all the way.

She knew that two of the ninth-grade students—Chuniaev and Golotsvan—had committed a murder. Danaë accidentally overheard their lively chatter, their voices brimming with real euphoria. The boys were cheerfully, ecstatically exchanging impressions. The Creator himself, it would seem, had experienced such rapture in the first hours after the creation of the world. But these two—Chuniaev and Golotsvan—had simply murdered a bum the previous night. With the aid of the homeless man they had been demonstrating to each other various martial arts strikes and holds, and finally martial-arted the man to death. Danaë also had previous opportunities to hear about this type of entertainment of the idle but energetic youth from families who considered themselves successful. The Perovo police took on the search for the homeless-cides with some reluctance. More precisely: they began the search reluctantly and then, after a few hours, dropped it completely. The Perovo police had much luckier corpses to track—ones with relatives and square-footage.

But the corpse of that bum did not vanish without glory: it had a short but successful career as an actor in an anatomical theater. The medical students showered him with bouquets of twinkling scalpels . . .

She was impressed that her students—Chuniaev and Golotsvan—were not only falling behind in every subject, while also, as it turned out, committing murders. This permitted her hatred toward them to acquire some firm ground. The testosterone was jumping out of Chuniaev's and Golotsvan's mouths, ears, noses, and even from under their fingernails . . .

Once, on television, she saw a news segment about a group of students who raped and murdered their phys-ed teacher. This happened somewhere on the outskirts of the city, which Danaë, a Muscovite, could imagine about as vaguely as she could the Flemish city of Brabant. Watching Golotsvan as he shuffled at the blackboard with his hands in the pockets of his wide jeans, which were covered with chains and trinkets, Danaë imagined him, with hands shaking, hastily unbuttoning his foul-smelling pants and throwing himself at her with his horn-shaped prick. She, Danaë, is lying crucified in the tar, naked, while Golotsvan's partners in crime hold her by the arms and legs; she struggles in their trap like a deer knocked onto her back. First Golotsvan, and then the rest of the goons, one by one, press against her with their unwashed genitalia, toss on her for a bit, then sprinkle her with what God gave them, and . . . experience a piercing guilt. Then, ashamed, they break her neck, or choke her with a wire, or stab her to death with penknives . . .

"And that's all you deigned to learn, venerable Golotsvan?"

"I didn't have time, Dana Innokentievna, my cat had kittens last night."

"How many did she have?"

"Six. Would you like a kitten, Dana Innokentievna?"

"Take a seat, Golotsvan. You get a 'satisfactory.'"

"Why 'satisfactatory'? Please, Dana Innokentievna—"

"Take your seat."

Grumbling under his breath, with his lower lip jutting forward, Golotsvan went back to his seat, jangling the chains and trinkets on his foul-smelling pants. His hands in his pockets. Danaë picked up a piece of chalk and turned to the board.

"Jewish bitch . . ." Golotsvan muttered.

Without turning around, Danaë grinned at the mouse-gray smoothness of the chalkboard. A thought came to her: *What would happen if I take this here piece of chalk and on this very blackboard write something really special. Like, for example, "May you all be damned." What would happen? Probably nothing. They'd all exchange glances and squeeze out puzzled little smirks, like lambs catching a whiff of the fire being lit under the spit. Besides, they were all damned long ago.* And she was too. Danaë herself had been damned even before the students sitting in this classroom. Because she was older than them. Almost

three times older. There's your arithmetic for you, in a literature class. In the Perovo neighborhood. In a state school,
in the city of Moscow, compared to which Brabant was just a
pathetic little village of five houses and one toilet.

It would be natural to assume that since Danaë had a father,
she also had a mother. Danaë didn't like assumptions, particularly if they came from strangers. First of all, the mom she did
in fact have at some point, she had no longer. Second, Mom
loved her little Danaë for only a very short time: from zero to
nine years old, plus the nine months that she spent carrying
her daughter in her womb. And when the nine years were
over, Mom placed a big down pillow on her sleeping daughter's pretty little face, and then sat on top of it. Dad had lifted
Mom off the pillow—and thus also off the red face of their
daughter—just in time. After that, Danaë never saw her mom
again. With the exception of that one time, which she had
mostly forgotten: she and her dad had, it seems, visited Mom
in some sort of yellow basement that smelled like medical syringes. Now, of course, Danaë knows all too well, and had
known it for twenty-plus years, that the awful trick with the
down pillow secured for Mom her demise in the mad house.

"Mom loves you," Karaklev assured his nine-year-old
daughter as she cried herself to sleep. "She just needs a little
medical treatment and she'll be with us again. Mom loves
you."

"And do *you* love me?" Danaë asked, smearing the tears
with her little fist.

"And I do too," Dad replied, taken aback that she would
question his feelings. "Very, very, very much. Daddy loves his
little pea, his clever girl."

* * *

Innokentii Karaklev was becoming more and more capricious, more cancerlike. More foul-smelling. Worst of all, Daddy started to recount aloud his past life, and specifically those moments that a healthy person would not only not recall, but would actively try to forget. The long period of dying had debased him. Instead of becoming more pious, he was transformed into a cynic to a degree that is rarely found among the camp of dying organisms. This is what Innokentii Karaklev said to his daughter Danaë on that day it rained cats and dogs, such a heavy, pounding rain that the pigeons caught in it received concussions. The neighborhood of Perovo looked like a boundless, cracked aquarium into which poured the water from a thousand hoses in the sky.

"I slept with your mother. I did it with all my passion. I drilled her and drilled her and then you emerged from her belly like a wild troll from a mangled cave . . . Admit it, my child, from the very beginning you never liked it here."

"No, I liked it here. From the very beginning. You're mistaken, Daddy," Danaë answered, listening with one ear to the hammering rain. "Fools like you are always mistaken. You're made of mistakes. You have a fatal error dangling right there between your legs."

Innokentii Karaklev watched the rivulets of rain running down the windowpane.

"Listen, child . . ." he muttered, swallowing dryly, "try to be . . . happy. I'm so sick of you being unhappy . . . I'm dying because of your unhappiness."

"You're dying because of cancer," corrected Danaë, sticking a cigarette in the corner of her smirk.

They were both silent awhile, thirty-five seconds or so. The smoke from Danaë's cigarette coiled around itself in the dark room like a scrap of seaweed.

"Do you know why I left your mother?" said Dad, scratching his sunken cheek. "Because of this one student. A handsome rogue. He was excellent at poker, had a thing for chemistry and water polo. Yes sir, my little pea, he always had jokers in store. His glass vials often exploded from overheating, and he swam in a mauve swim cap. Your mother found us—I was on my knees, polishing his . . . with my mouth . . ."

"His *what?*" Danaë turned to stone.

"His *that!*" He made a strange noise and squinted his colorless eyes at his daughter.

"Daddy . . ." Danaë stonily sounded out the words. "Are you saying you were a homosexual?"

An astonishing picture took shape in her mind: her dying father sucking the penis of Golotsvan, the flunk, the murderer.

"That's how it went . . . sometimes. And who didn't get into some of it? In one's youth, in the barracks, after a bout of drinking, in one's dreams—"

"Did you actually love my mother?"

"Yes, my little pea, yes . . ." Innokentii Karaklev nodded his hairless head. "You are the result of a grandiose love, a gale-force diffusion. The cells were jumping out of our bodies and mixing together. Such passion, it shook the atmosphere. Those were breathtaking, mind-numbing times."

"And what about that student?" Danaë asked, watching the column of ash crumble from her cigarette onto the rug. "What was his name?"

"Andrei. Yes, yes. It was a breathtaking passion." Her dad smacked his lips and purred like a cat. "Absolute diffusion. Overflowing excitement. To near suffocation. More a miracle than a passion."

"Did you love my mother?" Danaë prodded in a steely voice. "Answer me. I don't understand." She now imagined her dad's hairless head laboring over the perineum of the flunking murderer Golotsvan.

"I loved them both very deeply," answered Innokentii Karaklev. "And about twenty others. I loved everyone. And every time it was a miracle."

Danaë took a drag on her cigarette and fixed a vacant stare on the window. A lustful blush broke in crimson across Golotsvan's cheeks, his eyes turning back in his head, his moans encouraging her dad's frail, hairless head with its decaying mouth.

"And me?" Danaë asked almost inaudibly.

Her dad's wrinkles suddenly turned smooth and he answered: "You are my little pea. My favorite book. Plus Louis Armstrong. And Fellini. Plus my favorite *olivier* salad. And all the Egyptian pyramids and the ruins of the great castles. You understand me? You are also the lily pads on the pond where I swam when I was just a little kid . . . Plus God, whatever He may actually turn out to be. My little pea. Danaë. Come here, give me a kiss."

Danaë quickly crushed her cigarette butt in the ashtray, walked over to him on legs she could barely feel, and pressed her cheek into Daddy's lips.

"You too," she whispered, "dying one . . . Daddy . . ."

Golotsvan was done. But the rain in the neighborhood of Perovo wasn't about to finish. Danaë moved to the kitchen, leaving her dad to stare out the gray window covered with heavenly moisture . . .

She struck him with a meat hammer, with the burled side. Danaë knew beforehand that just once on the head wouldn't be enough. Neither would two. During the process she realized that it would be enough only when she had lost count for the third time. Then she stood there listening, without looking. She imagined a monitor with a wan green image of her dad's threadlike pulse. Then she dropped the hammer, went to the kitchen, washed her hands, went to the hallway, grabbed her bag of notebooks, came back to the kitchen, sat down at the table, and began grading papers. After a half hour she was sick of it. She moved into her dad's room, turned on the light (it had grown dark outside, but the rain was still pouring down), and peered at him. Innokentii Karaklev was sitting in the same armchair, but tilted over on his side so that his knuckles were trapped against the rug. His thoroughly beaten head was glazed in its own juices.

Danaë decided to leave everything as it was, at least for now, until she took a bath with some fragrant salts. Salts always had a positive effect on her body. Sitting on the edge of the tub and looking into a mirror, Danaë pronounced: "This is easy."

Later she was told that she'd gone mad. Just like her mom. Those who said it were right. She knew it and she'd reply: "And you're all bastards, bastards, all of you." It's possible that she was right too.

CHRISTMAS
BY IRINA DENEZHKINA
New Arbat

Translated by Marian Schwartz

J acob hung there, his shoes scraping the parquet floor spasmodically. "Papa, stop!" he rasped, trying to untangle the string of lights around his neck, while German, suspecting nothing, kept pulling the garland tighter and tighter thinking there wasn't much time left and the house decorations still weren't finished.

There should be a comma after "tighter," Yulia noted in the margin, then set her pencil down and rubbed her temples. As usual, the words were swimming before her eyes. They would keep swimming for another half hour, until Yulia put on her coat, picked up her purse, and left the publishing house. She put drops in her eyes. I'm going to have to move on to glasses pretty soon, she thought sadly.

As Yulia left the Barrikadnaya metro station, the heavy glass doors swung closed behind her with a loud wallop.

She heaved a distraught sigh, her head finally clearing after the stench of the sweaty underground crowd and their identical faces, on each of which she distinctly read: *IhateyouIhateeveryone.* Her black sweater was stuck to her body, the harsh wool bristly. What was it knit from? It pricked her armpits and back.

Yulia wiped the sweat from her forehead and made her habitual motion of smoothing down her jacket.

Her wallet was gone.

She had her cell phone. Here it was, on the right. But her wallet was missing.

Frightened, Yulia looked from side to side, feverishly trying to figure out who might have relieved her of her salary and bonus and where, when, and how.

Yulia moved forward on cotton legs and leaned her shoulder against one of the vans selling burned *chebureki* and sausages wrapped in pastry. Any other time the smell of the tainted meat would have turned her inside out, but the thought of the money drowned out every other consideration.

How was she going to live now?

Go to the police? Yulia laughed nervously. A lady walking by, wearing a gray puffer coat, gave her a nasty look and sent a tut-tutting curse her way. Rush back, down there, into the bowels of the underground, wrest her money back (from whom, dear Yulia?), howl . . . ? Pretty funny.

She gathered all her strength and walked on. Toward her building.

She moved past the *chebureki* and pirated-CD vans, past the crazy Gothic high-rise with the gargoyle faces. She gazed, sick at heart, at one of the faces, which looked down on her haughtily. Yulia sighed and plodded on. A frigid wind whistled down her jacket collar; her scratchy black sweater wasn't keeping the cold out. She stopped next to the American consulate, but she didn't have the strength to take another step forward, even though it was just a few more meters to her building. A dreary line stretched out from the consulate door. *Jacob took the hacksaw and, panting, began sawing off his mama's head. The hacksaw was hard to work, and the sweetish spurts made Jacob frown* . . . The words raced through Yulia's mind.

A guard with a badge bore his little piggy eyes into Yulia, and his muscles tensed to lunge. Yulia came to her senses and hurried on.

She tumbled like a sack into her apartment, having begun to slump in the elevator. Now she was sitting, drained, leaning against the doorjamb, moaning softly, and tears were pouring down of their own accord, dripping on her jacket.

Her Siamese cat ran up on his soft paws. His slanted blue eyes watched Yulia carefully.

"Barsik," she moaned faintly. "Sweet Barsik . . . I got robbed. Barsik. We have nothing to eat and nothing to live on."

Barsik rubbed his round head against Yulia's leg. And meowed.

Her phone rang. Yulia took it out of her pocket with trembling hands and pushed the button.

"Yulia darling." It was Oleg.

"Hi," she answered, trying to buck up, wiping away her tears and getting up from the floor.

"How're things, my dear?" Oleg sang sweetly.

"Kind of . . . strange." Yulia tried to quash her sobbing. "Today they fired our second proofreader . . . Mikhail Ivanich . . . You don't know him. And he . . . he left calmly enough. But when I went into the metro . . . I saw . . . imagine, Oleg, he took a running jump right . . . right in front of a train."

"What?" Oleg gasped, though there was more curiosity in his voice than concern.

"He took a running jump . . . He was standing in the middle of the platform . . . and when the train started coming out of the tunnel . . . he jumped."

"Are you kidding?"

"No. Also . . . you know . . . when he jumped he knocked over a stroller . . . and he and the stroller . . . fell."

"What was in the stroller?" Oleg's curiosity was growing.

"A child," Yulia sobbed. "And then . . . when the train pulled out . . . Mikhail Ivanich and the stroller were lying there on the track . . . Mikhail Ivanich was still twitching, but the child didn't have a head . . . There was just the horrible scream of its mother."

Yulia caught her breath. It must have been someone in the crowd that gathered who stole her wallet.

"What happened then?" Oleg asked.

Yulia felt like telling him how she'd been jostled in the crowd, how someone's cold insolent hand had slipped into her pocket for her wallet. Not that Yulia knew exactly what kind of hand it was, hot or cold, but that was exactly how she thought of it: someone's cold, bony, malicious hand.

Jacob started twisting her arm out of the shoulder socket but got nowhere; he hadn't sawed all the way through the flesh . . .

Jacob again! Yulia was getting angry.

"Nothing," she replied with a sigh, and got a grip on herself. "Nothing else. I feel sorry for Mikhail Ivanich. But everything else is fine."

"Good," Oleg said quickly. "You know, I'm hungry as a wolf! I'm on Paveletskaya right now. I've got some business to do. I'm selling a picture. But I'll come right over after that."

"All right." Yulia nodded and ended the call. She thought sadly, *So this is what we've come to.* There was no food in the house. No money whatsoever. Yulia was one of those people who drags out the last three or four days before her paycheck and by payday has absolutely nothing left in the house.

Oleg, however, had one quirk: food. There always had

to be some. And food always meant meat. Salad wasn't food. When Yulia met Oleg Bekas at his gallery and got to talking to him over a cup of coffee with brandy, he immediately informed her of this quirk. That—dinner not being made—was why he'd left his wife (now his ex) and his infant child. The baby's name was Sevochka Bekas and his wife's was Marina. Oleg came home from the gallery one day and there was nothing on the table. Marina's brown eyes stared at him guiltily as she held Sevochka, who was burning up with fever, to her breast. "Sevochka got sick," she said. "I didn't have time." Oleg gnashed his teeth, turned on his heel, and left. Softened by the brandy, Yulia nodded, as if to say, *Rightly so. What kind of a wife doesn't cook for her husband?* "You have to understand, I'm an artist," Oleg explained. "I'm not some low-brow proletarian. I have the right to put myself first." Yulia nodded.

A week later she learned from common acquaintances that on that fateful day Marina picked up Sevochka, who was still burning up with fever, wrapped him tightly in her robe, and went out to the balcony barefoot. It was snowing, and Sevochka quieted down and peeked out of her robe. Snowflakes were melting on his cheeks. "Pretty?" Marina asked. Sevochka goo-gooed approvingly. Marina climbed onto the railing, holding her son to her breast, and from there, from the sixteenth floor, to the dumbfounded looks of the group smoking on the next balcony over, she jumped.

When she first heard this, Yulia just shook her head. Foolish woman Marina. Who jumps off over men?

But right now she was ready to do the same thing. Pick up Barsik, hold him tight to her breast, and leap from her sixth floor, right in front of the dumbfounded visitors at the Metelitsa casino. Because she no longer had the emotional strength to be left not only walletless but also Oleg Bekas-less.

Yulia worked as a proofreader in a publishing house. Her only connection to art was through grammar. For days on end Yulia read other people's words very, very carefully. And corrected them. She felt like a worker who hammers a nail into a wall to hang a painting that gives off a divine light. But what kind of light does a nail give off? None whatsoever. Oleg was an artist, though, and canvases came to life in his hands. Even a sheet of notebook paper. Yulia couldn't do that. She could only go word by word, like an infinite rosary, barely penetrating the meaning of what was written.

She fell in love with Oleg once and for all (though she had never believed in love at first sight and in her youth had often snickered at her more naïve girlfriends). With Yulia it was all very simple. Like him—hook up—go to a café—go to bed. Love? Who cared about love? As long as he had a fat wallet and a generous nature. Maybe that's why Yulia hadn't been through any emotional upheavals before Oleg. She hooked up and split up with a cold heart and a clear head. Like a chekist. But here was Oleg. An artist. A creator. Someone from another world where they don't hammer nails but drink to Brüderschaft with God almighty . . . Yulia saw him in the gallery and fell hard. Her heart broke off and slowly dropped to the pit of her stomach.

Yulia went out on the balcony. The lights of New Arbat spread out right there in front of her. Here was a huge building with a web of lights like an open book. Here was a casino in the shape of a ship; here was another casino, and another. Expensive cars, lots of people. Sometimes Yulia dreamed of flying from her window and landing right on that ship burning with blue lights—and then sailing off to distant lands, where she and Oleg would live together in a cabin and have three children.

Jacob climbed onto the stepladder and tried to hang his mama's head on the Christmas star, but the star was so fragile, and his mama's head was so heavy, that . . . The words raced through her mind again and Yulia mechanically finished up: *that the boy couldn't hold it there and the head came crashing down, cracking loudly on the parquet floor.* Yulia didn't feel so good. Usually she didn't remember all the words to the texts she proofread, and now there was this flood. I'll ask them to give me a different novel, she thought. And I'll give this one to Mikhail Ivanich . . . Damn, he's gone . . . Everyone's gone . . .

Yulia let out another sigh and looked at the clock. She had approximately an hour and a half until Oleg's arrival. She went into the kitchen and opened the cupboard. Then the refrigerator, and then the cabinets over the sink. The old fairy tale about Roly-Poly came to mind. I'll scrape the bottom of the barrel, Yulia chuckled to herself. Her soul was being torn to shreds.

Her search was crowned with a near-empty bottle of sunflower oil, a piece of dried-out French bread, and an almost full bottle of vodka—Yulia gave Barsik vodka compresses when he was sick. She mechanically twisted off the tight lid and sipped some vodka straight from the bottle.

Jacob sat down on the chair and looked at her intently. His blue eyes said, Come on. It's so easy. Easy as pie. *Anna fidgeted.* "Maybe we can leave Thomas alone?" *she asked.* "Do you want to spoil the whole game?" *Jacob scowled. He fiddled with the cord of his checkered shorts.* "No," *Anna answered in fear.* "Then stand up and do it," *Jacob said gently.* "And don't forget this."

Compresses for Barsik.

Barsik.

Anna went over to Thomas's crib. He was looking at his mobile. "Jake, I can't get to him," *she said.* "The crib's too high."

"I'll bring a chair!" Jacob responded. A minute later Anna was climbing onto the chair and looking down at Thomas. "So pretty," she said softly. "Of course he's pretty," Jacob agreed. "But that's completely beside the point." "Yes," Anna said. "Is the water hot enough?" Jacob inquired. "You understand what I mean when I ask if the water's hot enough, right?" "Yes, Jake. It's boiling." Anna raised the kettle, screwed up her eyes, and upended it on Thomas. A piercing shriek filled the nursery.

Yulia shook her head, driving out the terrible thoughts, and took another swig of vodka. The thoughts returned.

What's the big deal? Yulia thought. The big deal is that I would never survive Oleg leaving me.

She gave herself a good shake and stumbled into the bathroom on wobbly legs. A second later she came out clutching a mop.

"Puss puss puss," Yulia called faintly, glancing around the room.

Barsik jumped out from behind the couch. Yulia caught him in her arms and moved out to the balcony. There she lay the cat on the tile floor. Barsik stayed there obediently, watching her with his slanted little blue eyes.

"I'm proud of you," said Jacob. "Don't howl." "I can't not howl. This is Thomas after all. He's still little and it hurts," Anna said, weeping. Jacob hugged his sister. He glanced at his little brother screaming in anguish in his crib with a piece of red meat where his face had been. "You see, Anna, he shouldn't suffer. We're going to save him." Jacob moved away from his sister and took the screaming Thomas out of his crib. He put him on the rug. "Did you bring what I said?" "Yes," Anna answered obediently. Jacob took the golf club from her hands. He stepped back a little and took aim. He raised the club high over his head, then lowered it with a whistle at Thomas's head, which cracked like a watermelon.

Yulia placed the mop handle against Barsik's neck. Then she held onto the railing and jumped with all her might on the handle. There was a crunch and Barsik's eyes popped out of their sockets and a wheeze tore from his throat. His little pink tongue jutted out to the side.

Yulia exhaled violently and nearly ran to the kitchen to crush the grief inside her with vodka. The firewater lashed her throat. She was sobbing.

"Don't cry, Anna," Jacob said calmly. "They'll buy another rug, and I tell you, they aren't going to yell at you. Now it's your turn." "Jackie, let's watch television," Anna said. "I don't like playing with you anymore."

Out the window, the ship-casino was bathed in blue lights. In the kitchen, Yulia skinned the carcass convulsively, tossing the fur onto an opened newspaper.

Oleg arrived at 9 o'clock. By that time Yulia had washed, made herself up again, and put on a red dress. She was a little unsteady from all she'd drunk, but Oleg didn't notice.

He lifted his nose, inhaling the aroma of the roasted meat. He slipped off his jacket, ran a handkerchief over his bald spot to wipe away the sweat, and as a final gesture smoothed his beard.

"What's for supper?" he asked cheerfully, giving Yulia a pat on the cheek.

"R-rabbit," she hiccupped.

"Excellent!" Oleg rubbed his hands and hurried into the kitchen. He sat down on a stool.

Yulia served him pieces and he ate it, crunching the bones and smiling contentedly, like a cat. The oil ran down his beard. Yulia sat across from him.

"Do you know which painting I sold?" he asked triumphantly, nodding at his briefcase.

"Which?"

"*Rusty Evening!*"

Yulia shuddered. *Rusty Evening* had been painted in blood. Oleg was so proud of his conceit—to create a painting two by two meters using only blood. He had bought syringes at the pharmacy and Yulia had given him blood in a skin ointment tube. It had made her head spin, but Oleg had been so pleased. "It's all right," he'd said. "You can take a break tomorrow. I have my mom and sister too." His sister was all of twelve. Oleg was very proud of the fact that the picture had "virgin blood." He drew human figures with it.

And now some "rich wuss," as Oleg put it, had bought their blood.

"Listen," Yulia groveled through her embarrassment, "since you got paid so well, can you lend me a little money?"

Oleg frowned. "I see," he said nastily. "The female wiles are here. I know these crass women. They need money, not love." He stood abruptly from the stool.

"No!" Yulia cried. "I'm not like that! I just . . . I just . . . They held back our pay. The crisis . . ."

"You have to be thriftier, Yulia," Oleg preached, dropping back down on the stool. "Let this be a lesson to you. I can't pay for your mistakes, understand? You have to save for a rainy day."

Yulia nodded, scared. Oleg relented.

"Come here!"

Yulia rushed into his arms, breathing in his painfully intimate smell, realizing she couldn't go on without him. She wanted to tell Oleg that something terrible had happened to her. But what would he say? She pressed up to her beloved's chest. *Anna and Jacob went into the bathroom. "Do I have to undress?" Anna asked again. "No need for that, I don't think," Jacob* replied. He took the cord he'd prepared beforehand out of the pocket of his checkered shorts. "Anna, you have to get in the bathtub." "Okay," Anna nodded obediently. "Just promise me, Jake, that our game ends here and we can go watch television in the living room." "I promise," Jacob said. "The game will end . . ."

Oleg turned off the light and was now trying to separate Yulia from her red dress, but the clasp wouldn't yield. Oleg growled lustfully, tugging at the zipper.

Jacob quickly tied one end of the cord around the drain grill. Anna lay down on the bottom of the bathtub. Jacob tied her neck so that there was no more than five centimeters of cord between the drain grate and the girl. "Goodbye, Anna!" Jacob said, and he kissed his sister on the cheek. "Bye," Anna nodded. "Is this going to take long?" "I think fifteen minutes is all we'll need," Jacob answered, and he turned on the water.

Yulia burned with desire as Oleg ripped off her panties and bra, but she was trying to drive Jacob out of her thoughts. Oleg licked her belly, arms, and face—whatever he came across—with his hot tongue.

German balanced on the edge of the roof, trying to hold onto the New Year's garland that was slipping through his fingers like a snake. "Jacob!" he shouted. "Jacob, help me!" "I'm hurrying, Papa!" Jacob shouted in reply, stamping his boots on the roof—and with a running jump he pushed his father off.

Oleg thrust himself into Yulia, panting and moaning. Yulia tried to get into his rhythm, furiously driving him on. Goddamn you, Jacob, her brain grumbled angrily. Goddamn those novels! Goddamn this job! Goddamn this life!

Jacob carefully mopped up the floor in the living room and kitchen. He checked the chicken in the oven to make sure it hadn't burned, then went to his room. He looked at himself in the mirror. There was an ugly red mark on his neck. I can put on a sweater,

Jacob thought. He carefully removed his checkered shorts and put on the white pants he'd hung neatly on the back of the chair. He found his white sweater in his closet and went out into the dining room, where the utensils were already neatly set on the snow-white tablecloth on the oak table. He sat down at the head of the table. It's Christmas, *Jacob thought.* I'm home alone. Like in the movies.

The next morning Yulia woke up with a hangover and a nasty taste in her mouth. Her head was spinning. Oleg wasn't next to her. Yulia rose with difficulty and walked into the bathroom. The shower brought her back to earth. She moved into the kitchen and sat down on a stool.

Life was quietly returning to her—the street noise, her neighbor's scratchy radio, and the sound of the boiling kettle. Yulia drank plain hot water, then she went out on the balcony to clear her head. The casino-ship had turned out its lights and no trace remained of its nocturnal grandeur. Yulia smiled. Out of the corner of her eye she noticed a crowd of people below. She took a closer look.

On the asphalt, in an unnatural pose—his hands and legs turned out like a marionette—lay Oleg. Naked. Yulia blinked. Then she mechanically stepped back.

Yulia struggled for breath. She went back inside. Here they were, Oleg's clothes. Here were his shoes. Here was his briefcase. With trembling hands Yulia unlocked it.

The briefcase was packed with bundles of euros.

It will be Christmas soon, Yulia thought. *And I'm alone. With a stash of money. Like in the movies.*

Jacob smiled.

THE POINT OF NO RETURN

BY SERGEI SAMSONOV

Ostankino

Translated by Amy Pieterse

He acted as though he had received a divine certifi-
cate verifying the fact of his brilliance from birth.
While the other inhabitants of Literary House on
the corner of Dobrolyubova and Rustaveli were plunged in a
state of despondency that comes from the sense of a wasted
life, my roommate, Tatchuk, lacked even a hint of that over-
powering feeling of hopelessness.

Surfacing to earth out of Lucifer's cowshed, otherwise
known as the Moscow subway, on our way back to the dorms,
I felt, as always, dejected, stunned by defeat. He seemed, as
ever, pampered by good luck, an immutable, victorious smile
on his lips. I hated Azerbaijanis, Russians, Moldavians, Jews,
Tajiks, Ukrainians, blacks, and all other earthlings, forty thousand of whom passed through the vestibule of Dmitrovskaya
station every day (with marble facings the color of a dried
blood blister). He seemed to take no notice of the riffraff, cutting right through the crowd as though it were just a hologram
image of a human herd.

"What's with the gloomy face?" he asked as we were coming out of the underground crossing on Butyrsky Street. "It
wasn't my fault."

"I didn't say it was."

"No, but I can tell from just looking at you that you think it is. Honestly, though, you can't blame me for the fact that you didn't have a single manuscript in your file! That, my man, is just plain bad luck."

It was like this: the head of our university was approached by the organizers of a certain literary prize, who had requested a few examples of the more interesting manuscripts that the student body had produced. All of this (reading and submitting the text) had to be done in a matter of hours, because the deadline for novels and stories had almost arrived. They chose Tatchuk, myself, and one other student. They checked our files, but mine was empty. Unlike Tatchuk's, which was stuffed full of work. So I missed my chance. A month later, I found out that my roommate was a nominee for nationwide fame, and a tidy little sum of money to boot.

The 29-K trolley pulled up to the stop and we squeezed into the coach, filled with scum and lowlifes.

"Cut it out," he said, hunching up his shoulders squeamishly, shoving away the people crowding into the trolley. "If you want, I can help you get a job at *Profile*. Let's go there together tomorrow, I'll tell them you're a better man for the job," he suggested.

"What about you?" I said.

"Don't worry about it. I'll get a job in *Business Primer*, they're offering a better salary there."

While others spent months looking for a job, he always had a choice between four or five attractive offers. All he had to do was cross the threshold of an editorial office, and the woman in charge went wild. "What a sweet young man!" He possessed qualities that piqued the sexual interest of young ladies and mature matrons alike: a sharply defined jawline, the playful brow of a caryatid, the sweet eyes of an angel, with the muscular hands and other features characteristic of a dominant male. If you only knew the way the girls at the university stared at him adoringly, burning with desire to give themselves to him.

But the newly won position had no value for him, and he ignored the obligations it entailed. In fact, he never stayed on with the same publication for longer than three or four weeks. Yet each time he found himself another job without the least bit of effort, as if Moscow employers were constantly creating new vacancies just for him. It was as though he had some kind of aura about him, like some sort of mythical deer with jewels pouring out of its hooves. Indeed, I owed several good jobs to his lucky charm.

We got out at 2 Goncharny Proezd, passed the bookstore named, quite idiotically, Page Turner, past Pharmacy and Optics, one right after the other according to phonetic logic, and they were soon behind us.

"Let's get something to eat," he said, nodding at the neon sign over the grocery store where young writers went to buy ingredients for breakfast and dinner (individually wrapped crab sticks and a packet of mayonnaise, occasionally allowing themselves some disgusting treat like liverwurst, or a string of glossy, suspiciously natural-looking pink hot dogs). He bought a pound of choice ham, half a pound of Dutch cheese, canned olives, and two bottles of Chilean red wine.

"What do you think?" he said as we were leaving. "Isn't it about time I started writing a new narrative, a story at least? I haven't submitted anything in a while, and spring is just around the corner—exams are coming up. I'd like to do a narrative using the stylistic techniques of Nabokov and combine that with the magical realism of Márquez. What do you say?"

"How about the sexual candor of Miller," I couldn't resist suggesting. "Maybe you can work that in?"

"No, not Miller," he said, flustered. "Intimacy is too vulgar in his writing. I would go for more refined love scenes. Nuanced, partly hidden in shadow. All of that *I screwed her* stuff you can save for your own writing. That's just your speed," he laughed. "The pornographic fantasy that never becomes reality."

When did this begin, and why did it always happen this way? At college they called us the twins from Novoshakhtinsk. We came to the capital together, and the only time we weren't with each other was in the bathroom. We had a deadly addiction to one another.

At last we came to our dwelling—a pale, carrot-colored, sooty, seven-floor building. You there in your faraway, big-time America, can you even imagine our Literary House, packed full of budding talents? Nope, it's only possible in Russia: a special university dedicated to teaching young people how to put words together, minding their congruity of course. Though invisible, the nearby presence of the Ostankino TV tower can be felt here in strange ways. They say that magnetic waves coming from that accursed needle are to blame for suicidal urges among the locals. In the case of our dormitory's inhabitants, the waves acted as a pied piper, enticing unrecognized literary genius into the realm of comfortable nonexistence. I think the whole thing is ridiculous. Magnetic fields have nothing to do with it.

Here we were in our room. An old-fashioned but functional refrigerator of a place, it sported fresh wallpaper, thick maroon curtains (that became a menacing blood-red when the light penetrated them at sunset and sunrise), a new hardwood floor, and prints of van Gogh and Bosch paintings on the walls that had been cut out of magazines by the room's former tenants.

Having scarcely entered, he sniffed the air and said, "Hey, how many times have I told you not to smoke in the hallway outside the door? You know I can't stand it, and you do it on purpose!"

"I was smoking by the staircase," I replied. "But you can't forbid other people from lighting up wherever they want. They still smoke at the end of the building by the window."

"It wouldn't hurt them to follow your example. Let's rip off the No Smoking sign from the college bathrooms! We could hang it up next to our door. I've dreamed of getting one of those signs for ages. Hey, you could snatch one, couldn't you? You've always been good at stealing random junk. Remember those books you stole from the school library? I didn't tell on you; I took pity on you then. Why should I ruin your life? I thought. It may seem funny now, but back then it was a criminal offense. You should keep that in mind. What would have become of you if you'd been caught? Now you're a student at an elite college in the capital, but you could have ended up in prison, a TB case coughing up blood . . . What are you laughing about? Cynic! You think you're off the hook now? You think that because no one's going to come after you now that you can take a deep breath and relax? What a fool you were, two years ago. What made you do it, anyway?"

"A thirst for beauty," I said seriously. "I loved those books with an almost sensual passion. The gold lettering, the leather binding. And when I ran my hand down the page, I could feel every letter, like Braille to the blind."

"You're supposed to love women with sensual passion," he chuckled. "Honestly, I think people like you have a knack for crime in your genes. You have the same lowly origins as the majority of people we went to school with. But you've done all right for yourself, you haven't become a plebeian like the thugs back home."

He'd had my number for half a year now, because I was guilty of childish mischief for which there was a very adult punishment. But was this the real reason I was so dependent on him?

It had all started three years before in the world of shabby apartment blocks, at our school in Novoshakhtinsk. It was a world of severe, crudely carved faces, a world of thieves, violence, and the ceaseless toil of a miner's existence.

A world of losers and scumbags with unblinking eyes who were trained to harass the new guy, and a world in which a merciless fate awaited them: high school, then community college, the army . . . then working the mines after that. Beer after work, soccer on the weekends. Or a short stint in organized crime followed by the inevitable bullet in the head. One day, out of nowhere, a boil appeared on the multiheaded body of the proletariat. An alien, with its head held high and a beaked nose: my present roommate, Tatchuk. He was insultingly different in every way. His clothes made the heavy-duty pants and jackets of those around him look like rags. His perfect, eloquent speech, the squeamish way he touched anyone else's possessions, even the inviolable, neat part in his thick jet-black head of hair.

He had everything I lacked in excess, bravery in particular, which he used to reinforce his inner *me*. In fact, he was almost disgustingly devoid of cowardice. Every minute of every day he had to answer the hateful stares and the all too predictable hisses ("Freakin' fairy!" "Faggot!"). And, indeed, he answered back, with his characteristic cool laugh and that remote smile that made you want to hit him, so full of superiority and righteousness.

He said that most people were like fish, only able to live in the waters they were made for. And if one day they decided to go deeper or higher than their stipulated habitat, they would most certainly kick the bucket. Just looking at him gave me hope that I might one day rise to a higher level of society *and* be able to avoid certain death at the same time. We became friends, and with that the possibility of easy ascension on the social ladder dawned on me; it was something like infatuation with an older brother who always protects and cares for you. And lo and behold! Never in my wildest dreams could I have imagined that things would turn out so well. We grew close, and he told me about how awful it was to be ordinary. He made me see that the two of us were not cut out for the wretched life of our town. And I believed him, like the ancient Argonauts believed in their specially invited guest, the favorite of the gods, whose sole purpose on the boat was to attract good luck.

It was a quiet evening at the dormitory. Suddenly, we heard cries of anger, plates crashing in the room next to ours, hysterical shrieks. We jumped up, sensing a scandal brewing. In room 620, Suskind had revolted. He lived there with Samokhin. Samokhin was always having friends over, drinking, hanging out with girls. Suskind, on the other hand, was an unsociable recluse.

"Enough, I've had enough of this!" Suskind shouted, his features twisted. He was screeching and squealing like a pig and smashing plates. "You bloodsucking swine! It's always, 'Suskind, who is this and who is that, and who the heck is Smerdyakov from Dostoevsky? Oh, that's right, Suskind!' And then they turn on the TV. 'Hey, Suskind, let's root for Lokomotiv!' I hate goddamn soccer! Picking on me because

I came from Penza, almost forty years old, to become a writer. Doesn't take much to believe in talent that's already been recognized. You try believing in *my* talent! And remember my name: Sueskin, not Suskind! Roman! Sergeevich! Sueskin!"

"Oooh! What an honor," Samokhin enthused sarcastically, and moved to pat Suskind's softly bearded cheek.

Suskind grabbed a knife lying on the table and shook it, wailing, "Stay back!" It was pathetic.

Fights are not a rare occurrence in our dorm. In the spring, tormented by lack of love, insignificance, and hopelessness, the bastards throw themselves out of windows. This whole place is permeated with reminders of the ever-present temptation of suicide—grates on the windows of the upper floors, metal nets stretched across the stairwell. The problem is that there are too many of us here. There are five hundred of us from every corner of this enormous country, five hundred losers, each one thinking he's a genius. Five hundred lonely voids, living hand to mouth on miserly government scholarships sent here by our parents back home. Only a few crazy geniuses and two dozen literary hacks would make it in the world. The rest are doomed to a life of total obscurity and wretchedness.

"You don't know the half of it, you guys," said Samokhin, when we had come out into the hall. "At night he tries to communicate with martians, honest to god. He says they want to take him away with them. Beam me up, Scotty! He could sink a knife into me at any minute, if his aliens told him to. As Samoilov wrote, if I remember correctly, 'This city is full of crazies, at least one in three is psycho. So speak to me softly. I might be one of them . . .'"

"'Don't be so sure that you're so smart,'" I finished. "'And I wouldn't jump to conclusions about which one of us'll come by a sharp razor first.'"

"So, Dima," Samokhin said, addressing Tatchuk on a different topic, "do you think you'll be the one who gets those five thousand greenbacks?"

"Who *else* but yours truly?"

How could he be so certain? It was as though his rich childhood imagination was furnished with its own personal universe that revolved around him alone (with a map of the stars on the ceiling and an army of teddy bears dedicated to their master). And then this perfectly polished cosmos expanded to the size of a three-room apartment, streets, schools, entire countries—and there was not one place his parent's love, backed up by their financial means, could not reach him. The outside world seemed to fulfill even his most extravagant desires. And so my roommate, who was used to all this, seemed to be able to force reality to conform to his expectations of it. This was, I suppose, his greatest gift of all: he made the whole world into a big-budget stage production in which he, Tatchuk, was the princely heir and future ruler. All other people were his servants—faceless minor characters whose only purpose was to serve their master and then disappear from his sight forever. In this world, respiration was the only thing that couldn't be counted on: my roommate suffered from chronic asthma, and was sometimes forced to use a fabulously expensive inhaler.

Back in our room, bare-chested, having uncorked a bottle, he surrendered happily to the nightly ritual of self-admiration. I bet nothing gave him as much pleasure as parading around the room with no shirt on. He could spend hours in front of the mirror, studying his own loving reflection in different perspectives and poses, enjoying a glimpse of his muscles, beautiful knolls beneath his satin skin. His narcissism was natural and justified, but it still got on my nerves.

"Just look at this six-pack," he said to me, stroking his washboard belly deferentially. "Here, touch it. No, come on, touch it! Touch it!" he insisted, indignant that I should take such a criminal disinterest in his amazing abs.

I left the room as if to go out for a smoke, trying to avoid this cruel form of sexual harassment. And I came face to face with Suskind, homeless like myself.

Oh, how lucky I was to have him: my guardian angel, the great and invulnerable Tatchuk! Ever since that train on the way to Moscow, when my bag was stolen with all my money and my passport. I was devastated. I wouldn't be able to register or sign up for classes. And then he came back (he'd left the compartment to throw out some garbage) and handed me my wallet. He had found it miraculously, in a trash can, with no money left in it, but my passport still inside. "What would you do without me?" he said. "I return you your name, your identity, and your future; don't take it for granted."

And so it went. Then there was the editing job at *Architecture and City Planning* magazine that paid three hundred dollars a month—money a provincial freshman could only dream of. The police trainees who found a crumb of hashish in the inner pocket of my canvas backpack, but who for some reason decided to let me go at the last minute for the ridiculous price of fifteen hundred rubles. The photo of us together on the first page of a glossy magazine, under the headline *Our Future Is Everything*. Not to mention the girls who flew toward Tatchuk like moths to a flame, and—praise the lord!—sometimes even bestowed their attentions on me. All my successes, all the publications, all the ills I managed to avoid were due to his presence at my side. It was with the greatest horror that I imagined what would happen if this deity were to turn away from me.

I went back to the room.

"Haven't you had enough of pounding those keys?" he asked, nodding at my ancient computer. "I need a new story too, you know. I already have a great name for it: 'The Point of No Return.' What do you think?"

"What is it about?"

"I still don't have it all planned out yet. Basically, it's going to be about two friends living in Venice. One is an aristocrat, although no longer wealthy. He works as a model for the leading fashion designers and writes brilliant poetry. The other is Gorlum. He is but a pale shadow, wracked with envy for the unending successes of his friend."

So that's what's going on, I thought. Our companionship, which had seemed not so long ago to be at least a kind of symbiosis, was now a glaring case of vampirism. Poor fool that I was, I had thought he had no ulterior motives for sharing his unending supply of good luck with me, that he did so with the same sunny generosity of all demigods. O the wretchedness of my soul and its innate servitude! I felt like the lowly lackey allowed to sit at his master's table, only to be thrust back in his place when the meal was over.

"So one day Gorlum decides to kill his friend. He thinks that by killing the first character, let's call him Martin, he'll solve all of his own problems, and at last fortune will come his way. But when the cunning plan is enacted and the murder has taken place, Gorlum realizes that his life has lost its meaning after Martin's death. Gorlum goes crazy. He starts seeing features of the master he so cruelly betrayed in different people walking by on the street. He starts running up to them, calling them by his friend's name. He begins to believe that Martin is still alive, and punishing him through his absence. It ends with madness . . . What do you think of the story line?"

So you think that my only purpose on this earth is to be your monkey, a mere dwarf in your court, Martin dearest?

"I feel I've heard this somewhere before," I said automatically.

"You're always doing that!" he exploded. "And when it concerns your own writing, you go hoarse defending the originality of your ideas. Have you ever thought that maybe the reason your work doesn't get printed is because you aren't capable of generating any original ideas of your own?"

"What about your work, why hasn't it been printed?"

"You're a lazy, ungrateful loser."

Like a greyhound on a leash, I began to quiver in anticipation of a fight. Now, finally, I knew what I wanted. I wanted to see fear in his eyes. But it wasn't so much fear as doubt that I was hoping for. I wanted to see him doubt his absolute right to demand and receive whatever came into his head.

"Listen," I said, lighting a cigarette and trembling with the suspicion that had so suddenly awakened in me, "your plot is all right, but it seems sort of unrealistic to me. I suggest you make a few changes."

"Don't smoke around me, you slob, have you forgotten? Put it out this instant!"

"In my opinion," I continued, inhaling, "talent seems to be distributed unfairly between your two characters. As a matter of fact, the story just doesn't seem believable or lifelike. One character is blessed so generously—as handsome as a god and as brilliant as Dante . . . Of course that happens in real life, but in a book it would appear too contrived."

"I said put it out!" He lunged at me, but began coughing, then snatched his inhaler, biting into it with whitened lips.

"On the other hand, if brilliant Martin can't put two words together on paper and is tormented by creative futility, it's a different matter altogether. The premise of our story is destroyed instantly; it has a deeper meaning."

Wheezing, he hit me, and I struck him back. I saw before me a sheep ready for slaughter, and with every blow I was hammering the sense of life's imminent end into him. All of a sudden, he gave a sharp start of surprise and threw his head back. I saw a fish that had fled the waters it was meant to inhabit and would end up floating to the surface with its belly torn open. I saw him as he was, weakened and made vulnerable by his own good luck, fed with its gifts to the point of surfeit and decay. His life, which had always ascended to new heights as though following a brilliant railroad track, had reached its apex and was now plummeting downward. I stood there in front of him, tempered and honed by defeat. I was used to it, just as a wolf is used to hunger and cold, and my face showed the coarseness and impenetrability of a pagan god.

"You'll pay for this!" he threatened, rubbing his broken nose, but it sounded as though he had merely sighed. Something had happened to him that was too serious and too deep to be manifested on the surface as a cry of protest or the convulsive shudders of limbs that refused to obey. I had hit him in his weakest spot, damaging his hermetically sealed protective armor. A cosmic chill, pitilessly indifferent to the reality of any single human "I," came rushing in through the air vents, filling my roommate's soul with the understanding that from now on, nothing was certain. God, he implored, could this really mean that I'm one of you guys now?

After that, my roommate kept his mouth shut for a long time. And I got to smoke without leaving the room. As soon as I appeared in the doorway, he would stand up and leave. The devil knows where Tatchuk was spending so much of his time every

210 // MOSCOW NOIR

day, but I heard some students say they had seen him walking alone down Rustaveli, past the stereotypical gray buildings, whose color leaves a sickening aftertaste of electrolytes, copper, rotten eggs, and the thick stench of burning rubber. He was out there alone in an antechamber of hell—not one with the splendor of purifying flames and endless volcanic eruptions, but one that was as cheerless and intolerably ordinary as an old cast-iron tub with a bunch of spiders crawling around inside if it.

With each passing day I felt my own life force becoming stronger as the vitality of my roommate ebbed. His female superiors at *Profile*, who had once so adored that "sweet boy," now demanded preliminary proof of his literary abilities and assigned him a test essay on "Why Smoking Is Good for You." That definitely got the better of him.

Rumor had it that doubts had been raised among jury members as to whether Tatchuk was, in fact, the author of the novel he had submitted. It was *too* mature, and *too* perfect. The piece far surpassed the abilities of a twenty-year-old. Without fuss, the jury thought it best to put forward a more humble candidate as winner.

Next, out of the blue, Tatchuk's parents refused to continue their generous financial assistance. It was then that the real reasons for his coming to study at our understaffed school in Novoshakhtinsk came to light. His parents had divorced. Both now had other families, and other children too.

The female students' once limitless admiration of Tatchuk evolved into little more than the ill-concealed fear with which one notices a crazy person on the city streets. He had become timid and unsure of himself, always muttering something incoherent and foolish under his breath.

The name itself, Tatchuk, suddenly appeared no more than

a mess of barbaric consonants. As though, lacking any other more suitable phonetic material, God had nailed together a magnificent church using the debris from an old wooden outhouse. How different than my own last name—Bessonov—a name that has been generally acknowledged as that of a future classic.

Besides, to be honest, I just couldn't be bothered with Tatchuk anymore. There were too many circumstances and events taking shape that were totally independent of him. I felt vaguely sorry for him, so far away, out there on the periphery of my needs, fears, and hopes. First of all, I'd fallen madly in love with a she-devil I met at the All-Russia Exhibition Center. Her beautiful face was enough to make my throat constrict like it was in a gentle noose, and my soul feel like it was being tickled by a dog's wet nose. Things were pretty much hunky-dory—riding the monorail together and the stuff of mushy romance like going up to see the view at Ostankino Park and Sheremetyvo Palace—until the day my sweetheart crossed the threshold of our dormitory room. By the time Tatchuk got back, my girlfriend already had her hand beneath my shirt and was brushing my lips with her own. So I have to say that my neighbor couldn't have chosen a more inappropriate moment to return. He sat down at the table with us, and I poured him half a glass of wine while my sweetheart continued, unperturbed, where she'd left off. As I allowed the nimble tongue, which might as well have been forked, to enter my mouth, I glanced at Tatchuk's tense, stoney face and sent him one last silent *Sorry*.

"Dirty whore!" he hissed, so that we jumped apart from each other. He stood up quickly and started rushing around the room, yelling that he didn't have to tolerate such animallike indecency in his own room. "Get out of here!" he cried. "If you don't leave, I'll go to the dorm supervisor!"

I shot up, doubling my hand into a fist. But when Tatchuk started coughing and groping for his inhaler in his pocket, I relaxed without touching even a hair on his head.

After I returned from walking her home, Tatchuk spoke to me for the first time since our fight.

"I'm in trouble," he said, with obvious difficulty. "It looks like I'm going to be kicked out of school."

"What makes you think that?"

"Don't pretend you don't know what's going on. If I don't hand in at least one new story by May, Urusov will expel me."

Well, I guess now is the time to confess everything. Tatchuk's writing had suddenly become remarkably bad. "It's weird," students would say. "How did he manage to write that brilliant narrative his freshman year? Maybe it wasn't his writing at all. What do you think?" My only answer was to chuckle vaguely and shrug my shoulders. What was I supposed to do, tell the whole world that I was the one who had scribbled down the notorious story for Tatchuk? That I was the one who had helped him along, correcting and rewriting most of it? We were fast friends back then, and I was totally convinced he had the golden touch. It was like we gave each other strength. I told him how to put words together, and through him I could stop feeling like such a loser. He made me feel like I, too, was somehow invincible, important, like we could make it if we stuck together.

"No," I said, "I've had enough of this. Do it on your own."

"I can't," he muttered.

"If you can't, you should transfer somewhere else. It's not *my* problem."

"I don't want to study somewhere else. I won't make it there either."

"Do you want to be a writer or not? Anyway, that's beside the point. Do you really think Urusov is such an idiot that he hasn't noticed anything? Just a couple of days ago he mentioned that our styles are strikingly similar. Get it? One more pretext is all they need to kick us both out of here."

"Please, just one last time!" he implored.

"Yeah, right."

"Then I'll just tell Urusov what happened, and you'll get expelled. If you write me another story, you'll at least have one more chance."

"Fine," I said. "Go ahead and tell him."

He stopped his pleading, but I had a feeling he was planning something. Just sharing a room with him became nearly intolerable. I had only just been able to stomach the royal, all-powerful Tatchuk of old, but this new one was simply too much to bear. He turned from a generous, merciful god into a backbreaking burden. His eyes followed me beseechingly. Where could I hide when we spent at least six hours a day together?

My instincts had not deceived me. Only a week later he pulled a stunt that had me itching with such fury that it took me all day to cool off.

"A month ago you broke my nose," he announced calmly. "The nasal septum was damaged, as a result of which I now have trouble breathing. Furthermore, my nose didn't heal properly, and now no one wants to be friends with me."

I stared at his unchanged nose. It looked fine to me: protruding, patrician, as always. Still, my roommate did look rather sickly. His cheeks were sunken, his eyes glassy with dark rings beneath them.

"I am in desperate need of plastic surgery. The operation costs ten thousand dollars. I have no one else to turn to. If you refuse to help me, I will have you thrown in jail. I will sue you for inflicting severe injury on me, and I have documented evidence to prove my claims."

"The money's over there," I said, nodding. "In the top drawer of the desk. Exactly ten thousand."

"I'm not joking. Have your parents sell their apartment. You should understand that my life is being ruined because of this. I have no other choice. Mark my words, you'll be doing time."

A nose injury, blown out of proportion into a worldwide conspiracy that cannot be proved or disproved—as long as you believe in it, it's true. But why was he indulging in this eccentricity, and what did he really need the money for? Was it a bribe? For whom? My god, could he really be so desperate as to believe that this fantastic sum could help him rise from the ashes? For us ordinary people (dorm dwellers), it would have been no more consequential than a mosquito bite, but for him it was a mortal wound. For the rest of us, unemployment, lack of money, obscurity, was the air we breathed. For him, it was a sign that his life was over, once and for all.

"You listen to me!" I shouted. "One more word out of you and I'll fix your nose for you myself, right here! Have *your* parents sell their apartment and shell out the cash to you! Or are you an orphan now?"

"My parents are unable to give me any money," he answered hollowly, as though his parents had died yesterday.

"And why is that?" I asked in surprise. "You are family, after all. And you've had it easy for three years, living off the money they send you. So what gives?"

"My parents are busy with their own lives now. They got

divorced, and I got left out of the picture, so I can't ask them for help anymore."

"But you think you can ask me for help?" I exploded. "Ten thousand bucks doesn't just materialize out of thin air, you know! What do you want it for anyway? To go to America? Or invest in Gazprom stocks and become a millionaire in six months?"

"I'm warning you, either you come up with ten grand or I'm taking this case to court."

"You can take it to the war crimes tribunal for all I care!" I stormed out, slamming the door behind me. What was I going to do with him? And how much longer could I keep this up, treating him like a normal human being? Get a grip! If we could sit down and have some vodka together, I might quote the words of a poor, homeless Russian poet who died in exile. He said, *It is cold to walk the earth; still colder is the grave. Remember that, remember, and do not curse your fate.* He wouldn't get it though. It would be like trying to explain that bread is bread. Somewhere deep inside, I knew: he was losing it. Something had to be done, an alert had to be sounded. The problem was that while his old swagger had not made him many enemies, it did little to win anyone over to his side either, so his fall was met with a general apathy. I was the only one he could count on. So I decided to go back in there and talk to him. I decided to say, *Come on, don't do this to yourself. You are healthy and strong as an ox! You're young and bright, well-educated and good-looking. You could be out there having fun and living life to the fullest, and you choose this instead?*

I went back inside, only to find him standing over my computer. I yelped like a wounded animal and rushed forward—but it was too late. With one press of a key, he had consigned my best piece to oblivion. Half a year of tense and difficult sleepless nights . . . I'll kill him! I grabbed a ceramic vase from the table and threw it at him, aiming for his head. I missed, and it crashed through the double-paned glass window. Then I went straight to the dorm supervisor.

"But you boys come from the same parts, don't you?" the supervisor asked me. "Why are you squabbling with each other? I don't have room vacancies at the moment. If you really want to move, I suggest you ask around. Maybe someone will agree to swap roommates with you."

Nobody wanted to swap with me; no one was willing to share a room with Tatchuk.

Each morning the sheets on my bed were twisted into a hieroglyph suggesting torturous insomnia. The reason: that maniac had acquired the revolting habit of getting up in the middle of the night and shuffling around the room like a somnambulist. My nerves were wound tight as strings, and it was like Tatchuk was pulling a bow across them. I always had the feeling that he was getting up stealthily, tiptoeing toward me. Perhaps with a pillow or razor in hand. I stayed on my guard, waiting for him to strike from behind. I think we both needed help. I found myself having to copy all the files in my computer onto discs that I secured in the desk drawer under lock and key. Things can't go on like this for long, I told myself. But it didn't get better. It just went on and on, in the same way.

Once, as I was returning home, I heard him through the door talking to someone on his cell phone. (It must have been his grandma—she was the only living soul willing to listen to his harping.)

". . . I filed my claim in court," he was saying. "He can't wriggle out of it now. You wouldn't believe how long it takes them to consider a case! I can't wait any longer. And guess what? That pitiful wimp managed to land himself a job as a copywriter at a publishing house. He's making five hundred dollars a month. Oh, and he has a book coming out soon. But I won't let him feel good about that when my life is such a mess. I want him to live in a state of constant fear. And I'm pretty good at acting insane. I think he's going to break down and help me soon. My life might be a mess right now, but that's all the more reason for him to have to suffer as well."

I went cold with fury. Whether in a healthy state of mind, from hatred toward me, or out of crazy envy of my latest successes, he was like a tick that bit deep into me and wouldn't let go until it had drunk its fill of my warm blood. They say you can't teach an old dog new tricks. That may be so, but today Dr. Bessonov is going to have to use a little shock therapy. I'm going to show him something that will make his latest strategy vanish—*poof!*—into thin air.

Late that evening, when Tatchuk left for the bathroom, I got hold of his inhaler and hid it in the top desk drawer. Then, after hesitating a moment, I locked the drawer and threw the key out the window.

"Sit down, we need to talk," I said as he came in the door. "It's time you went home. I've had just about enough of you, my friend. So I suggest you gather your things without a big fuss and go back to Novoshakhtinsk. I came clean and told Urusov that I'd been writing for you. The old man told me off a little, but said the papers for your expulsion would be signed in a few days."

"No, you couldn't have!" he cried. "I need my education . . ." Then he underwent a sudden transformation. He drew himself up straight and puffed out like a turkey, as though his sense of dignity had returned and was flooding him from within. He started pacing the room, and I watched him in his agitation. I experienced a cold, predatory curiosity, a sense of my own strength and the ease with which I could simply crush him like a louse.

"Tatchuk," I warned, "you had your chance."

He started coughing and turned toward me, jerking spasmodically. His face had gone purple, and his eyes were large and beseeching like a saint on an icon, or a bull in a bullfight. At first he didn't understand, as he knocked over mugs and glasses on the table, searching one surface and then another, grabbing at things, incredulous at not being able to find his priceless Swiss fix.

"What did you do with it? Did you take it? Give it back right now! Come on, give it to me . . . Be a man about it . . . It hurts, it really hurts. It hurts to breathe, I can't. Seriozha, man, I'm sorry, what do you want? I'm going to die, please. I'm sorry, I'm sorry." He was wheezing and sputtering, then he coughed out a few more words. He started to lose his balance, took a step toward me, then stumbled. He had to lean on the desk for support, and his hand seemed to go through the wooden tabletop like water.

I continued to sit there, ringing with numbness, as though I were not myself. I behaved with the same sweet aloofness with which a cruel child dissects a bumblebee on the windowsill, probing it's fuzzy belly with a needle until it spurts white pus like a ripe pimple. I found myself at the point of no return, where love is silent, and it was as pleasant and painful as returning to the cramped unconsciousness of the womb. Suddenly, as though I'd been yanked by the hair, I started at the seriousness of my insult to the world, and I slapped myself on the forehead. *What am I doing?* I snatched a kitchen knife and rushed to pry open the lock on the flimsy desk drawer. I fumbled for the miserable spray and rushed to my roommate's side.

"Come on, come on," I coaxed, "you don't have to be talented or smart or honest or good. It's enough to just be alive. Who are we, anyway, to refuse one another the right to exist?"

A day later, his body was found in a toilet stall in the left wing of the building. He was clutching an empty bottle of sleeping pills. By some cruel twist of fate, his body lay prostrate just beneath the words *You're useless*, which someone had underlined with a thick marker.

When a person loses someone close to him, it is common that he will feel tortured by a sense of responsibility toward the dearly departed. Friends give speeches in his honor. A bright, whitewashed image of the deceased is created, purified by suffering, which has little to do with the living person you yourself knew. This was exactly the way we, students of the acclaimed professor Urusov who gathered in the courtyard of the dormitory, recalled one who was truly talented, who suffered deeply in crisis—a vulnerable soul whom we ignored, abandoned, and paid no attention to, focused as we were on ourselves. Not that a long time was spent mourning. (It was, after all, the heat of May: sticky leaves rustled in the trees, and the hot air was as thick as the rubber ball we took with us to play soccer at Savelovsky station.) It had already been suggested, as though by chance, that there was no reason to torture ourselves because of someone else's frivolity and that the fellow himself was to blame. "It was so obviously his own fear of living," another colleague said.

I stood there trying to find the point from which we could go back to the past, but anger, or envy, or soul-killing apathy had numbed the senses, and, picking us up like chips of wood in a flood, had carried us toward the finish line. I couldn't find this point, or even picture it. And, more out of a sense of duty, not yet believing in the true, unparalleled reality of a higher judgment, I sidled off furtively, away from the others, mumbling silently under my breath, "God forgive me."

PART IV

WAR AND PEACE

THE COAT THAT SMELLED LIKE EARTH

BY DMITRI KOSYREV (MASTER CHEN)
Birch Grove Park

Translated by Mary C. Gannon

T hat dude, by the way, he never took his coat off," the girl told me. "For the first time in my life I did it with a guy in a coat. You know, an old coat, pretty gross."

A coat in the middle of a hot, stifling Moscow summer? I began to understand my client, the mother of this under-age creature. When a girl gives way to her fantasies to such a degree, her friends can deal with it. But not her mother. To the mother, a child will always be a child, even if that child has developed a habit of talking about sex with a definite world-weariness. That's when I get a phone call that goes, *Doctor, can you tell me if a normal person would think something like that?*

But, whereas you can lie to your mother and enjoy scaring her, you can't deceive a shrink. A professional will easily be able to detect whether an overripe teenager is merely fantasizing, or fantasizing while fervently believing in the fantasies, or simply . . .

Simply telling the truth.

"Did you tell your mother about that? About the coat?" I asked in a gloomy tone. "Do you realize that a normal person would never believe that? Look out the window—the concrete is so hot it's melting—and you're talking about a guy having sex in a coat. It wasn't a fur coat, by any chance, was it? Think before you tell your mother things like that. Or do you want her to pack you off to a mental institution after this?"

"Oh, so *that's* what this is all about," she said, and examined me with a long look. "Is that your diagnosis? All right, then. Let's go to the loony bin. Just let me grab an extra pair of pants, and off I go."

She waved her palm over her head in a circular motion imitating the flashing light of an ambulance.

Most of my income (not reported to the IRS) comes from single mothers who refuse to believe that their children have grown up. Not just grown up, but grown up to become coarse and ugly, so that if they're boys they contemplate throwing their mothers facedown on the kitchen table. And if they're girls, their mothers suddenly become spiteful, idiotic obstacles to achieving very concrete physical desires.

It's one thing when these are classic teenage fantasies, even if they border on pathology. (And they always border on pathology.) What I had just heard, however, was something completely different. Her eye movements, the tone of her voice, and the internal logic of the story attested to the complete absence of any fantasy. Yes, she said she'd do it with that guy for five hundred rubles in Birch Grove Park, which stretches from the Polezhaevskaya subway station to Peschanaya Square. Yes, she went with him to the end of the grove and waved a condom she'd pulled out of her pocket in front of his face. And then she was smelling the earthy, moldy smell of the gray overcoat, or even more likely a raincoat, that the man never took off in spite of the heat.

"He could've killed you, you know," I reproached her.

"He was all right," she said very convincingly. "Just wanted to get laid. Then again, *I* picked him. For his eyes. He had such—"

"Remind me how old you are?"

"What? So what if I'm fifteen? Does that mean I'm too young to want it, huh?" She opened her eyes, thick with makeup, very wide. "Oh, I'm sorry. I didn't know. My mom forgot to tell me."

"Okay, let me give it to you straight," I said woodenly. "If you're not careful what you tell your mother, *she*'ll end up in the funny farm, not you."

"Good riddance," replied the young creature in a sweet voice, and stared with disgust at my untrimmed beard and my baggy turtleneck sweater.

"Hold on a second. That means that I end up without a client, which isn't good for my business. Your mother needs professional help, not you; she's the one who called me, crying frantically and saying, 'Can you take a look at my girl? She tells me horrible stories. Is she crazy?' We need to calm your mother down or she'll be off her rocker in no time. Not you—her. Get the picture? So here's the deal: you made the whole thing up. I'll think of something to say to your mother. I'll say that you're fine for now, though you need to be under observation. And you keep your mouth shut about sex in coats. And at the same time you'll tell me about this guy—*dude*, that is—who goes around dressed like that in the summer. To tell you the truth, I'm more interested in him than you. Because who needs maniacs wandering around the streets of Peschanaya?"

"Mister, you're a maniac yourself," said my client's daughter, clearly enjoying herself. "He was a big, tall, funny guy, nice, with kinda faded hair. Still pretty young. Tan, like a construction worker or something. Maybe he'd just gotten out of the hospital and that's why he was wearing a coat. A weird coat."

"Oh, so now it's a *weird* coat, eh? Well, tell me more about the coat."

"The material . . . I've never felt anything like it before. It wasn't synthetic. Gabardine, or twill, or something else great-grandmotherish. A long coat down to his ankles. Big buttons. You know, like from a museum. Yellowish edges. And it smelled like it'd been buried underground for a hundred years. But the dude wasn't a bum. He was clean. I wouldn't do it with a bum, no way! You kidding? The dude himself smelled really nice, actually."

"Girl, just listen to yourself. You walk down an alley, see a man sitting on a bench wearing an overcoat . . . Okay, you think he's been in the hospital, but still . . . And so what do you do next, tell me again?"

I paid great attention to the pupils of her eyes, her body language, the movements of her head and shoulders.

"Nothing. I saw the coat, saw the dude. I wanted to get some action, so I batted my eyes at him and blushed like a schoolgirl."

"You *are* a schoolgirl."

"Well, I'm overdeveloped. So the rest is history."

I sighed and made a mental diagnosis. Teenage hypersexuality and an underdeveloped personality, with no pathology in my area—psychiatric, that is. I also realized that the girl's desire to torture her mother was spent for the day.

"Okay, to sum it up: you made the whole thing up and you're not talking about it anymore. Mom gets some peace of mind, and you, young lady—if you start seeing weird things, or if life starts to suck real bad all of a sudden, give me a call. I'll fix it all up for you. I mean it. We'll deal with the money thing later, a little bit at a time. And weird things need to be sorted out quickly."

"Dr. Weird," she said, and cast a sad glance at my sink filled with dirty dishes.

I walked to Birch Grove Park to get some fresh air and hide from the heat. And just to think a little.

After sunset, the squirrels went quiet in the branches of elm trees. Disappointed spaniels and dobermans hauled their owners back home; but pensioners remained seated in their usual spots, finishing their games of dominoes.

I peered across the park that was slowly succumbing to darkness. The girl hooked up with that dude somewhere not too far from here, and they went to most remote spot in the grove, which still hadn't been cleared of fallen trees after the disastrous storms of 1998. A person with an underdeveloped personality simply has no clue what a stranger wearing a long overcoat in hot weather can do to her.

Uh, wait a second—according to her, he hung the coat over his arm while they were walking, but put it on again before he laid her down on a concrete slab, took the condom out of her fingers, and rolled up her miniskirt.

She didn't make that up—that much was certain. So if this was the case, it was the guy who worried me. It seemed like more than just ordinary fetishism.

The local police station was located on 3rd Peschanaya Street, on the other side of Birch Grove Park. The precinct was a hole in a wall, splotched with shiny brown paint. The hole opened onto a short corridor that led down to a semibasement room, decorated in the best traditions of Brezhnev office style: cheap wall panels of faux wood, wrinkled linoleum imitating mahogany flooring, and painted white bars on the windows.

"Sexual predators? No, haven't had any of them in here in a long time," said the inspector with the fitting last name of Bullet. "It's good you stopped in, but I don't see a crime here. Okay, she's underage. *She* was hitting on *him*. No law against wearing an overcoat in the summer. Got anything else on him? No? Okay, I guess I could ask around. At least I'll be able to get off my butt, get some exercise. Come back in a week. You're a private doctor, I guess you know what you're talking about," he concluded skeptically.

And only three days later . . .

The flashing lights of the police car cast an unnatural blue pall on the gray stump of a body covered with a blanket. The figure lay on a stretcher that floated slowly into the yawning mouth of the ambulance. But I caught a glimpse of tangled hair and a wet forehead amidst the absurdly blue uniforms of the orderlies. Her face was uncovered, so she was alive. Inspector Bullet gave me a dark look and said, "The reason I asked you to come right away was that if she dies, I'm gonna have to interrogate your underage client. There's an overcoat here too. Looks like it's all true."

"I'd rather tell you her story myself," I said, thinking hard. "It would make more sense."

"Well?"

"Nice guy, funny, youngish, sun-bleached hair, tan, tall?" I asked.

"Far from it. Not very tall. The overcoat he wore dragged along on the ground behind him. The victim says the coat was strange, like something from the Stalin era. Other than that—well, maybe he was tan, maybe funny. Why shouldn't he be funny? So much fun to bash in a girl's head. They're probably gonna have to drill a hole in her skull. They say it's that serious. She went with him on her own at first, and then later she suspected something wasn't quite right . . . Yep. That's about it."

The investigation reached a dead end very quickly. Two construction workers, migrants, one tall and one short, who had been painting the building on the corner of 2nd and 3rd Peshchanaya Streets, vanished into a thin air. This greatly surprised their foreman, who couldn't locate his countrymen after returning from Moldavia. To find their whereabouts or prove anything was virtually impossible, since the photographs of the suspects that were soon faxed from their hometown, a place called Yassy, were only suitable for a trash can. So the building with the unfinished paint job returned to its peaceful slumber among the sticky lime trees and sounds of car alarms.

"We can't issue 'wanted' posters or arrest an overcoat without its owner," said the inspector. "But you know what I think? I think this is your department. After you stopped in the other day, I called all the old geezers from our precinct. They're better than any archive. Thought maybe there had been something like what you described two years ago, before I began working here. Turned out there was a case in 1973. Right here in Birch Grove Park. Then again, where else would someone work the walls with a girl? So there was this sex maniac who wore a wide-brim hat and an old-fashioned overcoat, who was always on the lookout for schoolgirls. Funny thing was that the girls didn't even hesitate. He took them to some broken-down barracks near Khodynka and made them wear white socks and a school uniform with a white apron. When he got busted, he threatened that the entire police force would have hell to pay when they found out who he really was. He hinted that he was some big shot in the Communist Party, or even one of the higher-ups in the government. To make a long story short, instead of going to jail, he ended up in a funny farm—your department, in other words. Never came back from there. He'd be in his nineties by now, I'd say. And he was a local, not a construction worker from Moldavia. Period. Case closed . . . What do you say to that?"

Quite frankly, I couldn't say anything at all, except a few standard comments about fetishism.

But fetishism isn't contagious. Especially when there's no direct contact. And fetishists rarely choose the same location twice.

Lighting up a cigarette, I sat down on a chair on the balcony and put my bare feet up on the railing. I had thought that I lived in one of the best neighborhoods in Moscow. Right next to the Sokol subway station and the large triangle of Bratsky Park, with its stately old lime trees. The park ends right at a lane of chestnuts, straight as an arrow, bordering an elegant square. That lane runs up to the famous Birch Grove Park, as big as a small forest. To live in a place surrounded by trees and green parks—what more could you wish for? Well, for one thing, that there weren't sexual predators roaming around in them.

But what could I do? I had (along with Inspector Bullet) very odd facts at my disposal. There was not one, but three maniacs, all strangely attractive to underage girls. The girls followed them willingly; my young patient even seduced him herself. Only one of them put up any resistance; but even she followed him voluntarily at first—a man she'd never seen before wearing an overcoat. She went with him to a remote, deserted corner of the park. And it was only when they got there that something happened she didn't like.

So, three maniacs. The second was short, since the coat

dragged on the ground. The first one was taller; the coat only came down to his knees. And the third maniac was already history—also featuring an overcoat, however.

If there's only one overcoat, then two different people would have had to wear it. As for the two builders from Moldavia, one of them could have just borrowed it from the other, and . . . and interesting things began happening to them.

But what about the 1973 maniac, who also wore an "old-fashioned overcoat," for god's sake? Old-fashioned even in 1973? When was it in style, then? The '50s? '40s?

The cigarette smoke drifted over the tops of the poplar trees, behind which stood gray brick buildings that looked like gingerbread houses. The clicking of a woman's high heels, fast and nervous, resounded on the concrete somewhere below.

The next day I went to visit the inspector with a silly question: had they found any link between the 1973 case and today's pedophiles from Moldavia? But, of course, there was no link. And, of course, no one wondered back in 1973 what had happened to the gray overcoat that the sex maniac wore to go skirt-chasing. Inspector Bullet had read in the 1973 file that the maniac had had a whole underground bunker, like an abandoned bomb shelter, right on the edge of Birch Grove Park. The police might have kept the white socks or the coat; but only the socks would probably have made good material evidence.

"What about the bunker?" I asked. "What happened to it? Where is it?"

"Who cares about the bunker, doc? When we come across a place like that, you know, a basement or an attic, we just seal it up and check the locks from time to time. So that winos or bums can't live there. I'm sure that was what happened to the bunker. Sealed up and forgotten. Come on, let's go. I'll show you why we have Comrade Stalin and his minister of internal affairs, Lavrentiy Beria, to thank for a good cop shop."

"Why Beria?" I asked absently, lost in my own thoughts.

Inspector Bullet didn't answer. Instead, he proudly motioned me to follow him down the corridor, where it ended at a plywood door. He opened it, revealing another door behind it. This one was made of heavy, rough cast iron, painted blood-brown. It had something like a ship's steering wheel, two feet in diameter, attached to it. No, it wasn't a ship's wheel—it looked more like the lock on a bank safe. I was standing in front of the door to a huge safe, the height of a grown man, covered in a slapdash way with multiple layers of paint. Numerous iron levers and knobs stuck out of the door—all parts of the locking mechanism.

"Does it work?" I asked in a grim voice, staring at the magnificent contraption.

"You bet," said Inspector Bullet. "We have the key, it weighs almost a pound. But frankly, none of us has ever felt like going behind the door."

He paused significantly, enjoying my confusion.

"No mutant rats or skeletons in rotten trench coats there, though," he added shortly, and wiped his large face with his hand. "But I suggest you don't go in there, either. Because . . . well, doc, I guess you've figured out this is an entrance to a bomb shelter. And our station is like the front lobby of the shelter. We're on the corner of Peshchanaya Square and 3rd Peshchanaya Street, right? We go into the bomb shelter from here, and using underground passages we can walk all the way over to the lane of chestnuts on your 2nd Peshchanaya. Think there's not a bomb shelter in your basement? It's just locked. But if you go down into the basement, sooner or later you'll end up in front of a metal door just like this one here. And behind it you'll find a passageway all the way to the Sokol subway station, or even the airport station, where the old airport use to be, on the former Khodynka Field. There was a secret subway line that went all the way there from the Kremlin. So, you go for a stroll underground, and when you figure you're lost, you start banging on this two-foot-thick door from the inside. But no one's going to open it, because even if someone's there, they won't hear you. It could get lonely, don't you think? Especially when it's pitch-black in there."

"You think Comrade Stalin and Comrade Beria wandered around in these bomb shelters?"

"Well, maybe they didn't. But all the gray brick houses on all the Peshchanaya streets have these bomb shelters. They were built by German prisoners of war. You know, 'You bombed 'em, you rebuild 'em.' They say that in the '50s, when Khrushchev set them free, they thanked everyone here for giving them the chance to return home with a clean conscience. And Comrade Beria, in addition to being the minister of national security, and then the minister of internal affairs, was also head of the prisoner camps. So it was all under his jurisdiction. The best buildings in Moscow are called Stalin buildings, but they should be called Beria buildings."

"That's all well and good," I said. "Beria and company—very interesting. But are you going to catch the maniac?"

Inspector Bullet sighed and looked at me unsympathetically. "At least the girl is alive. She says when he laid her down on some mossy hill, she changed her mind. And then he asked her to put on white socks, like a schoolgirl. Just like the other maniac. She didn't like the socks—too dirty. She began to fight him off. That's it. The case is basically closed. Not gonna dig up anything more on him."

"A hill . . . on the edge of Birch Grove Park, right by the concrete fence at Khodynka Field," I said with sudden clarity. "And who took her there? It was probably him. That's his place. Or *their* place? The same place as in 1973? And at first she followed him, as if . . . as if she were hypnotized. Right. See you, inspector; I'll be back."

"Hey, come work in the police force, why don't you? We really need a shrink in the department," replied Inspector Bullet.

The girl, Julia, gave me a much warmer welcome than her mother. The mother probably wasn't too keen on paying me for another session. She just sadly gestured with her hand toward the girl's room, saying, "Don't be shocked. Her majesty's wearing new clothes."

The red-haired Julia had dyed her hair jet-black and put on black and red lipstick. Metal trinkets of all shapes and sizes dangled from her wrists. A metal cross hung between her large breasts, which were virtually spilling out of her T-shirt, and were spotted with pimples.

"Come to lock me up in the funny farm?" she asked.

"They don't put goths and heavy metal fans away in mental institutions," I said. "Now listen carefully, sweetie. Two days ago, a man in an overcoat stinking of dirt cracked open the head of a young woman. The police are looking for him. Do you catch my drift? You have the ass of a grown-up woman and the head of a teenager. And when someone lowers a rock onto a head like that, and the brains begin to— Did you say something?"

In one quick, nervous motion, the gothic Julia lit a cigarette and stuck it to her mouth. Then she took it out, smeared with lipstick, and stared at me silently.

"So I need you to fill me in on some details, here," I said hastily, before she had quite recovered from the shock. "First, who was leading who? He you, or you him?"

"Him," she replied immediately. "He took me to the cement fence."

"You said there was a concrete slab. Was it hard?"

"Don't worry, it was soft enough for my butt." She was herself again, the first wave of shock already past. "It was covered with moss or something. It wasn't concrete, I mean . . . it was really old, more like a tuft of something in the ground. To the left of the path leading to a hole in the cement fence by Khodynka, the field. So it was real soft. Try it yourself. If you need company, I'll come with you. Doctors get a discount."

"One last thing. When you were going there with him, what were you thinking about? What did you feel?"

"What do you think I was thinking about? I was thinking about *that*," said Julia. "I felt a little high. I was like, you know, a little girl. Real curious. Like it was the first time. A big guy with a big thingy."

"Did you think those thoughts before?"

"I used to do a lot of things before. And now—hello, grown-up world."

I headed to the concrete fence, behind which the white towers of a whole new residential district, constructed on Khodynka Field in just under a year, soar up to the skies. The tops of the buildings bask in the sunset, and the fresh new walls glow pink, like the Cadillac Hotel. To the left stands the spire of Triumph Palace, the tallest residential building in Europe.

But all that is on the other side of the concrete fence. There, in a forgotten area of the old park, which is essentially a forest, twilight was thickening. An empty bench stood askew (what was it doing there—did someone drag it all the way over from the lane?), and weeds and burdocks grew on the tufty ground. Like gray mushroom caps covered with green mold, and slightly protruding from the ground at about knee height, there were two concrete slabs disappearing into the ground at a slant. A little farther on was another slab, level with the earth around it.

I thought I could make out something resembling small orifices, half covered in earth, by each slab. Passageways that once led down?

The slabs were covered with shards of broken bottles, sausage wrappers, and . . . a torn piece of foil—a condom wrapper.

So this was the place.

I had nothing more to do there.

Gray haze and a soft path silenced my footsteps. A shaggy dog emerged quietly from the bushes and stared at me with an unblinking, almost human stare, keeping a safe distance. Then it took two steps toward me. My heart fluttered in fear, but the the dog didn't come any closer.

For two hours I listened to a plump editor from *Sokol*, the local newspaper. She had suggested I do an interview on the topic of psychiatry, because "we do this with all the prominent people in the district." Then she talked about those who had died on Khodynka during the coronation of the last czar, when many people were crushed and their bodies were hauled away on carts. About Peshchanaya Square, which was built on a large graveyard for Napoleon's soldiers. The remains of the French soldiers were taken away, nobody knows where. A similar story about the dead in Bratskoye Cemetery: they were buried during World War I, and their remains were exhumed under Beria and Khrushchev, when the remote suburb of Moscow was turning into a beautiful new residential district. The bunkers on the edge of Khodynka? Those were located in a special area that belonged to the Moscow Military District—part of the defense line at the farthest end of the airbase. Airplanes took off over the heads of soldiers, their propellers droning heavily, and flew further west, to the railroad. Nothing interesting, apart from that. Stories about the living dead from the past? No, no; nothing of that nature. I would have heard. I left the editor and walked home through the empty treelined streets in complete silence, greedily breathing in the fresh air.

Parks built on human bones. Graveyards that no longer exist. An ominous name—Khodynka. More parks, couples with baby carriages, cyclists, poplars, lime trees. Graveyard shadows sleep peacefully among bushes and alleys. Sleep, O souls of long forgotten soldiers. Sleep in the best neighborhood in Moscow. You are welcome here, because all cities stand on the bones of the past. Carts, then hearses, rolled down these streets. These days, from the open balcony doors, you could hear women's laughter and music, and from the sidewalk you could see the tops of bookshelves and white ceilings with circles of honey-colored lights cast by chandeliers. A cat sat in the window and stared gloomily at the gray concrete below. The cat's name was Grymzik. He belonged to my neighbor, and I was almost home. And I needed to make an urgent phone call.

"Sergey? Hi, how's your precious health today?"

"Ah, good doctor! Nice to hear your voice. I'm great, actually. Physically exhausted, but glowing with mental health. I'm afraid I no longer make a very interesting patient. You're a regular magician, I'll have you know."

"Believe me, Sergey, no magic involved whatsoever. What

was it that bothered you? Depression and a couple of neuroses. Well, who wasn't depressed in the '90s? I used to have two patients who loved to discuss the benefits of suicide and its various methods with me every day. I didn't try to contradict them, and even participated in their discussions. What do you expect from someone who's been designing rockets all his life, and is then told: *Thank you, but we really won't be needing any more rockets.* Rope and a piece of soap is the only way out. And you . . . half the people in the U.S. take Prozac; and they had no major crisis or economic collapse to contend with in the '90s. So there's no magic to it whatsoever. But you should hear about my new patient. You won't believe it if I tell you. Actually, that's why I'm calling you. Do you still have your connections in the archives?"

"Oh, I never lost them. Still work there. Deputy director, if can you believe it. So the entire archive is at your disposal. What exactly are you looking for?"

"Well, you see, it's a very serious case," I said, improvising. "A fetishist, a rapist, most likely a murderer. Fixated on particular objects, locations, and events from the past. And particular names. I have a theory, which I thought you could help me test. Just promise me that you won't think I'm off my rocker when I start asking my questions. You wouldn't believe what kinds of nutcases there are out there."

"Indulge me," said the archivist joyfully. "What particular historical fetishes does your maniac have?"

"Coordinate number one is the area between the edge of Khodynka Field and the back of Birch Grove Park. Apparently, that part of the city is connected with some important people. And I'm talking famous historical people—from the Soviet era. Some bigwigs in the ruling party. Then there's a fetish, which is a summer coat, or an overcoat. Light gray, no belt, made from good material, like gabardine, worn by a man of above-average height. Do you think you could help me determine the exact era and style of an overcoat? It would help me figure out who he's fixated with. Because the bastard wouldn't tell me. So, the overcoat is coordinate number two. Then, since we're talking crazy people here, there's one peculiar detail: with him it's all about underage girls—white socks and all that nonsense. And that's your third coordinate. So, what do we get at the point of intersection?"

"Well, doctor, you're an intelligent man. You know your history. It's not what; it's *who*. Some concrete historical figure. But I'm curious. This guy—does he wear the old-fashioned overcoat and rape young girls in white socks?"

"Sergey, don't ask questions. Who's the psychiatrist here? Yet, indeed, you guessed it. Only the particular location is also significant here—the back of Khodynka Field and Birch Grove Park."

"But of course, my dear doctor. Let's begin with the overcoat. It's probably from the postwar era. In the '30s, the fashion was to wear military-style overcoats with a belt. Then, after that, up until the '60s . . . Well, take the photographs of the Soviet party during that muddy period between Stalin and Khrushchev, and you'll see about five overcoats like that in every picture. As for underage girls, it's perfectly clear. I'm sure you know who was infamous for meddling with them."

"Beria," I said under my breath, looking down at the dark treetops from the balcony. "Lavrentiy Beria."

"That's right. Of course, other party leaders have been know to savor similar worldly pleasures; but schoolgirls were Beria's particular preference. Well, not just schoolgirls; often women with specific figures and mannerisms. Am I using the correct terms?"

"Absolutely."

"Imagine a black car driving slowly along the sidewalk behind a girl with plump calves. Two men get out of the automobile and introduce themselves to her. According to some
sources, they just push her into the car and drive off to the
famous house on Sadovaya Street. Across from Krasnaya
Presnya, in case you didn't know. Other sources suggest that
the scenario was a little more genteel. They would talk the girl
into it first. If need be, they'd dress the teenager in a school
uniform, or sometimes a ballet tutu. Then they sat her on a
sofa and told her to wait. Dozens of books have been written about it; and just two months ago, some TV people approached me about it. They're going to make a program. Have
I told you anything you didn't already know?"

"The particular spot," I reminded him. "Our entire district was built by Beria. I know this already. He, of course,
always took off from the airport on Khodynka; but other people boarded planes on the other side of the field. What does
our maniac know about that other, forgotten part of the field?
And what does that part have to do with Beria?"

The archivist took a deep, noisy breath. "He knows something that very few people know, frankly. And I find it strange
that a maniac could get his hands on such information. It's
extremely difficult to come across. What's on that side of the
field now?"

"A construction site. Just like every other goddamn neighborhood in the city . . . New buildings crawling up to the skies
all over the place."

"And you want to know which building stood there before?"

"Can you tell me this over the phone?" I asked after a
pause.

"Yes, after Mr. Suvorov's novel *The Aquarium*, I can," the archivist reassured me cheerfully. "The Aquarium, the main intelligence directorate of the Red Army, stood there. Around it were various military fences, barracks, even tents, when the troops were training for the parades on the occasion of the Bolshevik Revolution. The area belonged to the military, in other words. That wasn't much of a secret. The secret, for a long time, was what was there underground."

"Do you mean catacombs, bomb shelters, underground tunnels?" I recalled the heavy metal door with the spindle wheel.

"That's exactly what I mean," said the archivist. "Back then they were building bomb shelters everywhere, and Beria was in charge of it. In the summer of 1953 they took him into one such bomb shelter at the far end of the airfield, just after Comrade Stalin died. That was where he spent his last days. How long exactly is difficult to say. They say that they executed him first, and prosecuted and sentenced him later, in December. It's possible, by they way, that he was executed in that very basement, right between Birch Grove Park and Khodynka Field. The site of his final orgasm, as it were."

"From the point of view of psychiatry, it's interesting that you would refer to an execution as a last orgasm," I said pompously. "Would you be so kind as to explain what you mean in more detail?"

"Doctor, not everyone's a maniac. Could you hold on a second? I'm going to go grab something . . . here. A memoir of someone who loathed Beria with all his heart. For various reasons. *The Bystander*, by one Mr. Dmitri Shepilov, minister of foreign affairs under Khrushchev. He was also in charge of culture, arts, and ideology in the Communist Party. He was, by the way, a handsome man who loved women. Ordinary women, mind you, not underage schoolgirls. The chapter is called 'The Battle.' And I quote . . . hold on a minute, I'm going to quote him where he talks about where they put Beria. 'And when he was told he was under arrest, his face turned green and brown from his chin to his temples and up to his forehead. Armed marshals entered the meeting hall. They escorted him to the automobile. It had been earlier agreed upon that the Beria would not be put in the internal jail in the Lubyanka or the Lefortovo detention cells: that could lead to unforeseeable consequences. It was decided to keep him in a special detention cell in one of the buildings of the Moscow Military District under surveillance by armed guards.' He's referring to your Khodynka; or, rather, the farthest end of it. Later the military closed some of the buildings there and gave them away. Oh, and here's the part about orgasms: 'He persistently from the depths of his memory recalled the most erotic scenes and relived them, voluptuously enjoying all the little details, in order to excite himself, seeking oblivion for at least a few precious moments. The supreme officers who guarded the door of his cell all day and night could see through the peephole how Beria, covered with a rough military blanket, writhed underneath it in spasms of masturbation.' What style, doctor! Note, however, that I wasn't quoting from the book. I was quoting from the original manuscript that I received from one of his publishers. Even though this was way after the Soviet era, the publishers had scruples about printing the piece about the military blanket, so they left it out."

A blanket, I thought. A military blanket. And clothes.

"Sergey, do you happen to know if they confiscated his clothing, too, after he was arrested?"

"Clothing? My dear doctor, not just clothing. Shepilov very clearly states in his memoirs that they they took away his shoelaces, his belt—even his famous pince-nez, so he wouldn't cut himself with the glass."

"And where did they take it all?"

"Oh, I wouldn't know. Does it really matter? I doubt they would have kept that information in the archives. Although, it's possible they might have written it all down in some official document somewhere."

On the other hand, I thought, it doesn't really matter. I imagined the military investigators fingering every little wrinkle of a light gray overcoat and then . . . then tossing it in some corner . . . and then . . .

Suddenly, I heard my mother's voice in my head. When was it? How many years ago did she tell me about the cold day in June 1953, before I was even born? It was a story about her and my father. They were sitting alone on some stone steps by the river, cigarette butts floating past, next to a tall Stalin-era building on Kotelnicheskaya embankment. They must have felt very happy on that short June night, when the sun rose almost as soon as it had set. They felt happy until the stone steps began to tremble under their feet.

Because tanks started rolling down the boulevard next to the embankment.

And my father—who had run off to fight in the war as a boy, and who ever since had been able to tell the difference between tanks on their way to military parades and tanks going off to war (portholes shut tight, armaments at the ready)—got up from the stone steps to watch. Then he went back to where my mother was and said somberly, "I think I'd better run home."

But it wasn't war. It was Marshals Zhukov, Nedelin, Moskalenko, and others, getting ready to enter the Kremlin and arrest the omnipotent minister of national security.

And arrest him they did. The troops under Lavrentiy Beria's command did not rise up in his defense. The door to the dungeon at Khodynka slammed shut behind him.

A cold, cold summer in 1953. A summer coat. An underground bunker that looks like a bomb shelter. Its roof, covered in moss, disappearing into the ground.

"Hello? Doctor, you still there?" said the voice on the other end. "I could tell you things that have come to light in other documents just beginning to surface nowadays. For example, Beria's not the only one to blame for the purges and execution of prisoners. After the war, he was involved in the A-bomb and nuclear power (glory be his name), and construction, and a number of other things. There were people whose hands were just as bloody as his. They were the ones who assassinated him. Are you interested in hearing more?"

"I am," I said honestly, "but not now. I have a crazy man walking the streets. Thank you very much, Sergey."

What happened after 1973 in terms of maniacs in overcoats? Nothing, really. They were dormant. Why was that? And why has that suddenly changed? I remembered the construction site, all the dozens of new houses that had risen up in the past few months on Khodynka Field. The large wasteland of the former restricted airfield was no more. It was crawling with . . .

Construction workers.

Construction workers clambering up and down the stairwells of the new buildings, dumping garbage by the surrounding fences, excavating . . . and excavating some more for the foundations of new buildings.

I had one slim chance left, and I used that chance the next day.

Because the foreman of the defunct brigade of two vanished construction workers from Moldavia was still occupying a lone structure in the next courtyard.

"So they're not coming back, eh?" I asked the foreman, and sat down on the porch next to him.

He shook his head furiously.

"Too bad," I continued. "Say, uh, they borrowed a book from me. . . about space invaders. You seen it?"

"No," replied the foreman mournfully, and again shook his head. "Haven't seen it."

"I understand." I was moving closer to my goal. "I just need the book. It's the cops who need the rapist. But the book is still mine, you see—"

"My guys are no rapists. They're good guys," the foreman said, finally able to muster a coherent sentence. "The book . . . go ahead and look around. There's no book in there."

I could hardly believe my luck. I went inside the little house where the construction workers had stayed. A strong, unpleasant odor from a portable toilet assaulted my nostrils. Then, in an instant, I saw a dull gray garment hanging on a coatrack right in front of me.

The rest was easy.

"By the way, I need to do a paint job," I said. "This thing here, is this your work coat? How much do you want for it?"

"That's no work coat," answered the foreman. "The guys left it here. You can have it. Instead of the book. Go ahead, they won't be needing it. They're not coming back. Their families keep calling and calling . . ."

Holding the gray overcoat at arm's length, I asked: "Where did you work before? Wasn't there a construction site over there? On the other side of the field, by that concrete fence? I believe that's where I met your guys."

"Oh, sure," said the foreman. "The finishing team arrived

when we were done over there. And we moved here. And now . . . we're done here too."

I remember at one point I felt the urge to bury my face in the coat and inhale the smell of a cellar and potatoes. It took me some effort not to do so. I threw it down on the landing in front of my door. I had no intention of bringing the thing into my apartment. I went inside and found a large shopping bag, put the overcoat in it, and left it in front of the door. Then I scrubbed my hands thoroughly. In a closet I found a bottle of flammable liquid for barbecuing and dropped it into the bag as well.

I was in a hurry. It was getting late, and I didn't want to leave the coat outside for the night. Someone might take it.

Then I was in that deserted edge of Birch Grove Park. An empty bench, and the remnants of the bunkers protruding from the ground.

I dumped the coat onto the surface of the nearest bunker, on the concrete slab covered with moss. I poured the liquid onto the coat and set fire to it with my lighter. Thick, oily smoke billowed up and gravitated to the concrete fence and beyond, where the floors of the nearby buildings mounted into the sky.

It burned very, very slowly.

"Now why did you do that?" The thin, tremulous voice came from somewhere below.

No, I wasn't scared. Even when I noticed that someone had been sitting on a nearby bench the whole time. It was . . . an old lady? That's right, just an old lady in a light summer coat and a funny straw hat trimmed with two wooden cherries. The red paint on one of them had almost completely peeled off. But her cheekbones burned with the same color, in an almost invisible network of blood vessels. When I saw those liver spots on her powdered cheeks, I thought in panic, How old is she? Why didn't I notice her before?

Or maybe she hadn't been there when I set fire to the coat?

"Do you think it's about the coat?" the old lady asked in a childish—no, not childish, but teacherish—voice, high as a violin string. "It was just fabric. Good fabric too. Very durable. That was silly. Just plain silly."

"No, it's not about the coat," I replied through my teeth. I had to say something, just to break the silence—and so I wouldn't be afraid.

"You haven't even seen him," the old lady continued, not paying any attention to my words, and staring vaguely in the direction of my sneakers with her light gray eyes. "You weren't even born yet in '53. Not to mention before that."

"Did you see him?" I asked.

"Just like I see you now," the voice went on. "Only closer, much closer. As close as can be."

And slowly, very slowly, she parted her thin, bloodless lips.

EUROPE AFTER THE RAIN

BY ALEXEI EVDOKIMOV

Kiev Station

Translated by Mary C. Gannon

"What's the story on your pal?"
"He was born, he suffered, he died."
—Dialogue from *Heist*, a film by David Mamet

If you ride out from the center of the city on the Filevskaya
line, a minute before Kievskaya, the train, whistling and
puffing, slows down and emerges out into the light on
the subway bridge. Your eyes try to take in the sharp bend in
the river, the angular, protruding architectural ruins along the
embankments, and the broad flat façade of the White House,
its flanks a bold invitation to gunfire from weapons mounted
on tanks.

On this day the picture seemed to be smeared like bad
reception on a TV screen with whitish rain showers, frequent
and driving. I frowned and hunched my shoulders, anticipat-
ing the discomfort, but when I crawled out from underground
into the station, it had already stopped. The darkened asphalt
breathed out a bathlike moisture, passersby shook off their
umbrellas fastidiously, and the returning sun was multiplied
in puddles.

I glanced at my watch and walked down the street, slowly making my way over to a fountain that looked like the remaining evidence of the recent shower; I wanted to turn it off. Some people had already sat down, sticking backpacks and plastic bags under their behinds, on the steps of this stunted amphitheater. Others peeled off their jackets or simply shook the water from their soaking heads; this hot spot for the young filled up quickly. I remembered that I had waited for Yanka here; I remembered that, stretching my hood as far as it would go and trying to light up underneath it, I had regretted my choice of meeting places. When the St. Petersburg girl had finally arrived, I took her to the new pedestrian bridge, where we blended in with other couples.

Together with them we staggered through the stuffy glass passageway from one side of the bridge to the other—I pointed with my finger, explaining that this was probably the only place in the city where you could see, more or less up close, four of the seven Stalin skyscrapers at once. Nodding at the MID building with a coat of arms on it, I explained that according to the original design it was to have been the only one without a spire. At the last minute Stalin announced that it looked too much like an American skyscraper that way. It was too late to change the design—the building was almost finished; but who would be the one to contradict Stalin's wishes? So they ran a gigantic metal rod through the top floors, and placed a ridge-roofed tower on top of that, painted to look like stone. After Khrushchev unmasked the cult of personality, he was reminded that it wouldn't be a bad idea to remove this idiotic detail of Stalin's gloomy legacy. Nikita snorted and ordered that it stay right there, as a monument to the tastelessness of the generalissimo.

On the left side we moved onto a path that led along

a high, grassy slope past the Turkish embassy toward the Borodinsky Bridge. Europe Square was now below and opposite us.

I like this place.

Here, the river and the open space in front of Kiev station leave a large expanse open to view. Here, you can really see the sky, which is rare in this capital city that squeezes you between enormous stone slabs. The view that spreads out before you here—the Gothic silhouette of the university on a distant bluff to the left, the palisade of mighty pipes on top of the Radisson, the spire of the Hotel Ukraine perpendicular to layers of lilac clouds—is one of those typical and utterly urban landscapes that create the face of a city, which Moscow, monstrous and vague with its eroded individuality, so lacks.

That's what I said to Yanka, trying to show her the city from its most presentable perspective, trying to be amusing and casual, not pressuring her. I knew my role and my place. When I met her a year before in her native Petersburg, I invited her out of politeness (but not only that, not only . . .)—I invited her (that is to say, *them,* her and Igor) to "visit us in our capital with no culture," promising to show them around and entertain them. Of course, they didn't jump at the opportunity—not because they had anything against me, but because in the absence of any other attractions in the city, the prospect of hanging out with me was not sufficient inducement to overcome a distance of six hundred kilometers. Then, suddenly, Yanka found a reason—the wedding of a college friend. The event was to take place over several days (the newlyweds belonged to circles that had money to waste on lavish parties). But the other guests weren't really to Yanka's taste; and that's when she remembered me.

Exceedingly pretty, with a slight, charming unevenness in

her features, and with that rare combination of intelligence and spontaneity, that balance of self-assurance and sincere goodwill that you sometimes find in people from very well-to-do families—smart, prosperous, and affable; that was Yanka.

During those three days, I mobilized all my meager resources of joie de vivre and sociability. My guest was as open and friendly as ever; she listened attentively and meekly tasted the shark at Viet-Café, but on the whole she seemed fairly indifferent. As I later became convinced, people who feel that they are equal to life's demands don't experience an excess of curiosity about the range of its phenomena: they already know exactly what they need from it.

I had absolutely no chance of ever landing on the list of things that those people wanted from life. Back then I hadn't abandoned my rock and roll efforts. Officially, I was supposed to be a journalist, which is how I presented myself (I was a freelancer). I was also acquainted with progressive, and sometimes even high-profile people; and I was, after all, a Muscovite. Theoretically, I belonged to practically the same circle as my female contemporary from the Petersburg theater crowd; the sense of insurmountable social and psychological distance was completely unfounded.

I felt not only a distance, though—I felt an abyss. In our relations, which seemed on the surface to be relaxed, there was something reminiscent of a conversation in the lingua franca of a Norwegian and a Malaysian who sit side by side on a flight in a transcontinental Boeing; however well-disposed they might be toward each other, they are still from different worlds. At that time, a little over four years ago, I had only begun to guess about the nature of that difference.

Yanka's generosity of spirit, which so impressed me at first, gradually began to disturb me. It was difficult, if not impossible, for me to share a perspective in which the world appears to be acceptably, if not optimally arranged.

I became suspicious of Yanka's self-sufficiency. I understood perfectly the origins of this feeling, since I'd had the opportunity to glimpse from afar the reality which the girl had inhabited for a long time already—the reality of her beloved theater, where she was highly regarded, with its well-established, intimate, exclusive company of actors. The same company was home, as well, to Igor; an amicable, handsome, easygoing guy who had a promising career ahead of him. In short, this world was so harmonious that at a certain moment it began to feel absolutely artificial to me.

Then I understood that I was merely deceiving myself. All I really wanted to do was expose the futility of affluence—so that I would see one advantage in my own deprived and uncomfortable existence. The advantage of authenticity.

A not uncommon compensatory trick.

Actually, all lives are equally real or unreal. The quality of everyday private and public loathsomeness in one of them affords no metaphysical bonuses to others.

It's just that for some people, everything in life works out. For others, it doesn't. And you can't draw any moral lesson from it. Other than: *Grief to the vanquished.*

I looked at my watch again and frowned. I couldn't do anything about my habit of turning up early for every appointment, whether important or completely inconsequential; even appointments with people who never show up on time anywhere in their lives.

And really, what's the hurry?

"But you can always try—"

"Look, Felix, Yanka was a very gregarious young woman.

She could have met up with anyone . . . Plus, it's been over a year already."

"Maybe you'll think of someone else."

"Oh, I don't know . . . Well, there was Pasha from Moscow— she met him shortly before that, I think . . ."

"Who's this Pasha guy?"

"Uh, what's his name—Korenev or something. Just an acquaintance. A long time ago, maybe five years ago, he went to Petersburg, and then, I guess, Yanka saw him in Moscow."

"So he went back to Petersburg?"

"Looks like it."

"What did Yanka say about meeting him?"

"Oh god, I don't remember . . ."

"Do you have any idea where he lives? A phone number?"

I walked around the square, stomped around on one spot, and sat on the damp stone. I started to smoke, paying close attention to my movements. I remember very clearly how one time, when she was watching me smoke, Tatiana mentioned that I had the gestures of an ex-convict. She didn't know anything at that time, though. She didn't know anything yet.

Feeling a moist caress on my face, I raised my head, but it was just the spray from the fountain.

Tin cans rolled around under my feet; empty beer bottles stuck up everywhere.

Suddenly, a dozen or so guys in orange pants sprang up out of nowhere and fell upon them. They quickly tossed the clanking bottles and cans into black plastic bags and hurled them into the maw of a toy tractor.

The struggle for cleanliness continued, apparently in an effort to live up to the name of the place—Europe Square.

Gleb, I remembered, was moved to laughter at the inscription on a plaque by the fountain: *As a sign of the strengthening friendship and unity of the countries of Europe, the administration of Moscow endeavored on such-and-such a date to create the ensemble of Europe Square.*

There was not much to be said about the friendship between the countries of Europe and Moscow—but most touching of all was the clear sense of identification of the bald mayor of Moscow and Co. with the European Union (immortalizing this was just as logical in Phnom Penh as it was in Moscow, in Gleb's opinion). We discussed the sacred conviction of our fellow citizens that they live in a brilliant European capital—as evidence for which they usually cite the number of high-end boutiques. Gleb, a dyed-in-the-wool "westernizer," said that the sincere incomprehension of the difference is the clearest evidence of the difference itself.

Having traveled from one end of the continent to the other and lived in London, with a multientry Shengen visa, Gleb considered himself to be in a position to judge and compare. As an indigenous Moscow resident, he just didn't like it enough; and he categorically refused to recognize it as a part of Europe. His basic argument was the flagrant disproportion of the size of Moscow to the human being, a point that was difficult to counter.

It was rare that anyone wanted to argue with him. I have hardly ever met a person with such sound and penetrating points of view. Also, his talent for expressing them with charm and panache, both verbally and in writing, made Gleb the soul of any gathering, and the star of liberal journalism.

Liberal, in his case, didn't refer to a position regarding civil society, but was a synonym for measured restraint. As a matter of fact, for Gleb, this restraint stood surrogate for political views to a certain degree—he wrote equally well, and with equal conviction, in both servile and seditious (and, naturally, glossy) publications. The logic of his ideas was so unassailable that even in the preelection hysteria, the most patriotic bosses didn't find fault with the author on the subject of his loyalty. Indeed, Gleb possessed the talent (without a tinge of sycophantism) of making every boss like him. I still remember back in school, where he and I became friends, how I looked on in amusement as the slightly wilted schoolmarms of a certain age fell involuntarily in love with the straight-A student.

Gleb began publishing at the age of fourteen; at fifteen he had already made it into print in the prestigious unionwide Soviet journals. At twenty he became the head of a weekly magazine, where I too—after trying to make a living as a homegrown punk rocker and from various meager supplemental earnings—got my first steady and meaningful employment (though I was never officially on the payroll).

Many people back then (and not just friends) said that I was a fine writer. In addition to everything else, I worked a lot, carried out all the assignments from the higher-ups, and got everything in on time. Nevertheless, both my articles and myself (no matter the subject, genre, or depth of pathos) were greeted (and published—if they agreed to publish them) by all managers with some vague initial skepticism, as though they were suppressing (and, later, no longer trying to suppress) the instinct to shrug their shoulders. When I asked point blank one day why they hadn't printed any of my reviews for more than a week, and some fat-assed jerk of a deputy editor muttered in slight exasperation, "You always pan everything, but, you know, people watch those movies and read those books; you just turn up your nose at them!"—I finally decided that it was time to call it quits.

And I did. For two years. Though I firmly believe this had nothing to do with journalism itself.

Of course, in a frenzy of self-searching, I acknowledged (according to an elementary logic) my own mediocrity. But to be honest, I never believed it. And I don't think it was only due to self-love. I knew I was good at what I did. The fact that no one needed it was another matter altogether. It was precisely my product that they had no need for. Someone else's—Gleb's, for instance—of the same subject and quality would be snatched up immediately.

I never understood why. I ultimately came to the conclusion that there was no reason. There are no rules, and no laws. It's just that some people make it in their jobs, while others don't. And this work has no objective value. More than that—*nothing* has objective value.

He should've been here already, I thought, looking around and trying to match a person with the voice from the phone yesterday—but none of the men there were paying any attention to me, and one of the two girls sitting right across from me frowned slightly and looked away.

"Dmitry?"

"Felix?"

"Yeah, Dmitry, hi. I called you earlier and you told me you saw Pasha last week."

"Right."

"Well, I came down from Petersburg just to meet him and I can't find him. People say he just dropped out of sight; no one seems to know where he is."

"Uh-huh, that's what I heard too; that he, like, disappeared, about a year or so ago. So I called around without much hope of finding him; but what do you know, I got

through right away. He's in Moscow. We got together at that
. . . what's it called, by Kiev station? You know, Europe Square.
We used to hang out there a lot. We used to cross the river
and drink beer on that slope, on the grass, with the view . . ."

"But you don't see him much these days. Is that right?"

"No, we don't hang out at all anymore. Almost two years
now. When Pasha got out we cooked something up together,
but we got busted pretty fast. Somehow, we never saw each
other after that."

"What do you mean, 'got out'? Did he do time or something?"

"Well, yeah. For something incredibly stupid . . . A few
joints, can you believe it? What bullshit—getting sent up for
something like that is truly an art. There was a raid. And he
hardly ever smoked. I shit you not, man, they dragged him in
purely to meet their quota. For a few measly sticks of weed
. . . but that's how it works here, right? They can throw you
in jail for anything they want. Article 228, section 1: *acquisi-
tion and storage*. The most they can give you is three years, I
think—and that's what they slapped on him. I don't know
why—the judge probably didn't like his face or something. He
did two of the three. Actually, it's really not that long; but
the pen did a number on him. He kind of jitters and jerks a
bit when he moves now. See, Pasha always gets, you know,
screwed over, somehow. Things never go his way. If you get
mixed up with him, you're gonna get caught red-handed, no
matter what. Not because he's low-down, or a cheat—on the
contrary, he's always honest; in fact, he's way too honest. He's
a real German, you know—a pedant. Just has bad luck, that's
all. I got burned once because of him, and I started to avoid
him after that."

"What else happened to him?"

"What *didn't* happen to him? I'm telling you. He never had a real, bona fide job; never had any money. He wrote for the papers—but he was never on any payroll. All his attempts at business failed. He wrote some kind of novel—same thing. Every publisher he contacted about it—eleven in all, I think— turned it down. Then, six years later or so, one publisher took it on. A minuscule print run; they paid him less than a thousand bucks. No one took any notice of it, naturally. Though Pasha himself said that's par for the course here in Russia."

"Why did you decide to get together again, if you don't mind my asking?"

"He left behind some documents for that company we registered two years ago. And I wanted to see him again—see how the years have treated him. I just wanted to find out, you know, if his karma had taken a turn for the better."

"So?"

"Well, same as ever. He's gotten really weird . . . he's drinking, I guess. Or shooting up. Not too good, anyway, from what I could see. But I tell you, I did enjoy seeing him. In the sense that, you know, nothing has changed. Because sometimes you think, you know, everything's okay for me, things are working out, money's piling up. You've got everything you need. And then suddenly something unexpected happens—just out of the blue. And, *boom*, you're totally broke, your pockets are empty. Or the meter's ticking. And so I took a look at Korenev, and, you know, I was convinced: if someone has bad luck, it'll always be that way. And if your life has always worked out well, most likely it will continue that way . . ."

"Do you know a Gleb Mezentsev?"

"A little. Through Pasha."

"Do you know what happened to him?"

"No . . ."

"He was in a car crash. Two months ago."

"Whoa . . . what happened to him?"

"He's in the hospital."

"Hurt bad?"

"Pretty serious."

"Hmmm . . . I guess that's how it goes."

"Pasha and Gleb were friends, weren't they? I'd like to see Pasha, to talk to him. Could you give me his phone number—the one you reached him at? I'm looking for him, but everyone says he disappeared . . ."

"His number? Sure."

I tossed my cigarette butt away, folded my arms behind my head, and stretched. A girl sitting directly across from me glanced over and then mechanically turned away. I just as mechanically slid my gaze above her head, a bit to the right: slid it along the concave façade of the Radisson, along the pseudoclassical colonnade of the station, along the bent stainless steel pipes in the center of the fountain, which were supposed to represent the horns of the bull who abducted Europa, according to the Belgian sculptor. A gift, you understand, to the city.

They'd probably be ashamed to erect something like that in the middle of Brussels.

A shaggy black dog gulped voraciously from the fountain. Little children waded in up to their knees. The girls sitting across from me finally stood up and walked by me, passing to my left toward the bridge, their heels clicking along. I thought to myself that if I had been here with Dmitry, like in the old days, an exciting little encounter with them would have taken place—at least a 70 to 80 percent chance of it.

I can't say that I really envied his garrulous nature. His

ability to get along with anyone, anywhere, at any time, and talk about whatever came up could be tiresome. But his very communicativeness bewitched me sometimes—in its universality and inexplicability. I couldn't figure out what attraction Dmitry held for people of all ages, social backgrounds, and IQs. He didn't have, say, Gleb's brains. He wasn't especially charming or handsome. He didn't have the rudeness that is so attractive to girls. On the contrary, Dmitry's manner and appearance were characterized by a faint, slightly intentional goofiness. A person without much education and wit, he played the role of an enfant terrible. And in this niche he enjoyed condescending but indubitable success, even when he behaved like a complete idiot. Everyone teased him, but at the same time they sought him out and called him incessantly (often without any reason whatsoever), and gathered around him in remarkably large, motley crowds. He affected people like a beautiful woman or free drinks: in his presence people began to chatter loudly, guffaw, and swagger. Guys gave themselves over as drinking buddies, girls as lovers. From the day he was born, Dmitry hadn't had to lift a finger to find either business partners or bedfellows—in spite of the fact that the guy never stayed loyal to either.

I was no different from his other friends. I was glad to drink with him, prepared to lower my standards of intellect and wit, and was forgiving about minor and not so minor character flaws; I generally took on a protective role, even when our social and financial status suggested the exact opposite . . .

I thought about our spontaneous encounter last week. There was something very strange, and at the same time very predictable, in the repetition of the classic scenarios of the old days—two people with a bottle on the grassy slope across from Europe Square. Right above the station we saw a golden slash through the gray clouds. Dullish rays fell in fan-shaped sheaves on the shimmery heights of the construction site, its signal lights winking on the straining arms of the giant insectlike cranes. (When we used to sit here back then, there weren't any cranes.) Below, from the Rostov embankment, a steady hum rose up, interspersed with bellowing horns and the gunning of engines. A Miller beer ad the size of a small building hung above the square, where everything ended for me . . .

We sat and drank, like before—both of us understanding perfectly well that it would never again be like it used to be. And then it dawned on me that Dmitry had started this phony demonstration of solidarity to prove to himself the absolute and fundamental inequality between us; two people who don't differ in any fundamental way, neither superior to the other, yet one of them receives everything and everyone without asking, and the other is shunned and doesn't even get what he has honestly earned. And neither one is to blame for this. And this is nobody's fault. No one is to blame for anything—actually, there is never rhyme or reason to anything whatsoever.

It's all just the way it is. For no reason. Just because. Just—because.

I looked up and met someone's searing gaze. A fairly unpleasant one. It belonged to a burly man who had suddenly materialized in front of me; someone of about fifty with the broad, crudely chiseled mug of a charismatic antihero. The fellow was walking toward me—uncertainly at first, but with every step more and more purposeful. I realized right away who it was. I was about to get up when the guy stopped abruptly, shoved his hand inside his coat, and, staring at me from under his brow, clapped a cell phone to his ear.

* * *

Kostya from the Criminal Investigation Department called; he was a great resource for Felix here in Moscow.

"Hello?" Felix answered in a quiet, curt voice, not taking his eyes off Pasha Korenev.

"You're trying to find out about Dmitry Lisin?" Kostya asked cautiously, his voice full of concern.

"Yeah."

"Were you able to see him?"

"Yes. Yesterday."

"Well, that's lucky," Kostya snickered. "Just in time."

"What do you mean?"

"Well, I happened across his name this morning. I thought of you right away. The report on the explosion on Sirenevy Boulevard came in from the eastern precinct."

"What explosion?"

"You haven't heard? At 2 Sirenevy Boulevard. It looks like a gas main burst. Several apartments were destroyed, three people died. One of them was Lisin. He lived in the apartment right above the one that blew up."

"A gas main?" Felix repeated slowly, looking at Korenev, who sat serenely in the same spot.

"That's what they suspect. The cause hasn't been determined yet."

"It wasn't gas, Kostya. I mean, maybe it was gas—but it wasn't an accident. It was murder."

"How do you know?"

"I just do," Felix barked, then hung up.

He approached the bastard, who stared calmly back at him and seemed like he was about to hold out his hand in greeting; but Felix's facial expression stopped him.

"Pasha . . . ?" Felix asked, surprised at the hesitancy of his own voice.

The bastard nodded. "Felix . . . ?"

A plain, pale fellow, who seemed paradoxically both younger and older than his thirty-some years. Absolutely average, a somehow ineffably unprepossessing appearance. At the same time, a certain detail that Felix didn't catch—probably something in the guy's eyes—triggered his memory of the words of the late Lisin: *He's gotten really weird. He's drinking, I guess. Or shooting up . . .*

They stood there facing each other—Korenev, calmly expectant. Felix suddenly realized he didn't know how to begin, or what to do. Or why he needed to see the guy so urgently . . . Since Felix had homed in on the creep, reason only intermittently guided his actions. The situation was dictated exclusively by emotions: Felix was impatient to see the monster, to stand near him, to observe him at close range—and to let him know that he knew everything. That this bastard had no way out—he would cringe in fear, he would feel terror so fierce it would hurt . . .

"My name's Shakhlinsky," Felix finally said, in the same strangled voice.

"Uh-huh," Korenev replied, nodding slightly to himself. Something flickered behind his eyes—but no, it wasn't fear.

"I'm Yanka's uncle," Felix added.

"Please accept my condolences," Korenev said after a slight pause, and Felix was ready to rip him apart right there. He knew why the son of a bitch had suggested meeting here, in a place full of people. He was afraid . . .

"I'm a colonel in the police force, Criminal Investigation Department."

"And what do you want from me?"

"You know what I want," Felix said, and mastered himself with a deep intake of breath. "They say it was several hours before she died. And you, son of a bitch, will suffer ten times longer, and worse. Do you think I'm going to send you up for this? No, you don't, of course." He struggled to assume a gentler expression. "You know there's not enough evidence. Only I don't need any friggin' evidence; I'm going to kill you myself . . ."

The bastard smirked. Felix could hardly believe his eyes—the guy was smirking without the slightest sign of fear.

"So you think I killed her?"

"And you didn't think anyone would find out? Right. No clues, and—the main thing—no motive. But I was lucky. Just by chance I learned about a few of your acquaintances. About what happened to them during the past year. The year when you suddenly disappeared. When no one could find you, except a few who died soon after. Or ended up as vegetables on life-support systems—like Gleb Mezentsev."

"Wait a minute—Gleb was in a car crash."

"Right. His BMW flew into a ditch after someone drove him off the road . . . It was a hit and run."

"You think I did that? That's crazy—I've never even had a driver's license. Although the fact that you single me out at all is kind of cool. You say you were lucky . . . ?" Korenev stared at Felix, who had a hard time not averting his gaze. But he held out, of course—the bastard lowered his eyes, and nodded. "So you decided I killed them . . . There's just one thing I don't get—why me?"

"Because you, motherfucker, envied all of them. Because you've been a sniveler your whole life. Because your life has been a pile of shit. Because you never got a fucking thing you wanted. Because you, you little shit, hate everyone who has it better than you, who lucks out—"

"Lucks out," Korenev interrupted. "What does that mean,

'to luck out'? You think you have the right to judge who's lucky and who isn't? Do you think there's any logic to anything? But of course. We always look for some rationale, some system to explain things. But we really invent them ourselves. Simply because we think in these categories; we don't know any other way. Only there is no system, and no explanation." Still staring, Pasha Korenev shook his head slowly back and forth. "They only exist in our own minds. That's what none of you want to understand. What I myself didn't understand for a long time. I kept thinking there had to be rules of some kind. And I tried to play by them! To do things conscientiously. To keep my word. Not let anyone down. I kept thinking if I was good to people, they'd be good to me." The corners of his mouth contorted. "But it's all a load of crap. There are no rules. Nothing depends on your personal qualities or the efforts you make. Either you're lucky or you aren't. Only *that*"—he suddenly took a half-step toward Felix, almost pressing up against him—"doesn't mean a damn thing. That's what I'm trying to tell you. That's why I come to all of you—so you'll finally start thinking about it. Rules don't exist here either. And even if you luck out all the time, it doesn't guarantee anything. Nothing. At. All."

"Mm-hmm." Now Felix moved forward slightly, forcing Korenev to fall back a step. "And you took the role of fate upon yourself?"

Korenev snorted in exasperation. "You're not listening. You try to attach meaning to everything. To find someone to blame. Naturally, it's easier that way, when there's someone to blame." He took another step backward, as if to observe Felix from head to toe. "But you must understand—there is no one to blame. And nothing you can do." Another step backward. And then, from the side, a group of loud, gesticulating young people surged around him. There was some minor scuffling, after which Korenev ended up about five meters away from Felix. Somehow following fluidly in the wake of the young people, he moved away, skirting the fountain. He quickened his pace, weaving in and out of people in the crowd.

When the bastard was about fifteen feet away, Felix started following. He had no plan—but he wasn't going to let the son of a bitch get away. Felix had to somehow lead him to a more secluded place, to set him straight or just tie him up and gag him . . .

In pursuit of Korenev, who maintained a fairly brisk pace and never turned around, Felix crossed the square and made it to the corner of the station—and there he realized the bastard was heading for the subway. He sped up, gaining on Korenev; but only when he was in the crowded vestibule of the station, only when he saw the bastard getting in line to pass through the turnstile leading to the escalators, did he look back at the ticket booth—a hopeless throng of people—and think: *I'll jump the turnstile.* Right then, however, he met the gaze of a cop on patrol. *Damn* . . .

Korenev pushed his way toward the escalator without having bought a ticket . . . He completely blended in with the crowd at the turnstile. Felix watched him descend underground—his feet, his waist, finally his neck and head vanished from view . . .

Rudely pressing against some heavyset lady (who cackled at him indignantly), Felix slipped through the turnstile. Pushing his way in front of everyone else, he hurried to the escalator, expecting to see Korenev rushing down the stairs.

The descent at Kievskaya is a long one; but the bastard was nowhere to be seen. *What the . . . ?* Felix scoured the length of the escalator with his eyes, oblivious to the complaints of the people whose way he blocked.

Gone . . . gone . . . Just like that . . . slippery bastard . . .

Shuffling around aimlessly for another minute or two, Felix sighed deeply several times then made his way back outside.

No big deal, really. He knew who to look for, and, thank god, he knew how to search. He'd been doing it his whole life. He never even considered the possibility that he wouldn't find the bastard again. And besides, Felix was always lucky . . .

Moving toward the parking lot where he had left the car, he came to the street. He waited for a lull in the stream of traffic and stepped out onto the pavement. In his pocket he felt a buzzing—then he heard the beep of his mobile. Felix hesitated, his hand scrambling around for his phone . . . Kostya from the Criminal Investigation Department. Felix finally managed to press the answer key, then turned his head at the furious sound of screeching brakes—but for some reason he didn't feel the impact of the blow at all.

"Hello, Felix? Hello! Hello!?" But after a short, sharp sound, he heard a steady beeping—the connection had broken off. Never mind; he'll call back.

Kostya stared at the monitor again. Huh, no way, colonel. That Pasha Korenev, the one the Petersburg cop was looking for, had died; according to a document Kostya had just located, it happened twelve months earlier. In the Sklifosovsky Hospital, in the intensive care unit. Fractured skull, swelling of the brain. They found him by the fountain on Europe Square. He had been beaten, and his wallet and cell phone were gone. That place was bad news, Kostya thought, always full of bums.

What a stupid death . . .

MOSCOW REINCARNATIONS

BY SERGEI KUZNETSOV

Lubyanka

Translated by Marian Schwartz

Nikita dozes off holding my hand.

Such a handsome hand he has. Strong fingers, smooth oval nails, nicely defined tendons. Light hairs, almost imperceptible, but stiff to the touch.

He's sleeping holding my hand, but I just can't.

I'm afraid of dozing off. It's like walking into cold water, slowly immersing yourself, diving headfirst and not knowing what you'll see on the bottom.

That Crimean summer I dove alone while Nikita watched from shore. Only later did he admit he was afraid to swim.

I wasn't afraid of anything. I was twenty-eight. Never before had I been as beautiful as I was that summer.

Nor will I ever be again.

Time has wrung me out like laundered linen and thrown me into the dryer like a crumpled rag. Back then I thought, *Time spares no one*, but now I know that's not so.

Time changes everyone, but men are grazed by a touch of gray, a leisurely gait, a solidity of figure. At least Nikita has been. As for anyone else, to be honest, it's been a long time since I've cared.

His hands have barely changed. Except that seven years ago a wedding ring appeared.

My skin is tarnishing, withering, covered with a fine fishnet inside of which the years I've lived thrash around like caught fish. My hair is falling out and in the mornings I look at my pillow, fighting the temptation to count them.

Once I couldn't stop myself. Now I know: 252 hairs, almost a handful.

I'm afraid of going bald. I'm afraid of my breasts disappearing in a few years, my belly sticking to my spine, my eyes sinking. Sometimes I feel like a living corpse.

Nine years ago I wasn't afraid of anything. Now I can't fall asleep out of fear.

But Nikita isn't afraid of anything. In those years he's lost all fear. *Blind swap?* as we used to say in kindergarten.

I didn't want to go to kindergarten. I was still afraid then. I thought one day my mama wouldn't come for me and would leave me there forever. Only later did I learn where that fear came from; it was the echo of my orphanage infancy, the first months of my life.

My mama told me the story herself. *You see, sometimes children are mistakenly born to people who aren't their parents. So they can take them to a special place where their real parents find them. The way we found you.*

I was six years old and I didn't know where children came from. I probably thought about a stork that might mix up his bundles, or a store where after a long line you could buy a child—and they might sell you the wrong one by mistake.

When I was ten, my papa explained: *The ancient Hindus believed in the rebirth of souls. I believe you are the little girl your mama couldn't give birth to.*

I knew by then that children came out of the belly, but I didn't really understand how you could not be able to give birth.

I no longer believed in the stork, or the store, but I believed in the rebirth of souls immediately. And I still do. I believe the soul travels back and forth through history, and can even be born several times in the same century, miraculously not meeting herself in a previous (subsequent?) guise.

I believe that. Or, rather, I know it. And that's why I lie here sleepless, squeezing Nikita's hand. I'm afraid to fall asleep.

In the filmy, viscous dimension between waking and sleep my past lives return. Men, women, children. They fill me until it seems like there's no room left inside for *me*.

I squeeze into a ball and try to push the past out—it was mine, it wasn't mine, it may not have existed at all.

No surprise I'm losing weight. I must think that if I shrivel up completely the ghosts will decamp and find themselves another receptacle.

Though I could get used to them. Ultimately, these are my past lives. I recognize them: the old lady twirling in front of a mirror; the man gazing at the river; the young woman hugging her pregnant belly; the man crushing out a cigarette butt; the soldier pulling a grenade pin; the naked man cooking breakfast; the little girl staring at the Black Sea; the man dropping to his knees in front of his lover.

They shout, laugh, cry, moan, and sigh . . . Sometimes I feel like throwing myself open, embracing them, and saying, *Come in, it's me, your unsafe haven, your future, reincarnation, rebirth. Don't cry, everything worked out fine, look at me, I'm much happier than you. My life is wonderful: a loving husband, a home, a car, a household, a full cup. They didn't beat me during their interrogations, my friends weren't killed, radiation didn't eat up my flesh, and I didn't wait to be arrested. I don't worry about money or survival, I don't worry about where I'm going to sleep tomorrow or what I'm going to eat. I can't remember the last time I was hungry.*

But the incorporeal ghosts sway in the stratum of sleep and swirl in the murky corners of my huge apartment.

They've already lived their own lives; they're not rushing, being sold off, drinking up the bitter water of earthly existence, or eating the bitter bread of posthumous exile anymore.

They're always hungry.

They're eating me from the inside out. My life is food for those I once was. They're gnawing at my flesh—and every month blood flows out, attesting that the feast continues, the ghosts are not sated, they are still unhappy.

Every month, following the phases of the moon, plus or minus a day, I receive the same letter: *You aren't going to have a child.*

Dozing off, we hold hands. My Kolya, Kolya-Nikolai. I want to sleep facing you, but every month that gets harder. You might even say we're sleeping for three, right? Only two months to go—and our bunny will be born. I wonder whether it'll be a boy or a girl. The old women in the countryside always guessed—based on your walk, the shape of your belly, and other signs.

Just think, it's been five years and I still can't get used to the idea that my Berezovka's gone. True, old Georgich's great nephew wrote last month saying they were planning to build a state farm in its place. I don't even know . . . I guess that's good. The cows will moo again and the chickens will run around, as if there'd been no war. You just look at it and it's all so horrible what happened; how are people supposed to live there?

I told Kolya about it, and he said, *So the fact that we're living in a dead soldier's apartment doesn't bother you? That's the way it should be. New people come to take the place of dead fighters.*

Except that we didn't have any fighters in Berezovka. Foolish Lushka hid two partisans—and that was it.

Nina looks at the street, lined with two-story wooden houses; an invalid on a bench is talking to two old women. The sound from a gramophone reaches her from a neighbor's window.

This is Moscow, the capital of the Union of Soviet Socialist Republics, the first worker and peasant state in the world. Marina Roshcha.

Nina gazes at her round belly and tries to persuade the boy or girl to hold on a little longer and not kick but lie quietly. The doctor said she could talk to him already. Or her?

Nina's waiting for her husband. She sits home for days on end, afraid to go out. Even in the daytime they could attack her on the street, take her money away, or just strip her. They could jam a knife into her, or a bullet. There are an awful lot of thieves.

Kolya says it all started after the war. Before, Moscow was different. But now that people have been taught to kill, they just can't stop.

Nina doesn't know how to kill. She only knows how to hide so she won't die.

For two months she hid in the forests, surviving on berries and occasionally digging up potatoes in Berezovka's charred gardens. At the sound of an engine she would fall to the ground, perfectly still.

Nina loved walking in the forest before. Her mama would laugh and call her *my little forest girl.*

Her mother burned up along with the rest of the village. Nina survived because that morning she'd gone out for mushrooms when the punitive expedition showed up. She hid out in the woods and didn't emerge until it was all over.

Until everyone was dead.

Kolya says he wouldn't have lasted a day in the forest. *I'm afraid of wolves,* he says. She laughs; he's probably not afraid of anything.

Nina is afraid for him.

Afraid they'll slit Kolya's throat to take away his gun.

Afraid Kolya will stop someone to check his documents—and the person will start shooting.

Afraid Kolya will go after a thieves' den—and be killed in a shootout.

Afraid Kolya will walk into a building—and into an ambush.

Nina says, *Take care of yourself, for god's sake. If only you could wait until the child is born!*

But Kolya replies, *I took an oath. If I don't stop them they're going to keep on killing. Pretty recently they butchered a whole family in Marina Roshcha. Even a tiny baby. Got away with 25,000 rubles.*

A huge amount. Kolya's salary is just 550. How long do you have to work to make that kind of money?

How old was the baby? Nina asks.

Still in its cradle, absolutely tiny, Kolya answers. *They killed him so he wouldn't cry.*

Why is he telling her this? Nina wants to hear one more time how after she gives birth Kolya is going to take time off. No, Kolya doesn't want to talk about leaving work, he answers

Nina. *Wait for us to catch them all, and then we'll start living well and happily!*

Nina doesn't believe it. She remembers how people used to say, *We'll drive Fritz out and then we'll start living well and happily.* Where is that happiness now? Now it's like seeing her husband off to the front line every single day.

Actually, it's her own fault. She knew who she was marrying. From the very first second. Only Kolya was so handsome in his new uniform, blue with red trim. His cap with its sky-blue band. His boots. The moment she saw him at the dance, she fell in love. Kolya later admitted he'd gone into the police force because of the uniform; they issued it for free and he liked wearing it.

There was a star on the cap, and in the center a soldier with a rifle at the ready. Nina liked that a lot too.

At the time Nina had only just arrived and she was afraid of Moscow. It was awful! Everyone cutting in and out, sideways, down the streets—and the locals pushing their way past, swaggering, spitting at their feet, not afraid of anything. You could spot them right away: soft eight-panel caps, boxcalf boots, and white mufflers.

Later Kolya told her those were the thieves. Crooks.

Why can they walk down the street like that with no one arresting them? Nina asked.

Well, you can't arrest someone for an eight-panel cap, Kolya laughed. *Don't worry, they won't be walking around for long. Too bad they've abolished the* vyshka. *But that's all right, if need be we'll take matters into our own hands*—and he winked.

Vyshka was short for *capital punishment.* Execution. It was abolished a year ago. Kolya says there's no one to chop timber in Siberia.

Nina thinks, *We're going to have a child—and how are we*

going to live? It's good the war's over. But still, are we really going to spend our whole life in the city? No forest, no real river. You can go to the big park, people dive and swim from the pier—but Nina feels shy. She swims like a country girl, after all, and in Moscow everyone must have some special style.

Nina sits home waiting for her husband. Sits and waits, worried, troubled, and afraid. She can't make heads or tails of what she reads, and they don't have a gramophone, or even a radio speaker; it's an old building. I don't know whether there were any televisions back then, but Nina and Kolya definitely didn't have one.

I'm sitting home too, and I'm waiting for Nikita too. I'm worried for him—even though I have no cause for worry. Nikita's business is peaceful and he drives carefully. I'm still worried, though.

I'd like to say, *I don't know if I could deal with being in Nina's place,* but I can't. She and I are one and the same, which means at some point I was sitting there like that, waiting for my husband to come home from work, bored, looking out the window, stroking my pregnant belly, afraid to go outside.

It's weird to feel other people's lives inside you. Snatches of other people's thoughts and irrelevant facts suddenly surface in my memory. Edible berries. The best place to gather mushrooms. How to climb a tree and get settled so you don't fall out at night.

And sometimes a tune gets stuck in my head and keeps ringing in my mind hour after hour. Sometimes I can even make out the words.

My dad the bigwig fucks his tart
Oh bastard me, I fuck my aunt

All the time, everywhere,
From midnight until morn
From one night to the next
And back again till morn.
My dad the bigwig only fucks 'em rich
Oh bastard me, I fuck 'em bent and humped
All the time, everywhere
From midnight until morn
From one night to the next
And back again till morn.

I know this is what the little boys sang when Nina walked around the yard. Nina heard this song, and now I hear it in my head. *All the time, everywhere, from midnight until morn*—and I don't know whether this song amused, frightened, or annoyed Nina. I get my melancholy from her. *All the time, everywhere*—that is, in this life and the ones before, around the clock, night and day, I sit in an armchair, on a seat, on a stool, and wait for my beloved to come home. And I'm afraid something's going to happen to him.

When I'm Nina, I caress my big pregnant belly. When I'm Masha, I paint my toenails over and over again, though I have no plans to go out. It calms me.

Kolya comes home and tells me how they picked up the Kazentsov gang a few days before, on a train, and how there was shooting. The gang had hidden out in the children's car but the conductor noticed them and called it in. It turned out they were hijacking cars. They'd ask a driver to take them out of town, where they'd kill him. Now they were the ones getting killed, at least two of them.

Kolya says there are too many guns in Moscow. Captured and brought back from the war, taken away from policemen, stolen from the Hammer and Sickle plant, where they're selling old inventory to melt down.

To make sure a policeman can't have his gun taken away, Kolya explained, the cop attached it to a special red cord. The cord goes up one side of his uniform, around his neck, and down the other side. The grip has a special loop where the cord is attached. Kolya explained and even showed me, but I still don't understand. Better they just take the gun. That way, if some crook decides he wants your gun, he doesn't have to kill you for it.

I'm really scared for Kolya. Since I got pregnant, I'm even more scared.

At first I was so glad we were going to have a child! I imagined him growing there, inside me. I went to the doctor once a month and the doctor told me when his little eyes appeared, and his little hands. I'm only sorry he's going to be born in Moscow and not the country. What kind of a life is this? Why did I ever come here? I must have known I'd meet Kolya. There's nothing else good here in Moscow.

I'm glad I didn't enter the institute. I'd have had to study— but before you know it, a little baby is going to be born and Kolya will come to his senses. We'll go away together, wherever we want.

I've been living in Moscow nearly a year and I still can't figure out what draws people here. In line at the doctor's I met a woman, also near her due date but older than me, her name was Marfa, also from the country, but she's been in Moscow a long time, from back before the war. She's a good woman and she reassures me, says giving birth isn't so terrible. *What's terrible*, she says, *is living, and even more terrible—dying*. Then I said, *Well, I know, my whole village perished*. And she stroked my head and said, *Poor thing!*—and for a second it felt like my mama was with me again. Though it's a sin to say so, of course, because I'll never have another mama. I'm a mama myself now. Only two months to go.

In line at the doctor's the women were talking about something terrible. They said you could get rid of a child for money. If you didn't want to give birth. In Berezovka they said that girls drank all kinds of potions to make it happen. I was little but I understood what they were saying. Well, a potion is understandable. But here apparently you could find a secret doctor and for fifteen hundred rubles he would take care of . . . well . . . it . . . everything.

Fifteen hundred! That's so much money! It's terrible to think who might have that! Here I am working out how to survive on 550 every month. For two—it's hard. And now a child as well, and he has to be fed.

I wish he could be born as soon as possible, my little bunny. If it's a boy, I hope he looks like Kolya. And if a girl, like my mama. I want her to have the same kind of eyebrows, and ears too.

I hope she's like my mama. I don't have anything left of her, not even a photograph. Everything burned up.

Mama would have been happy for me now. She must have been just as happy when she was dying. She knew I'd been saved.

Kolya laughs at me, but I know: there is a God somewhere. And my mama is with Him right now, on a cloud, watching me and seeing that I'm going to have my own little bunny, my own little boy, my own little girl—instead of her, instead of Papa, instead of Aunt Katya and Uncle Slava, instead of lame Mitrich and old lady Anfisa. Instead of our whole village.

Hurry up and get born, little bunny. I mean, get born when it's time, but don't make me wait too long. I'm a little afraid of giving birth. In Moscow you have to go to the hospital. There are strangers there and who knows what they might do. And people say there are doctor-wreckers around now too. And crooks probably.

Here she sits, day after day, little Nina from '48, getting heavier and heavier—and so is my heart. Because *all the time, everywhere, from midnight until morn*—it's the same old story, and I know what happens next.

Two weeks before the birth Nina puts jacket potatoes on the burner and suddenly remembers she's out of salt.

She goes over to Aunt Vera's, her neighbor.

She knocks and no one answers, so Nina pushes on the door and shouts, *Aunt Vera!* She walks in and she's struck by a cast-iron pot. They were aiming for her head but she managed to jump to the side, and then she hears a whisper: *Finish the bitch off!* She shields her unborn baby with her arms and starts yelling, but not loudly enough. When the second attacker strikes her in the belly, she screams loudly enough for the whole building to hear, the whole courtyard, even the street—and the sound barrels over the neighboring roofs, over the quays of the Moscow River, over the attractions at the central park, over the pavement of Red Square, over the Mausoleum's pyramid, over the Kremlin's stars, over the empty pit where the demolished temple once stood, over the wooden buildings built after the war, over the thieves' dens and lairs, over the police stations, over the prisons and penal colonies, over the subway entrances, over the movie theaters and cultural institutions—over all of postwar Moscow, over the unlucky victor city, over the kids without fathers, the women without husbands, the men without arms, legs, conscience, fear, family, memory, or love.

While Nina is still falling on the bloody ground, screaming and screaming . . .

One more blow and she would have been silenced forever. The attackers killed Aunt Vera and they could have killed Nina too. Smashed her head in, slit her throat, beat her with whatever came to hand—but they fled.

They would be caught two days later. Maybe they'd shoot someone during the arrest.

But Kolya was running down the street, holding the tiny body close, and the umbilical cord dangled like one more piece of red piping, and his whole handsome uniform was covered in blood. Kolya was running, cursing, weeping, and too late.

It was a boy.

Two years later they left Moscow. The state farm built where Berezovka had burned down gave them a house; a good muzhik always comes in handy in the countryside. And so they lived, until their death. Kolya trained to be a tractor driver; Nina worked as a milkmaid, poultry maid, and clerk at the general store—whatever opportunity arose. For a while she was even a kindergarten teacher. But not for long.

They didn't have children of their own. Kolya died in 1985, Nina a year later.

Sometimes I see her very old. Her hands are folded in her lap, she's sitting on a stool by the window, and the older teenagers, the girls and boys, are giggling on the bench. Music reaches her from an open car.

Nina has no one to wait for and nothing to fear. Her life is over.

Only in her head, like a worn-out record. *All the time, everywhere, from midnight until morn, from one night to the next, and again till morn* is like an obsession, an incantation, a promise that it will all happen again.

* * *

I doze off holding Jan's hand, but it doesn't matter. At night I dream of my lovers. The men I couldn't have. The boy from our school, a year younger than me, his curly fair hair escaping his school cap: a car ran him down right in front of his house, in front of his parents and nanny. The Menshevik agitator, his glasses shattered, his cracking voice turning into a short screech when a bullet forced the petals of a crimson rose open on his jacket chest. The Red soldier in the dusty helmet silently bowing over the corpse of his comrade who was captured by the White Cossacks; a star was carved on his salt-strewn back—a five-pointed star gone from red to brown. A fifteen-year-old kid shouting through tears, *Swine, swine!*, his ginger hair soaked with sweat and stuck to his forehead, so you wished you could run your hand over it. A stout man, temples lightly touched with gray, looking back for the last time before boarding that barge—a spark in his dark pupil, like a gleam of light, but from the other shore.

I doze off holding Jan's hand. It's a strong hand covered with fine faded hair, his closely trimmed nails edged in black. I kiss his fingers and imagine that this narrow dark stripe is caked blood, the congealed blood of the people he's ordered to be executed. I kiss his hand and think that this is the hand of someone who separates life from death, who splits human existence in two, the hand of someone used to deciding for others, whether they are to live or die.

My lips flick across his palm, travel up toward the bend in his elbow, and slip over the tendons of his forearms. When he makes a fist they tense, like a belt drive, and I feel the flow of blood, the faint pulsing, and my lips continue their journey, and I kiss his armpits, the hair smelling of grim soldier sweat, the only patch of real hair on his body, if you don't count the thick growth at the base of his mighty shaft, which rises down there somewhere. I forbid myself to think about that, run my tongue over his smooth chest, just grazing his nipples—and then Jan places his heavy hand on my back, and his nails start quietly clawing at my skin, always in the same spot, between my shoulder blades—*and even after who knows how many reincarnations I still swoon when Nikita strokes my back like that*—I swoon, and then I shudder, and my tongue turns downward, following the narrow path between his heaving ribs, crossing the puffy scar from the saber blow—*He did get me, after all, the snake, after I shot him with my revolver*—and run my finger over the scar, imagining some White officer drawing his sword against his killer with the cold fury of desperation, and at the same time I drop lower with my lips, to the rosette of his navel, and Jan puts his hand on the back of my head, urging, directing, hastening the now inevitable movement. My tongue goes into a spiral, feeling his great axis, around which my night revolves, rise higher and higher as it swells with blood. Finally, squeezing his two globes, I open my mouth and swallow the crimson head, sucking in air through fluttering nostrils, as if it were a line of cocaine, moving up and down, feeling the weight of his hand on the back of my head, the resilience of his cock between my lips, the trembling of his testicles in my hand, and the quivering of his powerful male body.

I've known the taste of quite a few men's cocks. My tongue and palate have learned to distinguish adolescent languor, animal fear, ominous hatred, trembling adoration, impatience, burning, itching, haste, the urgency of unspilled semen, the pressure of lust, and the spasm of passion.

Jan's taste is the taste of gun grease and machine oil. Viscous and sticky, it makes me shudder just to think of it. I hold on to his balls—easy to take, hard to let go—and feel his shaft moving in my mouth—the almost toylike barrel of a revolver, though not small—the taste of which so many have learned in years past. No, the huge hot barrel of an artillery gun, the organ of a machine of destruction, poised to fire, just waiting for the command.

I'm moving faster and faster, the hand on the back of my head won't let me rest, my lips itch with a sweet pain—I press my whole body to Jan, and from the depth of my heart rises the sacred word. It runs through my veins, flies up my throat, and opens my mouth even wider with the violent magic command: *Fire!*—and a sticky stream of semen explodes in my head.

At school, in scripture class, they taught us that the seed dies and yields much fruit. Jan's seed is dead and cools on my lips in a whitish film. The fruit it brings . . . they're beautiful those fruit—and tears run down my cheeks. Then he takes his hand from the back of my head, sits down on the bed, and jerks me toward him. I bury my sticky lips in his shoulder, and his hand lazily rakes my spine.

Then Jan starts talking. He recalls the Civil War, the Kronstadt rebellion, the Antonov uprising, the counterrevolutionary plots. He tells me how his day went.

His days pass with mundane matters. Compiling lists, dictating telegrams, and listening to reports, denunciations, interrogations, resolutions, and decisions. Now Jan almost never does the executing himself—*Let the others do some work*, he says. At the beginning of our affair I asked him whether he remembered how many people he'd killed, and Jan answered, *In battle doesn't count, and when they lowered me into the barge— there was really no one keeping score.*

Sometimes I tell myself, *Right now I'm crying on the chest of a man who has killed people without count*—and my heart pounds like a hammer. I ask, *Could you shoot me?*

Of course—Jan grabs me by the shoulders—*of course I could. I've shot men I slept with. They were traitors. I serve the Revolution, but you understand, Kolya, and the Revolution does not forgive treason.*

I don't ask him how many men he's slept with. I'm afraid he doesn't remember them any more than he does those he killed. I'm afraid of getting lost on his list, his long list, like his list of executions.

I don't ask him whether he's ever slept with a woman. That thought is unbearable: imagining Jan with a woman, imagining his mighty cock plunging into those fusty wet human insides. The female secretion is disgusting, like rust eating into the barrel of a rifle. I can't imagine Jan's seed, the seed of death, spilling in a woman's lap, that nauseating source of new life.

I'd like to hold Jan's cock in my hand and squeeze it with my lips always—to know that not a single drop of his seed would fertilize a woman. Small children are awful, their howls are a parody of passion, and their stinking diapers, strollers, and bonnets are the gloomy prophecy of old age's impotence, which I will not live to see.

One morning I'll see my cock dozing between my hips like a feeble worm. One evening, at the sight of a man's nakedness, it won't perk up and will stay wrinkled and pathetic. That's the day I'll realize my old age has arrived. And I'll ask Jan—because Jan will always be by my side, forever young—to add me to his execution list and—in memory of our love—finish me off himself.

Right now Jan almost never takes part in the executions. *I'm saving my bullets,* he jokes. *I have a dream about shooting a countess. A real live countess.*

When he told me this the first time I got scared. I imagined some high society love story: little Jan, an errand boy; the countess he lusts after (or who lusts after him); the old count who in the murk of the conjugal bedroom reveals to Jan the mysteries of homosexual love; a woman's silhouette in the doorway; the shouts, the hysterics, maybe the police or a lashing in the stables; the vow for revenge, underground cells, the party of Bolsheviks, revolution, war, Cheka, execution lists, my tears on his shoulder . . .

That time Jan reassured me.

You have to understand, he said, *I've never seen a genuine countess. Only in the movies. So I want to see how countesses behave before death, how they die, what color blood they have.*

Aristocrats have blue, I joked, but Jan didn't answer. I saw his cock stiffen up again, and in an onset of jealousy I squeezed it and Jan's nails dug into my back. Then he loosened my fingers and laughed. *What are you, jealous? Do you want me to take you along when we send her off to Dukhonin?*

Since then we've spoken of this often. Jan's dream has become my dream. We've imagined finding a countess: a spy infiltrated by White émigrés from Paris; an aristocrat in hiding who survived the Revolution in some out-of-the-way house, masquerading as a peasant, factory worker, or student. On the day of her execution she'll be wearing a white dress, holding a parasol, wearing black high-laced shoes on low heels. Sometimes we'll lead her down a brick corridor to the last wall, sometimes we'll take her out into the snow in the Cheka courtyard (they haven't executed anyone there in a long time, but in my dreams for some reason I see her walking, stumbling in the snow, across that courtyard), sometimes we'll take her out of town, to the Gulf of Finland. Even in his dreams Jan won't let me carry out the sentence myself—I just hand him the revolver and then he, squinting, slowly raises the muzzle and the countess turns pale, opening her parasol with a trembling hand or dropping it in the snow, covering her face in elbow-length white gloves. Jan always says, *Farewell, countess!*—and the seed of death bursts from his barrel, and her white dress turns red, soaked with blood, ordinary red blood, the same color as everyone else he has shot.

His dreams go no further than that shot, but in my visions I drop to my knees before him, kiss the revolver's smoking muzzle, and then carefully take the other shaft into my mouth, a shaft poised and ready to fire.

I doze off holding Jan's hand and think, *Today it seems like he isn't really with me, as if he's thinking about something else, not the Revolution even, but some other young man, a year or two younger than me maybe, a twenty-two-year-old beauty with curly fair hair.* Half-asleep, I see the three of us, then Jan goes away somewhere and my new lover kisses me on the lips—and then Jan's voice wakes me, and I don't understand right away what he's said, but when I do I squeeze his hand even harder—and fall asleep for real.

I've found her, Jan says. *I've found the countess.*

There'd been a joint meeting to fight banditry—the police, UgRo, and OGPU. When they were done, Jan went outside and saw a young woman standing with her elbows resting on a fence, almost stock-still, her entire figure replete with bourgeois refinement, the aristocratism of the old regime. She was out of place there, among the strong men in leather jackets. *I should ask for her documents*, Jan thought, but at that moment an UgRo officer he didn't know ran up to the girl, hugged her, and kissed her on the lips.

Jan walked away so as not to attract attention, only later he asked, *Who was that kissing the woman over there?*—and in reply he heard the man's name.

All the rest was a technical matter. Jan made inquiries and found out more about the man. Some Civil War hero, a fighter against banditry, a distinguished comrade. True, he had to dig deeper when it came to the girl. A student at the university—so Jan stopped by her department and checked her documents. Everything seemed in order, a worker family, but her name put him on his guard. He went to the address where her mother and sister lived. *My revolutionary instinct did not mislead me,* he chuckled. When the house committee saw his warrant, they told him everything. A former bourgeoise who started at the factory recently so she could get into the university.

The street cleaner volunteered to show him where they'd lived before—in their own house, it turned out. And there, not believing his own ears, Jan heard this: *The dead count's wife and daughter.*

I'll collect some more documents, he said, and I felt his fingers trembling in my hand, *and report to Comrade Meerzon that a representative of the exploiting classes concealed her origin when entering the university, and with criminal intent entered into a liaison with an officer of the workers and peasant militia. This means the death penalty, believe me, Vitya, I know how to write.*

I pressed my whole body to Jan, soaking up his trembling.

Why didn't you say something? I whispered. *After all, this is a gift for both of us.*

Yes, Jan replied gravely, *for the Revolution's birthday.*

The anniversary isn't until the next week, but I realize that Jan is already counting the days until his *Farewell, countess!*—when the crimson rose blossoms on her white dress.

He said *the Revolution's birthday,* as if the Revolution is a person, a woman he's in love with. I adore that chivalry in him, that obedience and sterility, the cold flame of unearthly passion eating him up from the inside. For Jan we are both the Revolution's lovers, and our intimacy is just an attempt to get close to Her; for him a new attempt, after years of war and execution lists, to replace death cries with cries of pleasure and the lead seed of the revolver with the seed of our love drying on my lips.

In the morning I watched Jan dress. He turned his back to me and I gazed at his butt, rounded and resilient, gazed at the scar between his broad shoulder blades . . . Aroused and trembling, I ran over and kissed the back of his neck.

Jan smiled over his shoulder.

Not now, Vitya, I have to go, and so do you.

Yes, I went to work too. A boring office job. If it hadn't been for meeting Jan, my life would have been as flat as the papers I sorted through. I despised my job, though Jan did say, *This too is service to the Revolution.*

I got dressed and wanted to leave with him—but Jan wasn't going to wait for me.

In a hurry to see your countess? I asked.

Our countess—and he smiled in the doorway.

I often think those words were the greatest avowal of love in my life, a magnificent epilogue to our romance, the farewell moment in a string of nights that smelled of semen and gun grease, long nights we shared the way we shared the Revolution, that stern Virgin; the way we shared the countess, the snow-white lamb doomed for slaughter in Her name.

Jan didn't come back that night. Sometimes he was kept late, but he always warned me in advance. After midnight, tortured by suspicion, jealousy, and fear, I ran all the way across the city to Lubyanka Square. I imagined the attempted arrest, the resistance of the counterrevolutionary conspirators, a foolish bullet, and a bloody rose on his broad, hairless chest.

I asked the guard whether Jan was there and in reply I got, *Get out of here, contra!*, words that are doubly frightening on OGPU's threshold. Lost, I wandered off; turning the corner, I heard the sound of an engine. A car was pulling up and behind the wheel sat a young boy. I knew him; he'd brought Jan home a couple of times after nighttime operations.

Are you Viktor? he asked.

I nodded, hesitant to ask about Jan. But he told me without waiting for my question. Later I thought they might have been lovers too. The boy's voice held a sadness, and he told me the truth, which an OGPU agent isn't supposed to share with an outsider—unless, of course, something more connects him to that outsider than the nighttime street, the predawn hour, and the dim glow of the streetlamps.

We got a warning, he said, *that Jan is supposedly linked to the SRs and is planning a terrorist act. An UgRo agent reported that some petty thief happened to give testimony about this during a roundup.*

What nonsense, I murmured. *Jan has nothing to do with thieves.*

I don't know, the boy said. *They killed the thief when he tried to escape. But the UgRo agent is such a distinguished comrade—he fought in the Civil War and can't be doubted. He spoke with Comrade Meerzon in his office for two hours, and Meerzon personally signed the arrest order.*

In the camps people sometimes talk about how they learned of the arrest of their near and dear. Usually they say, *We believed they'd sort things out there and release him.* I grinned ever so slightly. That night I had no illusions. I knew how this machine worked. I knew I'd never see Jan again. I knew it was pointless to go see Meerzon and tell him that the UgRo agent's lover was a former countess and he had slandered Jan when he realized Jan was getting close to her. Yes, I knew it was all pointless. Pointless and dangerous.

If there had been roosters in Moscow, that night they could have cockadoodle-dooed without end. I renounced my love in a flash—I said, *Well, Comrade Meerzon knows better*—and hunched up, went to meet the graying dawn.

My love died before the bullet entered Jan's smooth neck, right where I'd kissed him for the last time. My love died. The man I loved couldn't sit in a cell or answer any interrogator's questions. He could only ask the questions himself, only lock other people up in cells, with every movement asserting the great invigorating power of revolutionary death, which boiled in him like an eternal spring, gave strength to the roots of that mighty tree, filled with sap the strong shaft that swelled between my lips.

After Jan's disappearance I was gripped by a dreary sadness, as if the whole postcoital tristia our nights had never known had simply been biding its time. My dreams were pale, colorless, like the pages of the daily newspapers with their reports about new achievements, new construction, and new enemies. I went back to my hopeless, faded existence, now even more insipid than before I met Jan. Even young boys and men didn't excite me now, as if deep down inside I had found a secret inner courtyard where I made the very possibility of intimacy and love face the wall.

One day, at dawn, I dreamed of a girl in white carrying a parasol and wearing high-laced boots. She was walking arm in arm with a man I didn't know who was wearing a leather jacket, and I had no doubt that this was my love's murderer,

Jan's murderer. I was reminded of the unbearable contrast between the white lace and black leather jacket where their arms touched. The man seemed my age, broad of shoulder, round-headed, and like many in those days, shaved bald. The glance he cast at the girl radiated tenderness, but the moment he looked away his eyes turned into two black circles, two endless tunnels, two rifle muzzles ready to fire.

I woke up. On my lips was the forgotten taste of gun grease and machine oil. For the first time since Jan's disappearance I started to caress myself, turned over on my back, shutting my eyes, and squeezed my hardening cock in my hand. I imagined Jan—his powerful hands and fingers covered in fair hair, the scars on his back and belly, the prominent tendons of his forearms, his hairless chest, the forgotten smell of wartime sweat; but the familiar features faded and through Jan's image his murderer peered imperiously, as if Jan had turned into that man, as if the murderer had swallowed Jan up. When the metamorphosis was complete, a thick stream spurted up and fell in dead drops on my belly.

The countess was a mirage, a fata morgana. A set trap, a temptation Jan could not resist. The Revolution did not forgive infidelity; the Revolution's jealousy was worse than my youthful jealousy. The false promise to bring a lamb for sacrifice could not fool Her; in the secret order to which Jan and I belonged there was no place for women—only Her. Passion that did not belong to the Revolution could only be given to another man, as if to one's own reflection in the mirror, one's own double, one's own partner in the strict service of the cruel maiden.

I knew my turn would come sooner or later. I was going to pay for the dreams Jan and I shared; I would pay for *our* countess.

I waited for many years, and when the time came, I signed the investigation's protocol without reading it—but I didn't tell them anything about Jan, or our love, or the bewitching fata morgana who drew us into the fatal abyss.

Sometimes I think I didn't betray our love after all.

I was waiting for them to execute me, but times had changed. The Revolution required slaves, not sacrifices. They sent me to a camp, where I was certain I would die. I could die in transit, in Siberia, or at the colony; or, after the second arrest, in the transit prisons, in Dzhezkazgan or Vorkuta. I probably didn't perish because the death-infused seed I'd spilled into my throat so many nights in a row had filled me with strength.

In '56, during the wave of Khrushchev's rehabilitations, I returned to Moscow. I thought, *They've rehabilitated Jan too*. I thought I might learn the name of the UgRo informer, meet with him and look into his deep dark eyes . . . But I didn't try. What would I have done if I'd met the man? In my dreams I sometimes killed him, sometimes I had sex with him, and often at the decisive moment the countess would walk into the bedroom, a ghost, still very young, walk in and watch silently, and his mighty round-headed cock would soften in my lips.

Once I dreamed that the bullet—my lover's lead seed—would not let time waste my flesh. I'd been twenty-four—and the same number of years have now passed since I came back from Kazakhstan, although once again I thought I would soon die. The years have faded my memory of Jan, my memory of our love, my memory of the camp, the countess, and her round-headed companion, everything that happened in the last seventy-odd years. I've spent nearly my entire life alone; and in old age even the old ghosts refrained from violating my solitude.

I know this is how I'll die. Alone, in an empty apartment, the summer of 1980, the sixty-third anniversary of the Revolution's birth.

Death is a great cheat, a fata morgana. I once dreamed of it, but it slipped away, over and over. Eventually I gave up, weary, and backed off.

Now it's coming for me and I say, *Listen, I don't understand why I ever loved you.* In reply you squeeze my old fingers in your cold hand.

Is this really what I dreamed of half a century ago?

Too bad. You've taken so long to get here, I almost forgot how much I once loved you!

A little girl on Crimea's cliffs, a young woman from a burned-out village, an old woman in front of a mirror. A sailor floating down the Volga, a soldier pulling out a pin, an old man waiting for death, a man finding it for himself. And more and more new souls keep crowding in behind them.

All of them are me.

My god, so many! None of them are left—the son, the daughter, the heir, the heiress—no one is left, no one and nothing, there's not even anyone to remember, anyone to tell, anyone to utter a word to those who came after. No one sees or hears them.

Only me . . .

Masha weeps, she weeps for everyone who vanished without a trace, weeps and repeats: *Only me, only me* . . . and does that mean I'm their heir? Does that mean I have to bear all this, preserve these souls in my emaciated body, bear them eternally in exchange for my unconceived children?

I'm as alone as alone can be, Masha tells herself. I never knew my real parents, my mama and papa drove me out, I have no brothers or sisters, and will never have children. How will I carry this burden alone? Am I a medium or something? Did I summon up the dead? No, they came to me of their own accord, entered me the way a rapist enters a sleeping woman, a woman who has lost the strength to resist.

Oh well, if you've come, make yourself comfortable, eat me, enjoy. Here is my flesh, here is my blood, but no bread and wine are served here. Be my guests, only know it'll be a short story. Because I'm not going to be able to bear all this any longer.

I can't alone.

And I can't call for help.

I'll go to Nikita and say, *I hear voices, I have other people, dead people, living inside me.* Instantly his voice will become very patient, sympathetic, and upbeat. That voice will make even me start to think I've lost my mind and belong in a psych ward. It's probably better if I don't say anything at all.

Just so he's nearby, just so he doesn't leave, just so he holds my hand—and I'll keep quiet, I'll deal with the rest myself.

I'll say, *Wasn't it nice in the Crimea nine years ago? Remember I was still telling fortunes on the quay? Could that have been when it all started? Could that be where I let all these alien lives inside me, all these lost, dead, unfortunate, barren souls? But we were still having fun that evening, drinking wine, eating shashlik. We were young and foolish. Strong and confident. Maybe deep down I still have that strength, maybe it's enough at this age, what do you think, Nikita, eh?*

Don't answer, you don't have to. After all, you and I know ourselves how much we can withstand. Don't answer, all right? Just don't go away, please. Don't go.

I'll just hold your hand—we'll all just hold your hand—and maybe we'll surface, or maybe we'll finally learn to breathe underwater.

ABOUT THE CONTRIBUTORS

 **ALEXANDER ANUCHKIN** was born in Moscow in 1976 to a family of teachers. He has worked as a crime reporter for twelve years, in addition to writing for television. He is currently the anchor and chief editor of the *Essential (Glavnoe)* TV program. His debut novel, the political thriller *Gold Reserve (Zolotoi zapas)*, was published in 2009.

 **IRINA DENEZHKINA** was born in Yekaterinburg, a large industrial center in the Urals, in 1981. When one of her manuscripts was short-listed for the prestigious National Best Seller Prize, she drew significant critical attention from the Russian media. Her story collection *Give Me: Songs for Lovers (Dai mne!)* has been translated into twenty languages, including English. She still lives in her native town, working as a journalist, writing her next book, and raising her son.

 **ALEXEI EVDOKIMOV**, born in 1975, is one half of the author team Garros-Evdokimov, best known for their award-winning novel *Headcrusher ([golovo]lomka)*, which has been translated into eight languages. Their subsequent novels are *Gray Goo (Seraya sliz')* and *Truck Factor (Factor fury)*. Evdokimov has also published the solo novels *Zero-Zero (Nol'-nol')* and *Cinephobia.RU (TIK)*.

 **JULIA GOUMEN** was born in St. Petersburg, Russia, in 1977. With a PhD in English, she has been working in publishing since 2001, starting her own literary agency after three years as a foreign rights manager. Since 2006 Goumen has run the Goumen & Smirnova Literary Agency with Natalia Smirnova.

Alexander Strelets

 **ANDREI KHUSNUTDINOV**, born in 1967, writes in the sci-fi genre, although his prose has often been compared with that of Franz Kafka. He is the author of the novels *Danai Greeks (Danaitsy)*, *Huguenot (Gugenot)*, and *Table Rock (Stolovaya gora)*, the last of which was on the long list for the 2008 Russian Booker Prize.

Andrei Katasonov

DMITRY KOSYREV, a.k.a. Master Chen, born in 1955, has written for leading newspapers such as *Pravda, Rossiiskaia Gazeta,* and *Nezavisimaya Gazeta,* and other publications since the 1970s. An expert on China, he has lived in various regions of Asia. Kosyrev is the author of the spy novels *The Pet Monkey of the House of Tang, The Pet Hawk of the House of Abbas, Amalia and the White Apparition,* and *Amalia and the Generalissimo.* He currently resides in Moscow with his wife and two daughters.

VYACHESLAV KURITSYN, a.k.a. Andrei Turgenev, was born in 1965 in Novosibirsk. He is the founder of both the humanitarian conference "Kuritsyn's Readings" and the website Contemporary Russian Prose with Vyacheslav Kuritsyn. He is the nationally acclaimed author of a number of books of prose and poetry, including the much-praised *The Month of Arcachon (Mesyats Arcachon)* and *The Siege Novel (Spat' i verit'),* which was short-listed for the National Best Seller Prize and the Russian Booker Prize.

SERGEI KUZNETSOV was born in Moscow in 1966. In the late '90s he became a leading Russian film and pop culture critic. He is the author of a detective trilogy, *The Nineties: A Fairy Tale (Devyanostye: skazka),* and a futuristic novel, *No (Net),* together with Linor Goralik. His book *Butterfly Skin (Shkurka babochki)* has acquired cult status in Russia and has been translated into German and Italian. He lives in Moscow with his wife and two children.

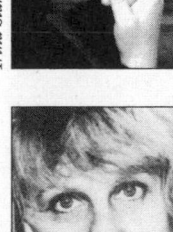

MAXIM MAXIMOV was born in Moscow in 1979. He has worked as a copywriter for several design and advertising agencies. He is the author of two volumes of poetry and is a fellow of the New Names program. He has published three novels: *Moscow Umbrellas (Moskovskie zontiki), We're Gone (Nas ne byvaet),* and *Far from Wrigley Gulf (Vdali ot zaliva Rigli).*

LUDMILLA PETRUSHEVSKAYA was born in Moscow in 1938. Her first work was published in 1972, only to be followed by almost ten years of officially enforced silence, when her plays and prose were censored. Petrushevskaya's novel *The Time: Night (Vremya noch')* was short-listed for the 1992 Russian Booker Prize and translated into more than thirty languages. Since then, Petrushevskaya has published over thirty books of prose, and her award-winning plays are produced around the world.

SERGEI SAMSONOV was born in 1980 in Podolsk. He works as a copywriter in a Moscow publishing house and contributes to the *Ex Libris NG* book review. His first novel, *Legs (Nogi)*, was translated into Italian. His second novel, *The Kamlaev Anomaly (Anomalia Kamlaeva)*, was short-listed for the National Best Seller Prize. Samsonov's most recent novel, *Oxygenic Limit (Kislorodny predel)*, was published in 2009.

GLEB SHULPYAKOV was born in 1971. His first collection of poems, *The Flick*, was published in 2001 and won the Triumph Prize. He is the author of the novels *The Sinan Book (Kniga Sinana)* and *Tsunami*, and contributes essays and criticism to Russian periodicals. He has translated the poetry of Ted Hughes and Robert Hass into Russian, as well as W.H. Auden's essays. Shulpyakov is currently an editor at the literary magazine *New Youth*. He lives in Moscow.

Maxim Kourennoi

NATALIA SMIRNOVA was born in 1978 in Moscow. After studying law and working as a lawyer, she moved to St. Petersburg to work as a foreign rights manager for a publisher. In 2006 she cofounded the Goumen & Smirnova Literary Agency, with Julia Goumen, representing Russian authors worldwide.

Alexander Garros

ANNA STAROBINETS is a journalist and scriptwriter. Her collection of short stories *An Awkward Age (Perekhodny vozrast)* has been translated into several languages. She is also the author of the novel *Refuge 3/9 (Ubezhische 3/9)* and the short story collection *Cold Spell (Rezkoe pokholodanie)*. All of her works have been nominated for the National Best Seller Prize. She lives in Moscow with her husband and daughter.

Kirill Tuchkov

VLADIMIR TUCHKOV, born in 1949, is an international correspondent for Vesti.ru, an online newspaper. His books have been short-listed for the Andrei Bely Prize and twice for the Anti-Booker Prize. His cyberpunk novel *The Dancer (Tantsor)* has drawn tremendous acclaim.

IGOR ZOTOV was born in Moscow in 1955. He has worked at the newspaper *Nezavisimaya Gazeta* for more than ten years, including as deputy editor in chief. He founded and for five years ran the book supplement *Ex Libris NG*. He is the author of two books and several hundred articles published in the Russian and foreign media.

Also available from the Akashic Noir Series

BOSTON NOIR
edited by Dennis Lehane
240 pages, trade paperback original, $15.95

Brand-new stories by: Dennis Lehane, Stewart O'Nan, Patricia Powell, John Dufresne, Lynne Heitman, Don Lee, Russ Aborn, J. Itabari Njeri, Jim Fusilli, Brendan DuBois, and Dana Cameron.

"In the best of the eleven stories in this outstanding entry in Akashic's noir series, characters, plot, and setting feed off each other like flames and an arsonist's accelerant . . . [T]his anthology shows that noir can thrive where Raymond Chandler has never set foot."
—*Publishers Weekly* (starred review)

PARIS NOIR edited by Aurélien Masson
300 pages, trade paperback original, $15.95

Brand-new stories by: Didier Daeninckx, Jean-Bernard Pouy, Marc Villard, Chantal Pelletier, Patrick Pécherot, DOA, Hervé Prudon, Dominique Mainard, Salim Bachi, Jérôme Leroy, and others.

"Rarely has the City of Light seemed grittier than in this hard-boiled short story anthology, part of Akashic's Noir Series . . . The twelve freshly penned pulp fictions by some of France's most prominent practitioners play out in a kind of darker, parallel universe to the tourist mecca; visitors cross these pages at their peril . . ."
—*Publishers Weekly*

ROME NOIR
edited by Chiara Stangalino & Maxim Jakubowski
280 pages, trade paperback original, $15.95

Brand-new stories by: Antonio Scurati, Carlo Lucarelli, Gianrico Carofiglio, Diego De Silva, Giuseppe Genna, Marcello Fois, Cristiana Danila Formetta, Enrico Franceschini, Boosta, and others.

From Stazione Termini, immortalized by Roberto Rossellini's films, to Pier Paolo Pasolini's desolate beach of Ostia, and encompassing famous landmarks and streets, this is the sinister side of the Dolce Vita come to life, a stunning gallery of dark characters, grotesques, and lost souls seeking revenge or redemption in the shadow of the Colosseum, the Spanish Steps, the Vatican, Trastevere, the quiet waters of the Tiber, and Piazza Navona. Rome will never be the same.